THE ALICE '65

OTHER BOOKS BY KYLE MICHEL SULLIVAN

General Novels:
The Alice '65
The Vanishing of Owen Taylor
The Lyons' Den
Bobby Carapisi

Fable:
David Martin

Adult Novels:
Hunter
The Beast in the Nothing Room
Underground Guy
Rape in Holding Cell 6
Porno Manifesto
How to Rape a Straight Guy

Out of print:
NYPD Blood

THE ALICE '65

Kyle Michel Sullivan

KMSCB, Buffalo, NY

Cover design by Jamthecat (©2021)
Photos via Shutterstock
Copyright 2018 by Kyle Michel Sullivan, dba: KMSCB
ISBN: 978-1-7344181-8-7

LIBRARY OF CONGRESS CATALOGING IN PUBLICATION DATA
Sullivan, Kyle Michel (1952-   )
The Alice '65 / by Kyle Michel Sullivan
Buffalo, NY: KMSCB, 2018 | Summary: A book cataloguer is sent to Los Angeles to pick up a rare copy of "Alice's Adventures in Wonderland" from the actress who inherited it, but she wants a favor, first...and turns his world upside down.
LCCN 2018901455 (print) ISBN: 978-0-9970007-5-7 (Hardcover: alk. paper) ISBN: 978-0-6921410-2-1 (Paperback: alk. paper)
ASIN B07C97J14G (ebook)
Romance--Fiction. | Comedy--Fiction. | Farce--Fiction. | Narrative--Fiction
PS3619.U4357 A45 2018
LC record available at https://lccn.loc.gov/2018901455

-- Acknowledgements --
Thanks to Carrie, Dawn, Joanna, Vicki, and Ian for helping me make the book as good and accurate as it can be. Without their assistance, this would just be another story.

Additional thanks to The Depraved Minds Club on GoodReads.com for giving me so much support. They help me keep real.

And a special debt of gratitude to Sir John Tenniel for being so exacting in how his work is presented. Had he not badgered Lewis Carroll into recalling the first impression of *Alice's Adventures in Wonderland*, this book would not exist...at least, not in its current form.

TABLE OF CONTENTS

(About the Author)

— ONE —

Had Adam Verlain known what was planned for him that Monday, he would have stayed home the entire week. But since one never can tell what the day will bring, he dressed in his usual suit and tie, made certain his Oxfords were bright and polished, slipped into his Mackintosh to ward off the morning chill and headed for the train at his normal time of 7:35. His russet hair had been neatened by the monthly visit to his barber, his pleasant face was clean-shaven, his brown-frame glasses were freshly washed, and his black rucksack held a notebook, sandwich, apple, bottle of water and a new copy of Sigrid Undset's *Kristin Lavransdatter* to read on the Underground, all of which gave off the impression that he was still at university and not someone approaching thirty.

He caught the 7:46 at Epping Station, changed for St. Pancras at Liverpool Street, then headed straight for Merryton College, where he was a cataloguer of antiquarian books. His specialty was incunabula and manuscripts in German, Latin and Greek, and while Merryton was neither the oldest nor the best-known university in England, he saw it as the perfect fit for himself. To begin with, it had a good reputation in the liberal arts and sciences. Secondly, their library of rare volumes was in the process of being expanded thanks to the recent addition of one Sir Robert Butterworth to the Board of Governors, who brought with him a tradition of valuing things based on how well they reflected on one's public image...or in this case, the university's. Third and foremost, Merryton had one of the best libraries of research materials on the subject of antiquarian books, anywhere, half of which had yet to be digitized for Internet access. Adam could track down when a particular volume had been written or printed, by whom or for whom, who had first owned it, who its binder was, who its later owners were, when and how often it had sold at auction — everything one might ask for, all without leaving the comfort of his department's building. So far as he was concerned, this was heaven.

Of course, there was one downside to the research library — it allowed him to become so engrossed in his investigations that were someone to ask him a question...well, first they would have to ask it twice, then he would take a moment, look at them with the expression of a curious kitten, remove his glasses, look at them a moment longer and finally say, "Sorry? What was that?" It was as if he had been in a separate world and had to go through a twelve-step process to rejoin this one.

His desk was situated in what was once the school's chapel, a shadow-riven room whose flagstone floor was partially covered by a well-worn Persian carpet and whose wooden ceiling was held in place by four-hundred year-old beams and braces. A wrought-iron candelabrum hung in the center, its electric bulbs twisted into the shapes of little flames that offered the barest illumination. Another fraction of light passed through tall slim windows of colorful leaded glass along two walls. It made more for darkness, true, but Adam loved how it bestowed upon the room a gentle aura of mystery, a feeling marred only by the set of four bland chrome and grey cubicles in the center of it all.

Adam's was number three.

On that Monday he entered at 8:54, as usual, to fire up his computer. He planned an easy start for the day — completing the provenance on a copy of Ludovico Ariosto's *Orlando furioso*. It was a special edition that had been translated into Latin, for some reason, and presented to King Victor Emmanuel in 1866. Adam's research had led him to believe it might actually have been transcribed for Pope Pius IX, who then passed on to the king. If true, that would greatly enhance its historical value, despite the last quire missing a leaf.

Adam had worked on nothing else for three days, spending more time in the basement where the research materials were located than at his desk. When Vincent, the department head, a man with the age and appearance of a Victorian ghost, had learned of this, he had stormed up to Adam, his face almost filled with color.

"We've a dozen books to catalogue with more on the way," the old man had snapped in his harshest headmaster tone, "yet you're still working on this one inconsequential volume?"

Adam had huffed. Granted, the book's red morocco binding was rather ostentatious in its use of gilt and design, but the possibility of a pope having presented it to a king at a time of major political upheaval was more than worth the effort. So he had responded with a simple, "Sir, I have never believed any book to be inconsequential."

Causing Vincent to jolt ramrod straight and snarl down at him, "Nor is this one more consequential than any other waiting to be cataloged. Be done with it." Then he had stormed off.

That was on Friday, last. Adam had already decided he'd dug as deep as he could into the book's history, finding nothing but hints and suggestions about its transfer from pope to king, so if Vincent thought he was ending his research due to his order it was of no consequence. Still he felt he was letting the *Ariosto* down. He picked her up and sighed, "You'd be just the right item for a pope to give a king before a war, so don't think I'm giving up on you; I'll unlock the last of your mysteries, eventually."

He set the book back on his desk and saw his computer was still thinking about waking up, so swiveled in his chair to look around as he rubbed a scrape on his chin, evidence of a rough rugby match with his mates on Saturday. The opposing team had been most emphatic about winning; Adam was happy to say they almost had not.

He stopped turning when he noticed a nearby beam of colorful sunlight illuminating some sparkling dust dancing on the edge of a shadow. This was such a gentle, elegant room, so full of history and wonder; it should have tables and cases of books and manuscripts to boast of, not these hideous blocks of walls in its center. Removing them and putting in a simple row of desks would provide it much more respect.

He was about to make a note for Vincent to suggest as much when Elizabeth, the lovely young woman in cubicle four, swirled in. She removed her coat and slung it over the top of her half-wall, every movement brisk, controlled and beautiful in a slim, blonde, London sort of way. Off came her high heels, which brought her down to Adam's height, and on went a pair of slippers as she said, "Bloody Eurostar; never runs on time when you need it."

"Were you in Paris?"

She held up a Chanel bag. "Weekend. Has Vincent been in, yet?" Then she pulled her hair into a ponytail.

Adam took a deep breath, catching the hint of a garden from her perfume, and shook his head. "You're safe. It's just gone nine."

"Thanks." Then she vanished behind her wall. A moment later, he heard her cry, "Bloody hell, my computer won't wake up."

That is when Adam's computer flashed that it would now allow him access to the database.

"Mine just has," he said. "Took its time."

"But you shut yours down; I let mine sleep."

"Best do a restart."

"Well, Vincent can't say anything if I don't have access to the server." Then she headed for the kitchenette.

Adam smiled, shook his head and turned to his computer to finish with the *Ariosto*. After that, he dove into a copy of Erasmus' *Morias Enkomion*, which had been sitting on the incoming shelf for several days. He broke for tea at 10:55, had his lunch at one and completed the provenance by three, just as his mobile phone chirped a thirty-minute warning of a meeting Vincent had scheduled with him.

He stood and stretched, still a bit sore from Saturday's scrums, then neatened his tie and carried the Erasmus to a short side hall while singing to her, in Greek —

> *I see a book*
> *Who's going to be took*
> *For Jeremy to photograph and put with all the rest.*
> *She's a lovely little book*
> *Who soon will find her nook,*
> *And she will be considered to be one of our best.*

He'd sung the same song to the *Ariosto,* in Latin. It helped make the book feel welcome to her new home.

He took the *Erasmus* into a room they called The Dark Chamber, a smallish square with thick shelves on the walls and two freestanding units in its center. Its bare illumination came from sconces fixed high above and a single oval window of colorful glass up near the ceiling. Here, newly arrived books waited to be archived or photographed, after which they were set on the center shelves for their journey to a climate-controlled vault.

The photography room was down the short hall from The Dark Chamber where a half-punk, half-*Eastenders*, much-tattooed lad named Jeremy had jammed his computer, table, camera, tripod and light kit into a space little larger than Adam's cubicle. He consistently whined about being cramped — which was no surprise, considering he was also four inches taller than Adam — and more than once he'd suggested swapping with The Dark Chamber. But Vincent always refused, making Adam very happy; he loved the room's tender play of dust and light and darkness, like it was wrapping the antiquarian volumes in the safety of shadows and silence. Jeremy would have destroyed that.

5

He placed the *Erasmus* on the *To Be Photographed* shelf then checked his phone to make sure of the time — and that his alarm was still set to remind him of his appointment; he had done it wrong more than once. But it looked all right. In fact he had time for an early cup of tea, so he popped across the hall to a kitchenette. After all, who knew how long this meeting would last?

He set the kettle to going and pulled down his mug — a black one with *A room without books is like a body without a soul (Cicero)* wrapped around it in white lettering. As he filled it, he caught a glimpse of Elizabeth slipping into The Dark Chamber with a neat drop-back box that contained a set of handwritten letters from Henry James to someone in the south of France. He thought it funny she was cataloging them since she had read none of his books.

"I tried *Washington Square*," she'd told him, "but his style is so arch. I prefer Virginia Woolf."

Adam was shocked. "But how could you *not* have read him?"

"Have you read every book in German?" she'd snapped. "Or Greek? Or Latin? Or made prior to 1501?"

"That's not the point, Elizabeth."

"Don't patronize me, Adam. I know Henry James well enough to make even himself sound ill-informed." Then she had worked on the letters all day without another word to him.

He had let it pass because it was now obvious that, while her specialty might be eighteenth through twentieth century literature, she was not a book person. He doubted she ever would be...though he was open to helping her learn...if she were interested.

He pulled down her mug and plopped a bag into it, calling, "Cup of tea, Elizabeth?"

"Tea?" she called back.

"Water's hot. Set in a flash," he said, pouring in hot water.

"Quarter milk, no sugar?"

"Just the way you like it," he said, dolloping milk into both mugs.

"Mmmm...no, thanks," she called back.

Adam froze. He now had two mugs of tea and only time enough to finish one. And they had to be drunk in the kitchenette; to take any sort of food or liquid back to your cubicle raised too great a risk of an irreplaceable book being damaged.

That is when Jeremy popped his head around the door and growled in his happy-puppy way, "Tea? You never make me any."

Adam blinked and responded, "Didn't know you drank it."

"So what about that bloody *Erasmus*? Been on the shelf a week and you're the Greek-meister and — "

"She's set to photograph."

That is when Hakim, their unctuous, fastidious, self-proclaimed office manager, popped in to snap, "The provenance better be right, this time."

Adam huffed. Once, when researching a manuscript copy of Richard Wagner's *Die Nibelungen* for The Arts Council, he'd neglected to put an umlaut over a "U" in his transcription from the German. Never mind it was he who realized it and informed Hakim before the provenance was sent over, the man now acted as if Adam's work was constantly riddled with errors.

Adam meant to respond with an off-hand, *Of course.* Instead he shot Hakim a glare — and noticed Elizabeth passing with a thick volume bound in vellum. He bolted over.

"*Wait, that is* Die Schedelsche Weltchronik," he said, in German. "*The one found in Romania.*"

The book had caused quite a stir around the department — an original *Nuremberg Chronicle* by Hartmann Schedel, created at the end of the fifteenth century and considered the first and most exquisite example of how illustrations could be integrated into printed books. This copy had been discovered in some attic in Bucharest and was being offered to Merryton for sale. Photos had been sent and most of the staff thought it was a legitimate copy, Vincent included.

This had been good enough for Sir Robert, who was more than a little perturbed when Adam insisted the binding did not look original and the photographs were of leafs too easily reproduced. Sir Robert had overruled him and now the book had arrived for consideration.

"*I planned to work on this, tomorrow*," Adam continued, still in German.

"Adam — English," Elizabeth sighed.

He was so used to being reminded he was speaking another language he merely asked, "Why're you taking her? She's outside your area of expertise while mine is perfectly suited — "

"Vincent asked me to," she replied.

"Why would he do that?"

Hakim snorted. "You disagreed with him."

To which Elizabeth added, with acidic sweetness, "And Sir Robert, neither of whom likes being contradicted."

Adam huffed. Sir Robert had also put down a substantial deposit to guarantee the purchase because he felt it was too good an opportunity to pass up. He would not like being made to look foolish, but if the book did turn out to be a later facsimile and not a first impression, she would be worth a fraction of the owner's asking price.

"Elizabeth," Adam said, taking the *Schedel* from her, "you must already see the binding is not contemporary to the book. More like eighteenth-Century, at earliest, and — "

He looked inside and huffed, again.

She had put her initials *EB* on the front endpaper, in soft graphite. It was meant to show by whom the book was catalogued so Jeremy could note it in his log before he shot photos of it; then it was to be carefully erased. But it was not supposed to be done until the book *had* been catalogued.

Adam cast her a glance of reproach then tenderly shifted

to the title page...and saw that he was right; it had been slipped into the volume with such expert care only one tiny crinkle barely showed in the paper. "Here you go; her title page is affixed — "

"Adam," Elizabeth moaned, "it's a thing, not a person."

He cradled the book in one arm and carefully held the page up for her to see what was blatantly obvious, to him. "But look at the base of — "

"Oh, give it here!" she snarled, whipping the *Schedel* closed, clipping his nose with a corner of the front board and making him yelp. She yanked the book away as she snapped, "Hakim's right. Half the time you've got no idea what you're talking about." Then she stormed off.

Jeremy snickered as Hakim glared at Adam, obviously thinking him fully incompetent. This was not to be borne. When he was right about a book, he was right, and he knew a massive mistake was being made.

He strode into The Dark Chamber, aiming for an ancient lift situated in a back corner...and rubbing his nose to keep from sneezing. While the lift was brutally slow and barely large enough for a man and a book cart, it was still the best way down to the research library. But its door and gate were manual and loved to catch your fingers, so one had to take extra care when getting in and out. Still, if the book he needed was down there he'd have no trouble proving his concerns about the *Schedel*, now that he'd looked inside her. So he yanked the lift's door and gate open and —

"Now, Jere, one of those is mine."

He turned to look past the shelving to see Jeremy framed in the doorway with both mugs of tea in hand. His expression was as innocent as the angels on high as he said, "Sorry, duchess. Last I heard, no means no."

"And I'm sure you heard it just last night," Elizabeth sneered, appearing in the doorway with him. "Here, it's my cup."

"Come and take it," he cooed.

Before he could even think to try and stop it, Adam sneezed, causing Jeremy to cast him a sly glance...and a wink...as he backed down to his room. She followed him.

Adam sighed and absently closed the lift's outer door. He was not surprised a woman like Elizabeth would fancy Jeremy. She could look him straight in the eye, when in heels. Plus you never knew what he might do from one moment to the next while the track of Adam's future was straight and obvious till the age of death. Deviation not allowed.

Adam shook his head and closed the inner gate — and it pinched into his left thumb. He yelped and saw he was bleeding, so he pulled a handkerchief from his suit pocket and wrapped it around his finger. He had clean bandages in his rucksack, so he would get one when he came back up. Then he set the lever to basement and started down.

Oh, well, he told himself, *at least the day couldn't get any worse.*

— TWO —

The one drawback to having the research library in the basement was how dark and dreary it could be. Electric lighting had been added a hundred years ago, when the shelves were much fewer, but had not been expanded. That left some corners and side sections in shadows so deep one had to use a portable lantern to see or read the books' labels.

Elizabeth had nicknamed it The Dungeon and hated to go down there for fear of rats or mice. Adam thought she was being too dramatic; he had yet to see evidence of vermin and, besides, they had Henry-Fourteen to handle them, if needed. He was a ginger tomcat named after the thirteen preceding him, and he was always happy to greet one as the lift door opened. Then he would wander off to be content in some dry corner till it was time for his supper.

So as he entered The Dungeon, Adam provided Henry with his ritual scratch and stroke, something he was sure the cat saw as a toll for passage into his domain, then he focused on finding a *Karmann Book Auction Records*. He had noticed a reference to an auction in the year 1958, when preparing to do provenance on the *Schedel,* and the *Karmann* might direct him towards the correct one...if a copy of the book had been offered, that year.

But was it where it should be? No, though that was not

unexpected. Bill, an older archivist in cubicle number two, who always wore jumpers and ate nothing but soup, was in the process of scanning and digitizing the entire library. When not photographing a book, Jeremy was tasked with collecting the volumes Bill wanted, bringing them up to him and then re-shelving them once the man was done — something he did with little enthusiasm. Or ability, if Bill's complaints were not exaggerations.

During a recent conversation between the man and Elizabeth, he had raised the probability that the lad once attended a school for those of *limited intellectual capacities* in Barking or Dagenham or some such place. Adam didn't intend to listen in, but it can be difficult not to hear what's being said when voices in normal tones drift from a cubicle next to yours, and he had to admit that while Jeremy's photographs were excellent he was hardly the brightest when it came to mundane tasks.

Such as re-shelving.

After much searching and using his phone's light on several occasions, Adam found the book he wanted two units down from where it should be. Sure enough, a *Schedel* facsimile had been offered for auction in Spain. *Caballero House*. Aisle twenty-three, around two corners into the darker regions of The Dungeon.

Naturally the one he needed would be on the top shelf, which necessitated the location of a ladder and more use of his phone's light, it was so dark. Then he sorted through the catalogues as if he were digging for gold...and almost heard what he thought could be the soft drifting sound of his name. However, he was too upset at how poorly the catalogues had been handled to pay attention.

Shoved into their holders upside down, backwards and sideways? *Not* acceptable. And just how difficult was it to count? Sixty-two did not come before sixty-one but was after, while sixty came after fifty-nine which came after fifty-seven which came after —

Wait. Where was fifty-eight, the catalogue he needed?

Not in the other upright boxes holding catalogues. Nor was it lying across the top of any others or on the shelf below. Finally, he sensed an irregularity in the darkest shadow at the back of the shelf so shone his phone between them...and could just make out a pamphlet had become jammed behind the rest. He shifted the boxes to free it, careful and easy, and there was *Caballero House*'s 1958 catalogue, its cover half folded over. Meaning it was now permanently creased! That angered Adam. There was no excuse for doing this to a book, not even an auction catalogue. He made a mental note to have a serious discussion with Jeremy about it then did what he could to smooth it over.

This time he did hear a vague and wary, "Adam? Adam?" He cast it aside because now he had his proof, so if anyone needed to speak with him, they could do so upstairs. He jumped down from the ladder and —

"There!" Vincent rushed over to him.

Adam yelped and nearly leapt back up the ladder. But he caught himself, then caught his breath and said, "Oh — Vincent...we...uh...we should revisit that *Schedel* and find out what the seller's trying to — "

"Hakim told me everything about that. Have you been down here all this time?"

"Just a bit," Adam said. "Our meeting's not till half-three."

Vincent's expression grew exasperated. "It's now past four."

"But I set my phone's alarm to remind me." Then Adam looked at it and saw a little bar at the top of the screen flashing, YOU'RE LATE - YOU'RE LATE - YOU'RE LATE. He had inadvertently flicked it to mute when he turned on its light. He grimaced. "Sorry, sir. I...I was just locating information on that Romanian *Liber Chronicarum* and — "

Vincent's exasperation shifted to the purest irritation. "Elizabeth's doing provenance on that. What about the *Ariosto*?"

"It's all set and I've done the *Erasmus*, as well. Jeremy's about to photograph them and — "

"Then you're free."

Adam laughed. "Free? Sir, we've a dozen more — "

Vincent raised his hand to silence him. "Come upstairs," he said, his voice as tight as a violin string. "And please leave the catalogue, there's a good lad; Elizabeth can do her own provenance."

"But she doesn't like to come down here. Rats, you know."

"We don't have rats, Adam, and if we do that is Henry's concern, not yours. Come along."

Adam hesitated, but Vincent was sharp and ramrod straight so he climbed up and slipped the catalogue into its box, with care...then put more in order, they were in such disarray.

"Vincent, if Jeremy is going to re-shelve these items, he should at least learn the alphabet and have some awareness of numeric sequencing."

"Adam! Come!" Vincent's tone suggested he was ready to unleash a slew of refined words meant to slice one down to one's knees with gentle contempt, so Adam huffed, sorted two more catalogues, then jumped down and let the man lead him away like a trained dog.

The path they took back to the lift was more direct but entailed heading down a narrow side hall with some ceiling pipes that were so low even Adam had to duck to avoid them.

Vincent did not look at him as he asked, "When did you use your passport, last?"

Adam had to think about it before saying, "Three years ago. When you sent me to *The New York Public Library*."

He had gone to review a collection they had received as a donation. The donor had wanted an independent evaluation of it for tax purposes, but he had not liked the value determined by the local dealer the library had engaged. They had reached out to The Arts Council UK who, on Vincent's recommendation, had asked

Adam to do the job. Adam had balked at the idea of travelling, but Vincent had insisted.

"I want us to work more closely with The Arts Council," he had said, "and to refuse this commission would not be the best option."

So Adam had reluctantly gone...and found the collection to be nice, though nowhere near what the donor thought its value to be. Until he discovered a complete Samuel Johnson's *London: A Poem* tipped into the back of a rather worn copy of the man's dictionary. With annotations in Johnson's hand! Those few pages had doubled the value of the collection, so the donor had been pleased, the library had been pleased, The Arts Council had been pleased, and what was best — Vincent had allowed himself to smile.

So as they neared the tiny lift, Adam continued with, "I had to get an emergency issuance. I didn't have one and — "

"Then it's valid and you've been to The States," Vincent said in too-cool a voice. "Care to go, again?"

Adam huffed. "God, no. New York was madness. I was almost struck by two taxis, a lorry and four bike messengers as I was crossing Fifth Avenue. With the signal."

"You'd be off to Los Angeles, this time."

Adam knew the city was big and wide and open but still had to ask, "Is it saner than Manhattan?"

"Doubtful," said Vincent. "But we've acquired a book and — "

Adam gasped, jolted up — and slammed his head against a low pipe. He yelped, in pain.

"Careful, there," said Vincent, more perturbed than concerned.

Adam nodded and before he could even think to silence himself blurted out, "Is she *The Alice Sixty-five*?"

Near color exploded across Vincent's face as he stormed up to Adam. "Who told you about that!?"

Adam took a step back, regained his breath and rubbed

his head a bit, for all the good it did. "I...I just heard. Heard someone..."

That *someone* being Jeremy, who had found out an extremely rare 1865 copy of *Alice's Adventures in Wonderland* was being offered for sale to Merryton. He had whispered the possibility to Elizabeth, a fortnight back, like a lover cooing in her ear. Had she been a book person she might have reacted with more interest instead of merely saying, "When it arrives I'll take care of it, like I did the *Appleton* printing."

That was just after Jeremy had taken a surprise photo of Adam working on a fine edition of Blake's *Albion*. "For the webpage," he'd said. Which was irritating because Adam had been lost in one of his research journeys and hadn't been given a chance to so much as comb his hair. What made it more-so was, Jeremy had then taken one of Bill, carefully posed and holding a cup of soup in the kitchenette...though that was not the least bit unusual; Bill did love his soups.

Vincent calmed himself, straightened to his full height, careful to keep between two low pipes, and said, "I wanted it kept quiet till the book was here. There's a bloody Australian after it, now, and he's been more than adamant."

"Christopher Meillon," Adam snorted.

Vincent glared down at him and snarled, "It's a pity the provenance isn't as detailed as the gossip in this organization."

"No, sir, that's my conjecture," said Adam. "I read where he was seeking one for his collection. Not because she's a book but because she's rare and expensive, and *he likes things like that*. I thought it would be a travesty if he got one."

Vincent almost smiled. "On that, we agree. Did you know he actually contacted Sir Robert and offered to pay us not to accept it?"

"No, sir, but I'm not surprised. Some people have far too much money."

"How he knew we were in negotiations is...well, quite troubling. Fortunately for us, Sir Robert ignored him. Now the paperwork's been signed and it's ours. Done and dusted."

"Oh." Adam felt vaguely dizzy so it took him a moment to continue. "Sir, are we certain about this?"

"Adam..." And Vincent's voice carried a warning.

"But I'm always leery when some person discovers a book worth two million pounds in their attic and — "

"Casey Blanchard is not *some person*," Vincent shot back. Adam's confusion regarding her was obvious in his expression, so Vincent continued with, "You have seen *Ilithium Four*?"

Adam jolted back and banged his head on the same pipe. In the exact same spot. Tears filled his eyes.

Vincent all but growled, "Adam, please, we're still trying to get funding to have the pipes redirected."

Which had been on the agenda since before Vincent was born.

Adam made no reply. He had avoided the film because the book it was based on was a lovely 1980s reimagining of von Grimmelshausen's seventeenth century novel, *Simplicius Simplicissimus*, into a futuristic world in a distant galaxy. He bore no interest in witnessing the desecration of a now-classic work of science fiction.

His dislike of the film must have colored his expression, because Vincent gave him an arched smile and continued with, "Purist, are we? I'll lend you my copy to watch on the plane."

"I hardly think I'd want to — "

"As you will be en route to meet a young lady who was the lead actress in the film," Vincent said, his voice lowering to an icy tone, "some of us would consider it good manners to be able to discuss her work with her." He continued towards the lift. "Do you have a portable DVD player?"

"My laptop, sir," Adam muttered, following him. His head still hurt and he could already feel the beginning of a knot, but far worse had been done to him whilst playing rugby so...

Vincent nodded. "As for the book you are to collect, it

was bequeathed to her by her grandfather, not *found in an attic*. I've seen numerous photos of it, inside and out, so I am certain it's a true first impression. Is that acceptable?"

No, it wasn't, but after the back and forth about the *Schedel* Adam knew it did no good to argue with Vincent when he was as tight as this. Instead, he said, "Sir, wouldn't it be better to send Elizabeth? It's her area, and I'm certain *she's* seen the film."

Vincent stopped just as they reached the lift but did not look back at him. "It — it would be just another book to her, as we both know. Is that really what you want?"

"No, but...but you know what that book means to me."

Vincent let out a heavy sigh as he said, "Yes, and I wish I could send someone else. But you...you understand the importance of this acquisition, and you would treat her with the reverence she deserves."

"If you want reverence, send Hakim."

Vincent shot Adam a look of pure incredulity. "Are you mad? It would take him a month to plot out his journey, despite the itinerary already being settled, and do *not* suggest Jeremy; he would trumpet this from the rooftops and we prefer everything be done with as little fuss as possible, and at once, while Bill would panic at the thought of not having his soup for one day."

"But, sir — "

"Adam, I understand," Vincent said, his tone growing gentle, "and I would make the journey, myself, but my...my doctor has prohibited me from flying. I am sorry to force it upon you but I...I believe the book is in a Solander case, and you know what those can be like. So go. Get the *Alice* and bring her straight back. You needn't — you needn't even stay the night. Your itinerary's on your desk."

"Vincent, please..."

"It's already settled," Vincent snapped, his voice tight, again. "Ticket's in your name and to change it would be prohibitive, in cost." He put on a smile he did not feel. "But once you've turned the book over, you're free till Monday."

He opened the lift and stepped inside. Adam hesitated then followed him in, closed the door and the gate — and almost caught his thumb, again.

Vincent eyed the bloody handkerchief as he said, "Have a bit more care." He shifted the lever to the ground floor then, as the lift slowly lifted them up, added in a voice that was far too cheerful, "Supposed to be a lovely weekend. You're involved with that girl in I-T — Nora, isn't it?"

Adam shook his head, which was a mistake because it made him feel a bit nauseous. But it kept him from telling Vincent he was behind the times by two years. And a month. And three days. Well...at four twenty-two it would be three days. And that was still three minutes away. Not that Adam was paying attention.

"She's no longer with Merryton, sir."

The man looked at him. "Oh? But aren't you sharing a flat?"

"Not anymore."

"Oh. Well. Young people are always breaking up and getting back together. You come from Epping, right? Why not invite Nora to stroll the forest? Or take her down to Brighton? Go bathing on the beach, at Hove. See if you can rekindle things."

"She's married and about to have a child," Adam murmured, a headache building, part from his collision with the pipes, part from memories of Nora and part from his upcoming journey. "As for the beach," he continued, "I, um, I avoid it. Why go if you can't swim?"

That finally removed Vincent's forced smile. "Oh. Yes. Why go anywhere, then?"

"That's always been my thought, sir," Adam said, his voice soft as a shadow. "And you know why."

Vincent grimaced and said no more.

— THREE —

Adam did not merely dislike the idea of travelling, he hated the thought of leaving London. He was comfortable here, understood how the city worked and felt safe. In New York it had been as if he had traveled to another planet, not just another part of civilization. But Vincent seemed certain the journey would be easy and straightforward, so Adam determined he could tolerate it for a day.

He planned to wear a suit on the flight, but his mother talked him into a nice shirt, neat trousers, loafers instead of Oxfords, and a light jacket. She had been to Los Angeles so convinced him by saying, "They consider this upscale form."

"If I put a tie with it..." he said, still not quite convinced.

"Adam, you said you're not leaving the terminal."

Adam nodded. "They're bringing the *Alice* to me, there."

"Then casual is best and looks smart on arrival. When *do* you arrive?"

"Just before two pm. The flight back is just after nine."

"That's a long time at the airport."

"I've got my laptop and Vincent lent me an adaptor. And there's my book. I suspect they even have food, drink, and most of all — security. Just what you'd want with two-million pounds in your rucksack." He paused then sighed. "Maybe if Da'd had security..."

"Adam," his mother whispered, "what's done is done." Then she continued in a normal voice, "Too bad you won't see any of the town. Los Angeles is lovely. Haven't been there since the Olympics, but I'm sure it hasn't changed so much."

He smiled at her. "I'll post you a card."

She dropped him off to Heathrow, the next morning, and he was soon ensconced in a more-space seat on the aisle. A pleasant punk couple named Julie and Manny Marshe-Croton sat beside him with their punk toddler, who smiled like an angel under his blue-spiked hair but had dark eyes filled with danger. Julie and Manny were tattooed, pierced, of neon-green hair, on the larger side...and had bubbling personalities, which put Adam at ease. David, his oldest brother, had gone snarly punk for a while and was quite the terror when Adam was twelve. Only later did he admit his version was more a middle class way *to bed the birds who love a bad lad but won't marry one.* Now he was about to have his tenth anniversary and third child, so his hair was cut short, his shirts had collars and his pants had belts instead of braces.

Adam half-smiled at the memory then settled in, his aging MacBook resting in his rucksack, atop his lap, and Vincent's DVD of *Ilithium Four* in hand. He was still not at all sure about his mission, but as he had said to himself consistently since being shanghaied into the trip, "It's for the *Alice.*"

Then a flight attendant touched him on the shoulder and said, "Excuse me, sir, you'll need to put those things under the seat in front of you. Doors are closed and we're about to taxi out. And please fasten your seat belt."

He nodded to her and smiled to the punk child next to him, who smiled even more sweetly. Then Adam bent down to slip his rucksack under the seat —

And the brat vomited on his back!

Adam yelped and bolted up, bent over like an old man, and was about to rise when another flight attendant raced up and held his head down.

"Don't," she cried. "You'll get it all over and we're on a twelve-hour flight, and it already smells something awful! Remove your jacket."

"How?" he cried back. She was holding his head practically between her knees, not exactly the most appropriate position to be in. Or comfortable.

"Hold out your arms," she said. "Go on! Straight out!"

He did as she asked, taking sort of a diving position. The first flight attendant scurried over to awkwardly roll the jacket up his back and over his head so it could be pulled off by using the sleeves. Then she shoved it in a white bin bag and said, "Much better," as the first one mopped up the little that had spilled.

That is when a male attendant called over the intercom, "Please stay in your seats! We're taxiing!"

The second attendant patted Adam's arm and said, "We'll clean it best we can and return it to you once we're airborne. Now buckle up."

He nodded and sat, casting the punk child a wary look and receiving a joyous smile in return.

Julie leaned over, also smiling. "Sorry, Sweets. It's his first plane ride and his tummy's weak." Then she tickled the little beast and did a singsong of, "But we're going on the *Hollywood Death Tour*, going on the *Hollywood Death Tour*, going on the *Hollywood Death Tour*, right, Sweets? Get your tummy toughened."

The child gave a wicked laugh.

Adam forced a smile then buckled up and settled in, using one of his Mother's karmic mantras to try for calm.

I prefer to live with ease.
Stress is no one's friend.
If I smile it brings me joy.
Breathe and breathe, again.

Which helped in no way. So he just closed his eyes as the

pilot came over the intercom to say, "Attendants, please be seated. We're cleared for takeoff."

Moments later, the jet turned, the engines whined to full throttle, and they started down the runway —

And the brat let loose in his lap.

****

Julie and Manny were very apologetic — and embarrassed, once they learned Adam had brought no extra clothing beyond a pair of briefs and socks, and those only at his mother's insistence.

"I'm not staying," he had told her, "so why would I need an overnight bag?"

"Just a change and some toiletries," was her reply. "You never know what might happen. Flight gets canceled. Delayed. Earthquake. On impulse, you decide you love LA and want to live there forever."

"When have I ever been impulsive?"

"Adam," she'd sighed, then she had stuffed the briefs and socks into his rucksack, and the look on her face had dared him to remove them. Now he was glad he hadn't.

Fortunately, the Marshe-Crotons had done carry-on; so they lent him hole-riven jeans and a shirt with a frayed British flag as its breast pocket. Unfortunately, Adam was three sizes smaller and five inches shorter than Manny, so they also lent him a set of braces to hold the jeans up. Then Julie wrote their home address on the back of her business card so he could return them, once they were done with their death tour.

The moment the flight was at cruising altitude, he used the lavatory to clean up and shoved his soiled clothes into the same bag as his jacket, then he made certain it was tied good and tight. When he got back to his seat, he saw Julie had moved next to him and the brat, now referred to as Dumpling, was seated on the other side of Manny...and was still smiling at Adam with his wicked eyes.

Adam ignored him and focused on the front of Julie's card to find she did henna tattoos — or *Mendhi*, her preferred term. They had a nice chat about its history, which extended over lunch, then she managed to convince him painting a design on his left hand would be fun.

She had little baggies of both henna and jaguar mixtures in her purse, like she was planning to decorate a cake, so squeezed thin lines of each on the top of his hand and used a tiny brush to work up a gleaming mandala with half the face of a peaceful wolf worked into the design.

"Lovely skin," she murmured as she worked. "Tight. Unblemished. On the pale side but that enhances the look."

"It's brilliant," Adam said when she was done. "Almost three dimensional."

"It will be once it's had a chance to cure. Careful not to smudge it before it's dried."

"Does the design have a meaning?"

"Awareness and adventure."

"Brilliant. And so quickly done."

"It's me living," said Julie. "Fairs. Streets. Run down the Brighton Pier wherever we feel like. Manny's the sales pitch; I'm the slave-labor." She winked and pointed to her Facebook address on her business card. "I post our schedule on there."

"You do well with this?"

"Well enough. I'm in Los Angeles to buy more mixtures. We're staying at The London. Swing by; I'll do the other hand. No charge."

Adam grinned and said, "I'm turning straight around, but thanks."

She shrugged and laid back to get a nap as he plugged in his ear buds and prepared himself to face the movie.

Adam had read *Simplicius Simplicissimus* during his first

24

year at university. In the original German. The story began with the Thirty Years War, which cut Germany's population by two-thirds and orphaned Simplicius. He grew up living with a hermit then traveled to France, Russia and a world inhabited by mermen, having mercenary adventures and heartbreak and sadness and joy along the way before finally becoming a hermit, himself.

The science fiction update split his character into male and female, which Adam had thought worked well-enough. Mar-Lee, the female, was the brains of the story as well as its heart; Creggan was the arrogant princely son of the controlling family on Ilithium 4, who was versed in the art of strategy and war. He dismissed Mar-Lee as being beneath him even though she proved herself smarter and more capable than he on many occasions.

After the story established their lives, corporate raiders from a neighboring star system attacked the family and their workers in order to take over the planet's resources. Their battles were fierce, but soon it was obvious they had lost, so Mar-Lee saved Creggan by knocking him unconscious and escaping the planet with him at the end of book one. In book two, they had a series of adventures across the galaxy, learning even more about how to fight before returning to their home world, ready to destroy those who had destroyed their loved ones. But then Creggan was killed in a battle with the raiders that nearly destroyed the planet, so in book three a weary Mar-Lee abandoned her past and wandered the stars to find understanding, only to see naught but more war and destruction before finally returning to Ilithium 4 to live out her life, alone.

The first half-hour of the film stayed true to the story until the raiders arrived and war began. The girl playing Mar-Lee as an adolescent was just right, as was the boy playing Creggan, though he was presented as more heroic and less foolish than in the book. Adam was hopeful.

Then they cut to Mar-Lee as a young woman, appearing out of billowing flames and wrapped in a protective cloak. She threw it back to reveal a face that would have caused Helen of

Troy to weep with envy. Sharp green eyes atop elegant cheekbones framed by short raven hair made her the personification of the warrior female, and her gaze told one and all she was a force no one could control. She stood still, for a moment, glaring around her, then went into battle mode.

Kung Fu-fighting battle mode.

Mixed with a healthy dose of *Resident Evil* gunfire, stunts meant to be spectacular, explosions worthy of a *Marvel Comics* superhero film, beautiful choreography, and slow motion bits as her cape danced elegantly behind her — the epitome of an Amazon Queen slaughtering her enemies.

The fight was all but over when a squad of rag-tag men burst onto the scene, led by Creggan, a big, buff, towering figure of perfect masculinity under flowing white-blond hair. Even Thor in all his majesty would have seemed like a gnome in comparison.

And what great comment did he make upon arrival? What soaring rhetoric did he offer? What wondrous words danced from his lips?

"You've been busy."

Mar-Lee looked around at him, barely out of breath, a tiny trail of blood from a single cut gliding oh-so-elegantly down her exquisite face, almost like a tear, and she asked, "What took you so long?"

To which he replied, "Traffic was a bitch."

Adam stopped the DVD, about ready to do as Dumpling Marshe-Croton had done. Apparently they had jumped to the middle of the second volume, slashing out the years Mar-Lee and Creggan had roamed the universe, all to keep the story focused on the fighting.

He would have left the movie at that point except for one small problem — a certain little beast had crawled across his sleeping father and over his sleeping mother to watch the video, even though he couldn't hear it, and had fallen asleep on Adam's lap. While rather inappropriate, Adam shrugged it off because it reminded him of his father's Jack Russell Terrier, Albacore, who would do the same thing when he was caught up in a book. So he carefully got his satchel, pulled out his copy of *Kristen Lavransdatter*, settled in, and would have been quite content.

Except Dumpling woke up, saw he had stopped the film and looked at him with those dark dangerous eyes.

"But you can't hear it," said Adam.

Dumpling's eyes did not waver, so Adam re-started the movie and let him have the ear-buds. The little monster watched about five minutes of it then fell asleep, again. So Adam turned it off, again.

And Dumpling woke up. Again. And looked at him.

Adam wound up running the film all the way through, twice, forcing himself to endure the silent image of Mar-lee and Creggan becoming lovers — something *else* that was *not* in the book, since both of them were only fifteen at that point in the story — but which kept Dumpling asleep. Until Adam felt something wet and warm trail into his lap and discovered someone was in training pants and still wet his bed. A lot. And since Adam was his bed...

This time the Marshe-Crotons had to lend him a full set of everything, and the flight crew made him sit on a rubbish bag for the second half of the journey, just to be safe. He also made certain another bag stayed between him and Dumpling.

So when Adam got off the plane, a jagged striped Polo shirt with a rat-nibbled collar hung on his torso, a pair of Manny's jeans — that looked like oversized clown pants with carefully shredded holes stripped in lines every few inches — whispered around his legs, and his simple black socks and loafers were so conspicuously wrong, he was certain he looked like a *Monty Python* version of a Scally-boy on holiday. He was now regretting not taking his mother's advice to the point of bringing his entire wardrobe; then he would not have been faced with passengers and customs officers looking away to smirk.

As if that wasn't enough, when he wandered up the ramp into the neon-style arrivals lobby of the international terminal —

his rucksack slung over one shoulder, his Mandala hand gripping its strap, the white bin bag containing his filthy clothes in his other hand — he saw people hanging over the wall above him holding signs and calling to those they knew, and more than a few pointed and snickered as he passed.

Once he reached the lobby, he looked around. And looked around. And looked around. Then he noticed an older woman by a window. She had what his mother would refer to as a handsome face, was about fifty, had dark hair that was cut medium-short and streaked with silver, and carried the floating stylishness of a Sixties Flower Child. She was focused on her iPhone, like a teenager, and held a sign reading *ADAM VERANE*.

Upside down.

He crossed to her and asked, "Is that supposed to be me?"

She blinked, looked him over with careful eyes and shook her head. "I'm waitin' for an Englishman," she said in a voice that carried a soft Texas drawl.

"I'm from London. Does that count?"

She took a couple of steps back to give him an even harsher look of appraisal. "You're Adam Verane?"

"Verlain, but I suppose it's close enough."

She shook her head. "Not for me. Got ID?"

He pulled his passport from a rucksack pocket to show her.

She eyed it and shook her head even more firmly. "Okay, this guy don't look like *Popeye*."

Adam was not about to comment on the absurdity of comparing himself to *Popeye*, so he just said, "I have more documents from Vincent."

He squatted to pull a folder from his rucksack then offered up his letter of introduction.

The woman looked at it and gave a sigh larger and longer and deeper than any he had ever heard as she said, "Oh, Casey."

"So I am who I am?" he asked, rising.

"And that's all who you am," she nodded.

"But you — you're not Casey Blanchard."

She smiled and chirped, "Good call, since I'm Patricia."

"Is she on her way here?"

Her smile became a confused frown. "Honey, she's at home."

"Oh. Then you have the book."

"No, I just came to pick you up. Casey'll give it to you."

"Give it to me? How?"

"At home."

"Home?"

"Yes. *Where the heart is*? You know that phrase?"

"Leave the airport?" Adam gulped. "Can't...can't...can't she bring it to me, here?"

"Why should she?"

"Well...that's what I was led to expect," he said. "I...I'm due to leave on the nine-oh-five and — "

"Oh, I don't think so."

Adam blinked, taken aback. "Sorry, but I...I have an itinerary."

He showed it to her. Her frown deepened as she glanced between it and him a dozen times. Then she shrugged and said, "Still gotta go get it."

"Is there no other way?" She shook her head. He looked at his watch; it was past two. He hated to leave the airport but asked, "Is it far?"

"Just 90210."

Which was not an answer. "Have we time?" he asked.

Patricia's smile grew wicked. "The way I drive?"

****

The way Patricia drove was like a Formula One pro

handling the racecourse on the tiny curving streets of Monte Carlo. She whipped and wove her Tesla convertible around cars and trucks and limousines and pedestrians and seagulls as they raced down Century Boulevard and passed under the 405 to spin around to the access road (on two wheels) then zoom right at the fork to swoop over the hill to La Cienega. Adam was so focused on holding on for dear life, he barely registered the sky was a soft cloudless shade of brown and the mountains had a distinctly blue-gray hue to them.

"So is that the latest London style?" Patricia asked as she shoved her way in front of a Humvee and hit the brakes to avoid slamming into the rear of a sedan. "The clothes? The tattoo?"

Since they didn't stop until they were close enough to see the driver in front of them had dandruff, it took Adam a moment to give her an answer. "It — it's just — just Mendhi...um, henna ink."

"It's lovely."

"Thanks." He cringed as she all but rammed between two cars and pulled in front of a semi...that had to brake to keep from rear-ending her. "The clothes are, um, the child in the seat next to mine had a sensitive stomach. I borrowed these from his parents." Then he jolted. "Oh, since we're out and about, have I time to give mine a wash?" He held up the bag.

"Dry cleaner can have 'em back, in the mornin'."

"But I told you, I'm leaving on the nine-oh-five."

Patricia changed lanes to follow a motorcycle. "I say somebody's got somethin' wrong someplace."

"What? No! No, it's on my ticket."

"Bet you there's a typo," she sing-songed at him then hit the brakes to keep from slamming into the back of a delivery truck before absently adding, "But we got a washer and dryer at the hacienda."

"If — if you don't mind my using them."

"If you know how. Maid's not in till Thursday, and you need a PhD in computer science to work the damn things."

A chirping sound came from the middle of the car. Patricia glanced at the display to see who it was from, let a charming smile cross her lips and touched an earpiece as she drove even faster.

"Gotta get this," she said. "Won't be a sec." Then she continued, oh-so-sweetly. "It's Patricia. ... Oh, hellooooo. ... Yes, I figured you'd call back. ... No, honey. ... Honey, it don't work that way. If you do publish those photos we will sue you from here to China. And maybe you'll win and maybe you won't, but you will have one nasty legal bill 'fore it's over and no judge'll give you a penny in expenses by the time we're done. ... All right, if you insist. But you should know we've already put out the word, and the market's shuttin' down on you. Publish those photos and it's no more access to Casey Blanchard. I hope I'm makin' myself clear." She listened for a moment, the charming smile still on her face. "Great, honey. Glad you finally see reason. Buh-bye." She disconnected, all but growling, "Oh, God, that was better than a massage by Zac Ephron," then noticed Adam was looking at her with vague horror.

"Just to let you know," she said to him, now speeding down a wide avenue at twice the speed of sound, "this dick with a thousand millimeter lens took pictures of Casey swimmin' in the privacy of her backyard. In the middle of the night. Butt naked. He thought he'd make us buy 'em back or sell 'em to the European tabloids. Didn't work that way." Then she hit the gas even harder so she could sneak ahead of another convertible and zoom through a light that was just turning red.

All Adam managed to say was, "Rather obviously."

Patricia laughed. "I didn't come across too strong?"

He gulped. "No, you were — were quite pleasant."

"Good. I figure, if you're gonna destroy a body you should at least be nice about it." Then she cast a glance over him and cooed, "No matter how much fun it is."

Adam didn't bother with a response.

— FOUR —

Twenty minutes later, they turned off Sunset Boulevard to travel down a road lined by towering palm trees and thick dramatic shrubbery to an estate fronted by a vine-draped adobe wall that ran a hundred feet along the street and had a gated entrance at one end. As it opened, they passed two lean young men watching them, one with a camera, one with a video recorder, both leaning against a motorbike.

Adam looked back at them as Patricia pulled through the gate. She noticed and smiled. "Her own private paparazzi."

"They just sit there?" He asked. "All day? Waiting for Miss Blanchard to appear? Seriously?"

Patricia laughed. "Honey, who do you think she is?"

They sped up a curved driveway protected by evergreen trees and lined with low ivy-draped barriers to approach a long, pleasant, two-story Spanish-style house done in white stucco walls and clay tile roof. They stopped before arched double-doors of deep mahogany, simple in their design but projecting strength and, to be honest, more than a little condescension.

As he got out of the car, Adam looked around to take it in...and to give himself time to regain his footing on solid earth. The grounds were perfectly sculpted to feel warm and inviting while whispering leaves gave off an air of gentle isolation that he found quite appealing.

"It's like Epping Forest planted in the midst of London,"

he murmured. "Nothing around for miles and miles — merely everything."

Patricia led him inside to an open foyer that separated the house into two wings. The floor was terra-cotta, the ceiling arched high, and to his right were French doors of dark wood and beveled glass revealing a sitting room of modern elegance, all in earth tones. Huge framed mirrors flanked them and on the wall above hung two paintings done in a Giorgio de Chirico style. To his left was a heavy oak door at the base of a staircase that ascended to an open walkway, which joined the two sides. Plants of every size, shape and color filled spaces not taken by heavy tables, haunting sepia-tone photographs and nick-knacks of every possible style.

The foyer led under the walkway to more double-doors that opened into a space filled with comfortable couches, low tables and thick carpets atop a colorful Spanish tile floor, all of it focused on a genial stone fireplace. A small bar was nestled between that and a tight stairway that wound up and around the chimney. Another dark door was on the other side of the bar, beneath the stairway's landing, and the wall across from it had built-in shelves containing all manner of books. Translucent curtains were drawn across a massive window that looked out over a back yard that was even more garden-like than the front, pool included, of course. Dozens of potted plants made the room feel very cozy.

"It's like a dream," Adam murmured as he took it all in.

Patricia headed straight to the bar, saying, "Coffee? Tea? Shot of vodka?"

Adam just smiled and said, "No, thank you," as he let himself be drawn to the wall of books. "I'm tired and rather hungry. Not a good combination."

"Didn't they feed you on the plane?"

"Yes, but I'm the English breakfast sort."

"I could whip you up something."

"No, thank you," Adam said, already lost in the library. "I'll grab supper at the airport. Is the book in here?"

Patricia mixed a Tequila Sunrise, albeit with gin, as she said, "No, it — uh, it's somewhere else. In a box."

Adam let his fingers drift over the books as he asked, "Box?"

"Yeah. For protection."

"A Solander Case. Yes, Vincent mentioned it." Then he hummed as he continued with, "Oh, aren't we some lovelies?"

Patricia stopped and looked at him. "You talk to books."

Adam glanced at her, his face open and happy as he said, "Hmm? Oh, right." He chuckled. "They're my life."

"I like reading, too." She held up a small tablet. "I'm on Molly Ivins. Hometown girl, so..."

Adam looked at her and gave a gentle nod. "My mother has one of those, as do my brothers and sister. I prefer the feel of an actual book." He saw the Barnes & Noble limited edition of Kate Chopin's *The Awakening* and pointed to her. "May I?" he asked.

Patricia shrugged. "Sure, honey."

He reached into the back to pull the book out a little then gripped the sides to draw her from the row of other volumes, so very gentle as he said, "Have you seen her?"

"Seen who?" Patricia asked, watching him as she sipped her drink.

He slid the book from the slipcase to look inside, intense and tender, saying, "The *Alice* — um, *Alice's Adventures in Wonderland*."

"Oh, right," Patricia said, "Casey's book. Flipped through it on the crapper. Sure don't look like much."

"Crapper?" he asked, focused on the *Chopin*.

"Yeah, that thing where you take a dump."

Adam jolted then scurried over to her, the Chopin still open in his hands, his voice cracking as he said, "She kept her by the toilet!?"

"Don't listen to my mother. She messes with people."

Adam jumped and looked up to see Casey Blanchard

leaning against a bannister, next to the chimney...and he froze. In the film his main quibble with her in the role had been that she was far too beautiful to play Mar-Lee. Creggan would never have treated her with contempt, as he did, but instead would have been doing everything he could to make her his mate...as he finally did get around to, in the movie. But when she drifted down the stairs — wearing a peasant blouse, cut-offs and sandals, chestnut hair whispering soft behind her, deliberate confidence and poise emanating from her, no makeup, clear skin and a form suitable for any portrait of Diana — Adam saw that minimizing her beauty would have been an impossible task, because the only thing that kept her from being perfect was a touch of sadness in her eyes.

Before he had a chance to fully appreciate who he was looking at, Patricia drew his focus back to her by caressing his chin and saying, "I only mess with boys and only if they're cute."

"Sorry?" Adam asked, looking at her, lost.

Patricia just smiled and said, "Nothin'."

"So you're her mother?" Adam whispered.

"Didn't I mention that?" Patricia whispered back. "I'm also her entourage and guard dog. So be warned." Then she chomped at him.

Adam heard Casey sigh her own warning of, "Mom."

He hesitated, blushed, then returned his gaze to Casey to say, "Miss...Miss Blanchard, it's so nice to meet you. I'm...I'm Adam Verlain."

Casey gave him a cool look of appraisal, noticed his hand was extended and politely touched it as she said, "It's Casey. Vincent told us about you."

Patricia snarled a chuckle as she said, "No, he told me, and I told you, and you told me to tell him to tell us when Adam was comin', which he did and I did, and we misspelled his name."

"I called it from the e-mail, Mom," Casey replied as she walked around Adam, inspecting him.

He turned to keep her in view, closing the *Chopin* as he said, "Um, I...I've seen *Ilithium Four*. You — you were quite good in it. Captured the idea of Mar-Lee — "

"You're sweet," said Casey. "Don't move."

He hesitated then stood still as Casey continued to circle him. "It, um, it was a curious choice to make as a film," he said, "considering the depth and richness of the language and life it depicted and — "

"It made a billion bucks," she said, then added, "You're not exactly what I expected."

"Sorry?" He blinked, then grimaced. "Ah, yes-yes-yes, the clothes. They're not mine nor do I enjoy wearing them, but it's a long story and — "

"It's okay," Casey said, turning to her mother. "Orisi."

Patricia touched her earpiece and said, "Call the madman."

Adam glanced between them. "Sorry? I...I don't understand."

"You gotta change," Casey said. "Can't have you look like this."

"Of course. I just need to give my clothes a wash — "

"No. For tonight."

He blinked. "Tonight?"

"If you'd come in a suit, I might've let you wear that. But you didn't, so..."

He backed away from her, fumbling as he returned the *Chopin* to her case then put her back on the shelf. "Wait-wait-wait, there's been a mistake. My name is Adam Verlain and I'm, uh, I'm here to collect a book and return to London and — "

"I know," Casey said, "but it's in a safe deposit box — "

"That's the box I meant," Patricia chirped. "They're Solanders, in England." Then she said into the phone, "Orisi. Patricia. Call me, honey."

"No-no-no-no-no-no," Adam said, "this is not right — "

Casey focused on him, saying, "Adam, your plane got in too late to get the book and no way was I getting it out till you were here, and since tonight's the premier I figured — "

"No, there...there's been a mistake," he said. His head was beginning to pound and his stomach was NOT happy. "My...my return flight leaves at nine-oh-five, tonight, and I have to check in three hours before. I have an itinerary and we've arranged with customs to handle the import, at Heathrow, and — "

Casey cut him off by gliding up to him and putting a finger to his lips, soft and easy, then she said, "Mom."

Patricia nodded and tapped her earpiece and said, "Call Vincent."

"Vincent?" Adam said. "But I — he said I wasn't to stay over. I could go straight back. I wasn't even to leave the terminal."

Casey eyed Adam, wary. "Why would he say that?"

Adam rubbed his forehead and fought a fear that his insides were about to do a Dumpling all over Casey's carpets. He was supposed to have remained in the safe arms of airport security with his valuable cargo till he returned to London and was back in the comfort of his routine, all by supper, tomorrow, but now he was being told he was expected to remain in a city he didn't know doing God only knew what? It was all so wrong.

He barely noticed Patricia watching him, a smile on her lips that screamed she was about to raid the cookie jar. She slipped over to Adam, all but purring, "Casey, why *not* keep him like this?"

That made him notice her. He backed away like a skittish kitten.

Patricia continued with, "He's got a nice form, and this'd be an interestin' style choice. Just spike his hair a bit and get rid of these."

She snapped the suspenders off his shoulders. The jeans dropped halfway down his hips to reveal the elastic band of Manny's FTLs. Adam jolted back from her then tripped over the couch to slam to the floor and clip his head on the hearth. His world shattered focus as he bounced onto his side; for a moment he wondered if he was going to pass out.

From a thousand miles away he heard Casey scream. "Oh-my-god! Adam!"

Blood trailed across his face and splattered onto the Spanish tile, next to his glasses, and the only thought that came to him was, *I hope this doesn't stain.*

Then Casey was kneeling beside him. She pressed her fingers against the cut in his head and wailed, "You're bleeding! Mom, get a towel. Get some ice."

A clean wet rag appeared in Casey's hand and she held that against the cut. He could hear Patricia's voice echoing, "Adam, I am so sorry. I wasn't thinkin', and I'm used to guys knowin' I'm just playin' with them and — and are you thinkin'? You didn't crack your brain open, did you?"

He was unable to formulate an intelligent response to such a ludicrous question. His eyes were still shivering and unsure when Patricia knelt behind him, shoved Casey's hand aside and pressed a towel packed with ice over the cut, hard and fast. He yelped in pain and pushed her away.

"Sorry," he muttered as he took the ice and gently held it to the cut. "I — I'll be all right. Just...just give me a moment."

He started to get up but Casey held him down. "Stay put. We'll call EMS and — "

"No. No, please, I — I'm fine. I'll be fine. Thanks. Just — I just want to sit up."

Casey guided him into a sitting position as Patricia waved her hand up in front of his face, asking, "Are you sure your brain's not scrambled? Can you tell me how many fingers?"

He sighed and held up three of his.

She kept on with, "Okay...so how 'bout somethin' for the pain? Like Tylenol? Oxy? Bourbon? All three?"

He leaned back, saying, "Please, got hurt worse in rugby."

Casey almost laughed, in surprise. "*You* play rugby?"

"Just pub league." Then he added in a near chuckle, "But the scrums can be rough. Once finished a match with a broken finger."

"Oh, now was that bright?" Patricia asked in a momma-tone.

"That's what me Mum said when she reset it."

"Your mother fixed your broken finger?" Casey asked.

Adam nodded. "She was a Sister before she got married. A nurse. It was let her or hours in A&E waiting for a physician. I wouldn't have minded; I had a book to read. But Mum hates to sit." He wiggled his left index finger and forced a smile. "Turned out all right."

Patricia gripped his finger and wiggled it, to his shock, and nodded as if in agreement. Then she jolted and focused on her earpiece. "Oh, Vincent, hi. It's Patricia. Uh, there's a situation and, uh, Casey wants to talk to you."

Casey rolled her eyes. "Not now."

Patricia shoved the actual phone into her hand, growling, "It took three tries to get him to answer and they're eight hours ahead!"

Casey sighed and rose to her feet, saying, "Hi, Vincent. Sorry to call so late."

At the same time, her mother turned to Adam and guided him onto the couch, murmuring, "Here we go, honey. You sure you don't want to see a doctor? I mean, it's just a scrape and head wounds always bleed like crazy over nothin', so I don't think you'll need stitches or an MRI, but you sure you wouldn't like a couple puffs on a bong?"

"No," he said, even more wary of her. "Thank you. The ice is sufficient."

Casey began to pace. "Vincent, listen — wait, I can't hear you. Second." She turned the phone's audio up as high as she could and the noise of what sounded like a bar drifted from it.

"What's the trouble?" Vincent was barely heard asking. "Did you and Adam miss each other?"

"No, he's here but he says he's leaving tonight."

"Hang on, hang on, I'm stepping outside." The din of the pub lessened, to be replaced by city traffic. "Better?"

"Tons," said Casey. "Why've you got him leaving tonight? I told you he'd arrive too late to get the book out of the box."

Vincent actually sputtered, "Casey, I-I-I-I recall very strongly urging you to get the book from the bank, early, and bring it with you to the airport under guard and-and-and hand it straight over to him, where it would be safest and-and — "

She cut him off with, "That's not what I agreed to."

"Casey, please, I've known this young man all his life, and I made assurances to him — "

All she said was, "Vincent," but her voice nearly screamed, *Do you want the book, or not?*

There was silence...then he gave a long heavy sigh. "All right," he said. "All right. I'll arrange accommodations — "

Casey laughed. "Baby, c'mon, I got five bedrooms in this crib; he can stay with me."

"I seriously doubt Adam will agree to that. He's not exactly your normal sort, as I'm certain you've seen by now."

"Then you talk to him. Here." She offered the phone to Adam, saying, "It's Vincent."

He looked at her and accepted the phone...but looked like he thought it was about to bite him. Streaks of blood now smeared his face. Casey went to the bar to get another cloth.

"Sir?" Adam asked. "What's she talking about?"

"Just a...a slight change of plan, Adam," Vincent chirped in too joyous a tone, city traffic echoing around him. "Miss Blanchard wants you to stay the night, you lucky dog."

"But I can't. You know I can't."

"Adam, you sound far too much like Hakim, right now. *Travel plans must be followed to the letter* and all that nonsense."

"But I...I have no money or any idea how to — "

"Oh, for God's sake, it's not as if you're in the middle of Bangladesh — "

"Vincent! I didn't even bring a change of clothing."

Patricia patted his knee, making him jolt as she said,

"Honey, that's what madmen're for." Then she rose and headed upstairs.

Adam huffed, his breathing quick and sharp. He shifted into German to say, *"What? No-no, this is — my itinerary — you — Vincent, you said I wouldn't have to — that I'd be returning, at once, and — I would get the book and — and go, and I never wanted to come and —"*

"Oh, for God's sake, Adam," Vincent all but howled, "drop the bloody German! This isn't a sodding skit from *Monty Python*!"

Adam had to gulp in air to end the explosion of words. Casey eyed him, wary, as she handed him a clean wet towel.

"Now," Vincent continued, "do you like your job?"

Adam's voice shook as he murmured, "You...you know I do."

"Yes. Which is why I hired you over a more qualified candidate. I knew you would be good at it, and you've proven me right. However, you have also put yourself on the wrong side of Sir Robert, and he is suggesting we need to rethink a few positions. Yours included, thanks to your actions. But if you handle this properly it...it will look quite favorable for you."

It took Adam a moment to say, "I see." Then his voice dropped to a growl as he added, "But I told you —"

"I understand! You know I do. I knew your father quite well and I am very sorry to ask you for this. But understand me — Sir Robert wants us to have that book and Miss Blanchard cannot give it to you until tomorrow. So stay, you must. You're there, it's just the one night, and I truly do believe your concerns are ill founded and paranoiac. And, to be perfectly honest, I don't bloody care if you have to snog bloody Miss Blanchard in the bloody middle of bloody Beverly Hills while a hundred bloody cameras are rolling in order to get it! Do it! Bring us that bloody book! Do you understand me!?"

Patricia was coming downstairs with a first aid kit and heard everything. Her expression grew tight and filled with warning as Adam leaned back on the couch, ice still to his head, now at a full and complete loss for words.

"It's on your shoulders, lad," Vincent continued. "And, again, keep in mind — it's just the one night. Do you hear me? Adam? Adam?!"

Adam finally whispered, "Yes, sir."

"There's a good lad," Vincent said. "Set yourself up on tomorrow's flight and have the bloody airline bill the change fee back to us. I'll rearrange everything, this end. I'm ringing off, now, and ordering myself another pint. Or ten. Cheers to all." He ended the call.

Adam handed the phone to Casey, numb, whispering, "He said, *Goodbye*. To you both."

"So I heard," Patricia growled. "And I cannot believe he suggested you snog her in any way, form or fashion!"

Adam gave her a confused glance. "Sorry? What was that?"

"You know damn well what I mean, so — "

Casey sighed. "Mom...I think you're thinking of *shag*."

Adam jolted at realizing what Patricia was thinking and said, "Oh, no, um, snogging just means kissing. Nothing more."

Patricia's glare went wary. "You sure 'bout that?"

"Should one really argue British slang with an Englishman?"

She smiled and patted Adam's knee, saying, "Crap, I always did get those two words confused."

"When've you ever used them?" Casey snapped as she sat beside Adam then, in as comforting a voice as she could manage, said, "Adam, looks like there was a foul-up in communication, so let me give you some back-story. Okay?" His eyes still on Patricia, he gave a slight nod. Casey continued with, "Vincent and I've been FedExing documents back and forth for a few months, now — "

"Not to mention e-mails and phone calls and textin', oh my," Patricia chirped as she dug at the blood on his face with another wet cloth. He yelped, in pain, sat up, took the cloth from her, gulped a deep breath and began cleaning himself.

Casey stayed focused on Adam. "We finally got everything settled, but the flight you came in on arrived too late for us to get to the bank and pick up the book...and I do not want it in the house, overnight. I've had a couple of attempted break-ins and — well, I guess Vincent didn't really understand."

"But he said to bring her straight from the bank, with guards," Adam murmured. "So why not — ?"

"And call all kinds of attention to it?" Casey shot back. "You saw those guys camped by my gate, right?" Adam nodded. "The whole world'd know what's going on before your plane landed. You really want that instead of something nice and low-key?"

He gave her the slightest shake of his head.

"Exactly. So...I'm going to the premier of my new movie, tonight. *Eva Notorious*?" She gave him a look as if to ask, *Have you heard of it?* His blank expression told her everything, so she nodded and continued. "Well...I can't go alone. Doesn't look good. But last week I broke up with a — a dog — and can't go with him because he keeps barking like I don't mean it, and that would give him the wrong idea. He's an actor I worked with and is kind of dim about relationships."

"Dim," snorted Patricia. "He just doesn't understand how anyone could not wanna be with the super-perfect-super-manly Sci-Fi King of the King Fu crap."

"Mother!" Patricia looked at her in all innocence. Casey turned back to Adam. "Thing is, we both worked on this movie, so he'll be there, tonight. If I don't have a date or come with someone he knows is just a friend, he'll keep hounding me to get back together. But if he sees me come with another guy...I think he'll get the hint and find someone else's yard to dump his load."

Adam finished cleaning his face so Patricia took the bloody cloth from him. "Thanks," he said then turned to Casey. "Um, so you want me to attend this premier with you? Me? As *your* date?"

"Yeah."

"This was arranged with Vincent?"

Casey hesitated then said, "That was...was just a screw-up. In communication. This was something I came up with and, like I said, I just thought since you'd have to stay the night, anyway, you'd like to go. We'll get you a nice suit and you get to walk the carpet. See the movie before anybody else. What's even better is, you're not a Hollywood person. I...I think that would finally hammer the message home to him."

"This all sounds rather odd," Adam said as Patricia dabbed alcohol on the cut. He jerked away from her. "Ow, that stings."

"Means it's workin'," she smiled.

"Mom, please." Casey turned back to him. "Adam, you said you saw *Ilithium Four*."

"Twice. It put the child next to me to sleep — on my lap. But it did keep him from vomiting on me a third time."

A sharp laugh burst from Casey. "Nice to know the movie was good for something."

"Not really. He's still potty-training. This is my second change — in his father's clothes! Under normal circumstances I'd not be caught dead in this ensemble."

"Honey, what's wrong with lookin' like Popeye?" asked Patricia. "He's strong to the finish."

Casey shushed her with a wave of her hand. "Adam, you remember the actor who played Creggan? As an adult?"

Adam rolled his eyes. "I wish I could forget — him?" He looked at Casey, in horror. "Is *he* your former — ?" She gave him a shrug. "Oh, God, he was awful! The complete opposite of Creggan in the book! Swagger and stupid quips and-and-and-and idiotic faux sensitivity and — bloody hell!"

"Casey, this one's got good taste," said Patricia as she applied a fat lavender bandage to his scrape.

Casey ran a soothing hand across the back of his

shoulders as she said, "Adam, you'd be so perfect for tonight. You're somebody who's smart and different and the complete opposite of him. So c'mon, let me show you my town with people everybody wants to know and prove to my ex he means doggie-doo-doo to me. I can promise you it'll be a night you'll never forget."

He gave her a long wary look before he finally whispered, "Well, first I should reschedule my flight."

"Mom'll do that. I'll even throw in a first class ticket home, for your pain. You get champagne, caviar, classy crackers."

"No promises about the vomit," Patricia just had to add.

He glanced between them, still very unsure. "And you'll give me the book, tomorrow? And we go straight to the airport?"

Casey nodded, her eyes gleaming with triumph. "I'll even have an armed security guard from the bank drive us. In plainclothes, of course."

He finally shrugged an uncertain okay.

That's when Patricia's cell phone rang. She touched her earpiece, with a wicked grin and said, "Talk about timin', honey, here comes the madman." Then she leaned in close to Adam and whispered, "Be afraid — be very afraid."

His eyes grew huge and he looked like he was about to run.

And if glares could kill, Casey could have been guilty of mommy-murder five times over.

— FIVE —

Moments later, Adam was wandering through a room the size of his mother's semi-detached home and gazing out a sliding glass door on that sculpted yard. Well-padded chairs on swiveling wheels faced a desk that snaked around two-and-a-half walls and had six shelves of folders, five photos of a handsome middle-aged man, four humming CPU towers, three massive monitors, and two gleaming keyboards. A partridge in a pear tree was all it needed to be complete. The carpet was as thick as sponge and the plants were almost to the point where if there were two more the room would be its own ecological unit.

The dark fabric-covered walls were decorated with framed posters of films Casey had been a part of — *Minotaur, She Wakes*, *Minotaur 2, Mini Minotaur, Sky Knights, Blood Angel, Safe Haven, My Own Private Minotaur, The Wilderness Rule, Mine To Kill, Find Ray T,* and others. In the center of them all was a breathtaking poster for *Ilithium Four* in a Syd Mead style, imagining a world that Adam felt really should have been used for the paperback's cover in place of the rather pedestrian space-view one.

After a moment, Patricia rushed in to present him with a glass of fresh-squeezed orange juice and several cookies on a plate.

"Breakfast cookies, honey," she told him. "Very organic. Now — let me nuke you somethin'."

"If it's no trouble," Adam had said, his stomach rumbling. "I'd planned to eat at the airport and — "

"So long as you like Fettuccini," she chirped as she vanished.

Adam bit into a cookie...then he had to use a gulp of orange juice to chase it down, it was so dry. On top of that, the juice was so tart he felt it behind his ears, but it was food and manners forbade any complaint.

He looked at the desk, again, and smiled. Jeremy would have had kittens at seeing this, but not even one section would have fit properly into his little photography room, let alone the array of electronic additions. He focused on the framed photos, catching a resemblance between the man and Casey. Probably her father, he thought...but there was not one photo of the two of them together, so maybe not.

He turned his attention to a full-size corkboard mounted just above eye-level on a thick-wood door, where a photograph of Lando Grissom had been used for dart practice. His ice-blue eyes stared straight at the camera, and his too-square chin was outlined with a touch of scruff that whispered up and around his mouth in a vague goatee and added to a little smirk on his lips. His blond hair was well-coiffed and he appeared to be shirtless, with his muscular left arm flexed and his left hand behind his head. The photo's mix of light and shadow made every wrinkle vanish and gave his cheekbones the feel of a knife. Adam could see all of this despite the presence of dozens of dart holes in the photo, the sheer number of them making it obvious there was more than mere dislike happening here; he wondered if Casey had done the breaking up...or if Lando had.

Before he could make any kind of determination about it, a short wiry Terrier of a man dressed in white pants, white turtleneck, black boots, white hair and dark eyes burst into the office. Casey barely had time to introduce him as Orisi before he had manhandled Adam to the center of the room and begun to adjust him like he was a mannequin, part of which included yanking his cookies and juice away then picking at the holes in Manny's jeans as if he were trying to make them longer and wider. Obviously, the concept of personal space was alien to him.

"Jumpin' jeebus, son," Orisi barked. "Didn't your momma never teach you to stand up straight? Shoulders back. Tummy in. That's nine-tenths of lookin' good."

He ran his fingertips over Adam's cheeks then jabbed the bandage on his forehead and scrape on his chin. Adam was so shocked, he could not formulate a coherent word of protest.

"Gotta shave," snapped Orisi. "Not enough to call it scruff, though you could use some." Then he ran his hands through Adam's hair and growled, "No conditioner? And what's this bump?" He pressed on it.

Adam yelped and cried, "Hang on!" as he jerked his head away. "I struck my head, yesterday."

Orisi heaved a sigh to fill the ages with regret. "So much for shaving this crap off."

Which jolted Adam into saying, "Shave my — um, so much for something that was never going to happen."

Orisi just kept eyeing his scalp. "Dunno if I can fix it, though. And your skin — jumpin' jeebus. Have you never heard of exfoliates? May need to apply a base. Now — your fingernails." The man picked at Adam's nails and snarled at the bandage on his left thumb. "Self-destructive; just what I need." Then he jolted and looked at the design on Adam's left hand. "What's this?"

"It's henna — "

"I know that, but who did it? It's a class design."

Adam pulled Julie's card from his wallet. "She did."

Orisi grabbed the card and blinked. Twice. A third time. "Julie Marshe-Croton did this?!" Adam nodded. "*Th*e Julie Marshe-Croton?" Adam shrugged. "Meanin' she's here in LA?" Adam nodded. "Well now she's gotta do the other hand. Just one side throws everything off. It's good you're almost hairless; no need to wax." Then he jolted and spun Adam around. "Wait —

them's some hairy calves! *Do* you wax your butt?"

"What!?" Adam screamed as he spun back to face the man. "No!"

"We'll see."

"Sorry, we will not."

Throughout this, Casey leaned against the nearest section of desk, taking copious notes, while Patricia worked at one of the monitors, Adam's passport and itinerary in hand, the photos on the desk turned away. She finally piped in with, "Ticket's changed to nine-oh-five, tomorrow night." Then she cast Casey a cool glance. "You never let me go First Class."

Casey did not even look at her as she said, "When have I ever stopped you?"

"Not the point."

Orisi pushed between them and shoved Julie's card into Patricia's hand. "Find her! Bring her! Now, now, now!" Then he spun back to Adam and snorted, "Down the pants," as he whipped out a cloth tape measure.

Adam looked at him as if he were mad and said, "Sorry?"

"C'mon, son, hips, legs, and ass, gotta see what I gotta work with." He snapped the suspenders off Adam's shoulders. "Them things're only good for sellin' yourself on Santa Monica. Snap to it."

Adam grabbed the jeans to keep them from falling. "I...I don't understand. Why don't I just try some things on?"

"'Cause we ain't Walmart!"

"Well, what're you planning to do — make a bespoke suit for me to wear?"

"If I have to. Now — PANTS!"

Adam huffed. "Actually, they're jeans. Granted, they look rather silly, but still some form of denim. I think." He started to unbutton them, but Orisi yanked them to his knees to reveal that Manny's FTLs were boxer briefs of the purest white. Almost. And they barely clung to Adam's hips. Fortunately he froze in place and only squeaked a startled, "Careful," because if he had tried to jump away he would have fallen...and so would the undies.

Orisi staggered back, his too-tan skin going almost semi-tan as he cried, "Jumpin' jeebus!" Then he turned on Casey, snarling, "You couldn't warn me?"

"How would I know?" she shot back. "I just met him."

Of course Patricia felt the need to whistle and toss in, "But worth it for that butt."

"Here, now!" Adam snapped. "It's not like these are mine. I was soaked through by that brat."

"Then you should've free-balled it," Orisi snarled as he grabbed his cell phone, shaking, and hit speed-dial. "Not so embarrassin'." Then he growled into phone, "We got a stage four emergency. Need all back-up. Full force. Now, now, now." Then he pointed at Adam. "You in the tub. In!"

"Oh, God, do I still smell of it?" Now Adam felt the need to find a hole to crawl into. "But I had a wash on the plane! Twice."

Casey took him by the arm and guided him to the door holding Lando's much-mutilated photo. "C'mon, baby. In here."

He pulled the jeans partway up but still had to sort-of duck-wobble along, babbling, "They even let me use the first class lavatory, the second time. Had lovely soap, heated towels, was large enough to move around in, and the attendants were very understanding."

Casey put a tender hand to his heart and whispered, "Shh, baby, don't let Orisi get to you; it's all show. Just trust us, okay? It'll be fine."

Her touch calmed Adam in a way he found surprising. He took in a deep breath and nodded. "Sorry, I — I'm just not used to all this attention."

"I know. But it won't be for long."

"Cut the chit-chat and get to it," Orisi snapped. "We ain't got all day." Then he gave Adam's butt a swat, which startled him far more than it stung. Then the man frowned and swatted it, again.

Adam backed away from him, snarling, "Stop that! You're not a rugby mate!"

"But Patricia's right," Orisi said, almost smiling. "You *do* got a nice ass."

"When have I ever been wrong about that?" Patricia purred.

"Lando," he shot back. "Never seen such flat cheeks with so damn much hair on 'em."

"I thought he got implants."

"'Course he did. You think I'd let an Orisi man get by without somethin' to give him ballast?" Then he growled at Casey, "Now you — I assume you got the right stuff?"

"All courtesy of you, baby."

"Show me."

They vanished from the room.

Adam noticed Patricia smiling and shaking her head, so he felt emboldened enough to ask, "Is all of this really necessary?"

She chuckled and said, "Honey, it's LA. Best to go with the flow, 'specially when the bullshit's flowin' like it does with that man. Hell, *any* man." And the way she looked at him was quite discomfiting. She finally rose and said, "Take your cookies and juice with you. I'll re-nuke what I nuked. Maybe you'll have time to eat it."

Adam remembered he was ravenous, so smiled and nodded. "That would be brilliant."

"Won't take a minute. And honey, don't let anybody ever make fun of anything about you. Especially your, um, choice of undies." She winked at him and left the room.

"They're not mine!" he called after her. "I told you." Then he stepped out of the jeans, muttering, "That I'm in someone else's underwear — and that people have *seen* it — is beyond belief." He took in a deep breath and murmured, "But it's for the

*Alic*e, it's for the *Alice*," then grabbed his cookies and juice and continued into the bathroom.

****

Well...the bathroom put the office to shame, because even though it was a quarter the same size, it was so bright and open and joyous — with translucent tiles, and wash basins and mirrors covering one wall, and hanging plants everywhere, and soft light filtering in from skylights cut into the ceiling, and a floor of warm granite — it was like a conservatory. What was even better — a massive rectangle of a white tub within an even more massive maroon one sat in the center of it all. Adam was awe-struck.

He started the basin filling with just the right mix of hot and cold, then he wolfed down a cookie. Patricia brought in another glass of juice, saying "Fettuccini in four minutes and countin'," as she spun around and headed back out.

"Thanks," he said as he sipped at the OJ. Then he called after her, "This juice is very good. A bit tart, with so much pulp, but..." But she was already gone so he shrugged. "California oranges. Nothing like 'em." He sipped some more then finished undressing, draped his clothes over a maroon chair and slipped into the steaming tub. Luxuriated in it. "A basin as big as my bed," sighed from him. "Unbelievable." He began to feel very mellow. Perhaps this evening wouldn't be so bad after all, he thought.

Then Orisi burst in with several colorful bottles of stuff, snarling, "Here we go."

Adam jolted upright and managed to grab a facecloth to keep hidden as he snapped, "Hang on!" And gasped when he realized a woman was following Orisi in, and she was —

"Julie?!"

"Hallo, Sweets," she chirped, bright and happy, Dumpling in one arm. She tickled the little beast as she looked around and said, "Here, you go. There's the man whose life you thought you ruined. Who knew he was coming to this?"

"I wasn't. I was supposed to turn around at the airport."

"Jumpin' jeebus, would've been better."

"On that, we agree," Adam snapped.

Orisi turned down the hot water, snarling, "What's this steam for?"

"I like a hot bath."

"Why? You ain't no Dim Sum."

Julie shoved Orisi in the rear with a foot as she set Dumpling between the sinks. "Be still, O. He's a lovely man and for my work to work I need him calm. You tend to wind people up."

That is when Patricia entered holding a bowl of something offering an aroma fit for the gods — but Orisi shoved her back out of the room, crying "No-no-no-NO-NO-NO CARBS!"

"It's just a bowl of pasta," Adam said.

Orisi all but howled, "I still gotta get your measurements and I don't want 'em changin'! You wanna get all bloated? Do it on your own time! We're on Orisi-time, now!"

Patricia peeked around the door and said, "Adam, I'll bring you another glass of juice and some cookies. Keep your strength up." Before Orisi could explode she pinched his cheek and said, "Organic. No gluten."

"Keep my strength — ?" Adam cried. "I'm English. Have you seen an English breakfast? It's not cookies and juice."

"This ain't England!" Orisi roared, pouring red liquid into the tub.

Now Adam huffed. "What's that?"

"Gotta do something with that skin, son. Now — use these to cleanse." He held up a different colored bottle for each word. "Body." *Green.* "Feet." *Orange.* "Face." *Blue.* "Hair."

Cream. "And everything in-between. Each one's got its own story so use 'em all. Scrub-a-dub-dub!"

He plopped the bottles on a table beside the tub and grabbed the clothes off the chair as Adam held up a nicely-scented bar and said, "But I have soap, right here, and — "

"SOAP!?" Orisi spun around three times and turned four shades of unadulterated raw umber as he shrieked, "SOAP!? JUMPIN' JEEBUS, CASEY, YOU TRYIN' TO RUIN MY REPUTATION!? SOAP!"

He grabbed at the bar but it popped out of Adam's hand and plumped into the tub. Orisi dove his right hand in to search for it, making Adam jolt back and cry, "Careful!"

After whisking about in the water, with Adam close to crawling out of the tub to avoid him and Dumpling howling with laughter, Orisi found the soap, wrapped it in the Polo shirt and stormed out. "Casey, you better be able to explain this travesty to me!"

Julie grinned and said, in a coy voice, "Looks like I'm getting Manny's threads back, quick, quick. Good thing the hotel has a laundry."

Adam sank back in the water to look at Julie. "That man — am I correct in understanding you know him?" She nodded. "How could you possibly?"

"Went to cosmetology school together," Julie said as she pulled out her kit, "but obviously we branched in different directions. You'd never know he's from Hounslow, not Houston." Then she leaned in close to whisper, "Or he stole my boyfriend from me."

"And you're still friends with him?"

She nodded and pulled the stool and chair over. "Worked out good. I met Manny soon after and we've been together ever since. Soul-mates."

"How'd he find you so quick? And get you here?"

She sat next to the tub. "My Facebook page. The London's just up Sunset. Walk to the Roxy. Viper Room. Book

54

Soup! A bus straight to Hollywood. Rooftop pool. Lovely view. Posted photos. Here, give me your hand."

"Julie, I'm sorry but I'm neither comfortable nor calm, right now. Perhaps you should wait till I'm done to work up the mandala. I'm not one for being naked in front of people."

"You're a rugger-bugger but uncomfortable being naked?"

Adam huffed. "Do I look like a thick-headed arse? Besides, that's just me mates. Lads I've known forever."

Julie nodded. "No worries, you'll be covered," she said taking his right hand to lay it palm down on the stool. She dried it with another facecloth.

That is when Adam realized colorful bubbles were building in the water. Lots and lots and LOTS of them, building and building. Adorable and happy and advancing on him. Closer and closer.

He almost got out of the tub, naked or not.

He never had liked bubble baths. As a child he would push the bubbles away or would refuse to be set in the basin, which vexed his mother, no end. David had accepted them until he turned nine, whereupon they became very uncool, while Connor, the second oldest, had insisted on one every time he washed. Beryl, but a year older than Adam, had used them as her Zen time, something that could be massively inconvenient in a single bath home.

When Adam was six, Mum finally realized he liked to shower with a simple bar of soap and a washrag. She asked him why he preferred that and he told her, "I want done with it; I have books to read."

"You can read the book in the bath," Mum had said.

"Have my books near water? Mum, are you mad?"

She had left him alone, after that.

Adam sighed as the bubbles drifted over him like a blanket. He sipped some juice, bit into a cookie — and stopped in mid-chew. "I'm sorry," he said, "would you and Dumpling like a biscuit and some juice?"

"Thanks, I'm fine. Sweets, would you like some?"

Dumpling worked his way off the counter and toddled over to grab at the cookies, his black eyes never leaving Adam. That is when Patricia barged in with a fresh plate, saw what Dumpling was about to bite into, and swooped him up in one arm as she set the plate down. Then she took the cookie from him, grinning.

"Oh, I got something lots better for you, honey," she said. "Cereal! With bananas. And your own glass of juice."

Julie glanced between her and the cookie in Adam's hand and quietly said, "Thanks, Pat, but he likes tea with half milk and two lumps. And do you have porridge?"

Patricia gave her a completely blank look, so Adam grinned and piped in with, "Oatmeal."

Patricia brightened up. "Right! I use it for the cookies." She tickled Dumpling into giggles as she chirped, "I gots some straws-berries and blues-berries and honey, just like the three bears. You'll like it lots more." Then she carried him from the room.

"He won't vomit, again, will he?" Adam asked.

Julie relaxed and smiled. "No worries. Solid ground. And you are a very bad boy."

"Why do you say that?"

"You should think before you speak. Keep your hand still."

By this point, the mass of bubbles had covered Adam up to his chin, so he turned off the water and leaned back in the tub, forcing himself to relax.

"Why do people have bubble baths?" he muttered, deep and growly. "To me, it's as if the residue left on my skin is meant less to cleanse and more to fill my pores with petroleum by-products, thus enhancing the possibility of eczema."

"Manny and I love them, but we use a light soap and rinse off, after. Dumpling, he accepts."

"Too bad I've no access to a shower."

Julie looked around then nodded to the faucet. "What about those buttons, by the hot tap?"

Adam looked at a series of colorful dots atop the left edge of the basin. One had a shower icon next to it. "Do you think it is?" he asked, then looked up. "I don't see a shower head."

"Try it," said Julie. "Just keep this hand safe till it's dried."

"Where's Manny in all this?" he asked, with a sigh.

Julie cast him a sly look. "Next room, being Fan-Boy."

"With Casey Blanchard? He's heard of her?"

Julie giggled. "If he had known it was she you were coming to see, he'd have crawled into your lap before Dumpling had a chance and discussed her films and career the entire flight. Puts her on a scale with Angelina Jolie and Sigourney Weaver, he does. One of his mates let the cat out when he said, *Bitches who can beat you to a bloody pulp, and wouldn't ya love it*? Our first date was to see — which was it — *Sky Knights*, I think. It's hard to keep track. We own every one of them, and Dumpling has slept through *Ilithium Four* twenty-seven times."

"You might want to make that twenty-nine," Adam chuckled.

Julie whispered the first touch of henna across the tops of his fingers as she said, "I'm counting yours, Sweets."

"Oh."

"You really didn't know who she is?"

Adam shrugged. "I'm not much of one for film. I read. Prefer it. There's something permanent about a book. Steady. Comforting. But I can't really tell her that, can I? It'd be like dismissing her entire career."

"She's been around long enough to handle it. Manny says her first job was when she was ten, on a sit-com. *The Family Saint*."

"Mum and Beryl used to watch that."

"Played a neighbor's daughter. We have the first year on

Blu-Ray; that's all she was in."

"Dear God, Manny *is* mad."

"But he's my madman. Now hold still."

Then she began laying down the design's details.

****

Thirty minutes later, she had set the mandala and a car was returning her, a reluctant Manny and a sleeping Dumpling to their hotel. Adam drained the tub, found another dry wash cloth, turned his right hand palm up, draped the cloth over it and pressed the shower icon, using his left hand.

A tinkling version of *Singin' in the Rain* played as glass walls rose up between the inner and outer basins, then several ceiling tiles shifted aside to reveal tiny showerheads and water rained down on him at the same temperature as he'd used for his bath. He was just able to keep his right hand out of its way as he leaned back to let the whispery warmth cascade over his head and body. The sheer luxury of it was so overwhelming, so decadent, so off-kilter, he had to chuckle and say, "The rich are different, all right. They're their own bloody species."

At the end of the song, the water stopped, the walls slid down and the tiles flipped back in place, automatically. Adam dried off, found a bathrobe on a peg near the door, wrapped in that and returned to the office, still chuckling, to find —

Orisi was no longer alone. Half a dozen of his minions stood at parade rest, all in black turtlenecks, black trousers, black boots and black haircuts, looking so much alike it was difficult to tell the lads from the lasses. The only part of them that moved was their eyes, which followed the man as he yanked Adam to the middle of the room and briskly circled him, snapping like a drill sergeant, "We got zero to start with, people, so face — hair — nails — all of it's built. Careful of the mandalas." The only time he stopped pacing was to yank the robe open to reveal Adam's chest and sneer, "No need to wax."

Adam was feeling so mellow, he just sighed, pulled the robe back into place and muttered, "Careful."

Orisi responded by turning Adam around and yanking up the rear of his robe, snarling, "Ass, either."

Adam yelped and, of course, that would be the moment Patricia came in with another glass of juice to instantly chirp, "Oh. My. God."

Before Adam could even formulate a coherent thought, Orisi bounced at her with agitation, screaming "Out! Out! You know Orisi ain't no spectator sport."

She merely responded, "You are so full of shit," and handed Adam the juice.

"Thanks," Adam said. "May I ask — have my clothes been washed?"

She gave him a laugh. "Honey, I told you — I got no idea how the damn thing works."

"But I need — I mean, I can't wear trousers without underwear."

"No worries about that," Orisi crowed as he held up a pair of black boxer-briefs that looked nice and comfortable — except for the silver and black sequins making up a gloriously detailed fig leaf on the crotch.

Adam burst out a laugh. "You want to put glittery bits on my bits? Are you mental?"

The crew gasped.

Patricia backed out of the room.

Orisi froze.

And glared at Adam.

A wolf-like snarl crossed his lips as his face returned to that shade of burnt umber, and his voice grew terrifying in its quiet control. "Okay, son, we need to get somethin' understood, right here and right now. Every damn thing I do is considered, contemplated, crafted and created for conspicuous consumption, and why is that? Because I am Bernardo Giancarlo Michelangelo Orisi, not some cow-pokin'-steer-wrestlin' fool from Montana, and it is my God-given right to decide what is good, bad or ugly. *No* one else's! So it is impossible for me to be mad, mental or mendacious. In fact, you should be *thrilled* that I have focused the power of my abilities on you despite you being completely ill-suited for them, which means you now *owe* me for my benevolence. And because of this, you are *my* man, now, and my rules will apply to the rest of your life.

"Therefore, from this day on you will not eat carbs on a night when you are going to be seen by anyone but your mirror. Nor will you merely *wash*, you will *cleanse*. And you will never, never, EVER utter the word *soap* in my presence, ever again. Nor from this day forward will you just *try things on*! An Orisi man would not be seen DEAD in a department store fitting room; he has his clothing built to his frame. Every stitch of it, because we are not lumbering nouveau-riche fools who think a designer name is all that matters! No, we know the meaning of style and class, and we dress from the skin out beginnin' with designer briefs made from Egyptian cotton with a thread count of twelve-hundred, *min*-i-mum, followed by shirt, socks, pants, shoes and all the accouterments required. Then we stand up straight and present a positive, confident image to the world, for to do less would be an affront to me, and everything I stand for!

"And one last thing — you must understand this, as well — if you ever, ever, EVER let plain white boxer briefs near your ass at any time in any way, form or fashion, again, I personally will track you down and berate you to within an inch of eternity. And don't even begin to think I won't know, because I will. Do I make myself clear?" Then he whipped the briefs up like a black flag.

Adam downed the orange juice in one gulp and coughed, reminded himself, once again, "It's for the *Alice*," and grimaced at finally realizing he'd found his own private mantra.

He took the sequined briefs and discretely pulled them

on...to find they were surprisingly comfortable. Except for how odd the sequined area felt against his crotch. Then he straightened himself up, smoothed down his robe and calmly stood back in the center of the room.

Orisi circled him three times before he clapped his hands, triumphant. "Let's go, go, go people. We're makin' a man from this lump of clay, and we're late, we're late, for a very important date."

So off came Adam's robe and out came Orisi's tape measure as a gleaming tablet appeared in one minion's hands, and in quick-quick fashion Orisi snapped the tape here and there and around as he shouted Adam's measurements for neck, full chest, full shoulder, half shoulder left, half shoulder right, full back length, full right sleeve, full left sleeve, both biceps, both fore-arms, trousers waist, hips, front jacket length, wrists, front chest width, back chest width, trousers out-seam, trousers in-seam, trousers crotch, left thigh — at which point Orisi jolted and said, "Jumpin' jeebus, son, you sure you ain't a linebacker?"

"Rugby," Adam grinned at him. "Number 8."

"Do better as a prop." Then he whipped the tape around Adam's right thigh, and each knee and calf, and nodded, "Okay, Number 8."

"You couldn't tell from looking at me?"

"Eyes lie, numbers don't."

Adam would have argued the point, but he was so lost in all the figures being tossed around, he couldn't even think of what language to think in, at the moment. In fact, he doubted he'd ever be able to look himself in the mirror, again, without considering his measurements, let alone buy clothes off the rack. After all, who knew your arms could be different lengths or your waist slightly angular? It helped that he was finally well-beyond caring about being half-naked in front of a pack of strangers. He didn't even mind being jammed into a chair so the crew could attack his nails, both fingers and toes, with buffing and scraping and clipping, oh my, as they smeared a mask of lavender and lace on his face, and sliced and diced and buffed and burnished his hair before it was tipped and coiffed and yanked and grabbed and spiked and un-spiked and spiked, again, as a female minion sat next to him to touch his bare thighs with colognes to be sniffed at and moaned over and wiped off with an alcohol pad.

That is...until she trailed a bit too close to the sequins. But all Adam had to chuckle was a soft, slow, "Careful," like a whispery foghorn, to make her use his calves, instead, toying just a bit more than necessary with the hair on them...almost making him giggle.

Through it all, Orisi griped and grunted and growled and grimaced and snapped and snarled and adjusted and everything else anyone could think of as his crew worked and worked and worked and continued and continued and continued until he cried, "Enough!"

They stopped dead and stepped back, their hair wrecked, eyes glazed, pants wrinkled, turtlenecks askew, and a hint of sweat on their fevered brows. The walking wounded. Two seconds later, another minion arrived with a suit bag and carryall.

Orisi took the bag, held it as if it contained the purest gold, and said, "Now comes the true test."

He unzipped it, slow and easy, luxuriating in the sound of it opening wider and wider until he maneuvered it off the hanger to reveal — a nice navy-blue suit and pressed burgundy shirt with matching tie.

"Perfection," Orisi said as if in prayer. He hung it on the door then pulled black burnished Italian half-boots with thick but stylish heels from the carryall along with two small boxes — one holding a tie clip, the other a pair of cuff links, both with Amethysts set in.

"What, no belt?" Adam asked.

"Never," said Orisi. "Breaks the line." Then he froze, shrieked, "Wait!" and looked back at the shirt. He whipped out his tape measure to check the shirt's collar...and howled at the minion who'd brought the bag, "Two-and-five-sixteenths!? I told you two-and-a-quarter!'"

The crew collectively gasped.

The minion with the bag wilted.

"It looks fine," Adam murmured.

Orisi cast him a glare then turned back to the pathetic wretch and snarled, "Fix it!"

Out came tiny scissors, and needle and thread, and in five minutes the collar had been seamlessly reworked to the proper width then pressed with what looked like a hair curler. To Adam's shock, it *did* look better.

"Don't let it happen again," Orisi growled.

The minion backed away, bereft.

Adam slipped into the shirt, which felt nice and crisp, then worked on a pair of burgundy silk socks carefully matched to the shirt's tone, stepped into the trousers (no pleats), and tucked in the shirt. He wrapped the tie (measured at exactly one and an eighth inches in width) under his collar and prepped it per Orisi's snarl of, "Half Windsor." Then he slipped into the half-boots, which were zipped up by the bereft minion, before he let the man guide him into the coat, all the while wondering if this was what it was like to have a butler.

Once the coat was buttoned, Adam marveled, "It's a perfect fit."

Orisi snorted. "Like I said, we ain't Walmart. Wait here."

Then he led his minions from the office. Even from behind Adam could tell they were frazzled beyond belief.

"Casey," he heard Orisi growl, "you're payin' me triple, givin' each of my crew a shot of Stolichnaya, and if this was the *Golden Globes* I still wouldn't let him out of the house."

Casey's voice shot back, "You forgot why I'm taking him."

"Jumpin' jeebus, I never forget anything! But get yourself ready." He whistled and cried, "Adam. Come."

Adam barked like Albacore, laughed, then peeked his head out the door with the goofiest, sweetest grin he could manage and sang in a jokey, growly way —

> *Ooooooooooooooh, I'm an Englishman, that's for sure,*
> *Who's just had his first pedicure.*

He dissolved into chuckles and added, "Sorry, it's just I never knew I'm ticklish."

Orisi scowled at him and snapped, "Jumpin' jeebus, OUT."

"Don't see the point of a pedicure," he said as he stumbled from the office. "Got boots on. Who's gonna see my feet? And these heels — what are they, six-inch?"

"Three," said Orisi. "With inserts. Make you a nice, normal height."

"Feel like I'm on tippy-toe." Then he hiccupped.

Casey cast a harsh glare at Patricia. "Mom? Those cookies? That orange juice?"

Patricia put her innocent look. "He was so uptight, I — well, I got the cookies from your batch, Casey, not mine, so don't have any until I check 'em. Okay?"

Adam grinned at them then yawned, shoved his hands in his trousers pockets and leaned against the door's frame...

And the room went dead silent.

He glanced around, uncertain. "What? No hands in pocket?"

"Oh, no, no, no, honey, you keep 'em there," Patricia said as she took a picture of him with her cell phone. "Gotta record how gorgeous you are."

He chuckled, deep and easy, saying, "Away on. People don't call me gorgeous."

"Stop it," Orisi snapped. "An Orisi man always looks good and damn well knows it."

"Here," said Patricia, offering Adam the phone.

He took it and looked at it — and froze.

On the little screen was some stranger in a deep electric

navy blue suit with lapels like gleaming stilettos, a dark burgundy shirt with matching tie and handkerchief, and too-cool glasses sporting silver and black frames...through which he could actually see; how Orisi got those, he had no idea. His face was bright and clean, the un-bandaged scrape on his chin looked more like a sexy scar, and the bandage on his forehead had also become burgundy, making it part of the ensemble. The elegant boots and his hair — now in a killer cut with more than a hint of blond highlights — complimented it all.

All Adam could think to say was, "Bloody hell..."

"No kiddin'," Patricia chirped as she poured Orisi's crew their drinks. "Though a ten-thousand-dollar suit don't hurt."

Adam jolted. "Ten-fousand — uh — ten thousand? That's more than I spent on food, last year!" He pointed to the photo. "I-I-I can't wear this. What if I have to sit down? What if I have to pee?"

"Pee!?" Orisi snarled. "You're an Orisi man, now; we don't pee!"

Adam huffed. "Why not? Trousers've got a zipper."

"That's just for aesthetics!"

"Don't pee, then; piss," Patricia said, nice and happy as the soft whoosh of a text being sent whispered from her phone. "Took it long enough," she muttered.

Adam looked at his photo, again. "What? What was that? What'd you do?"

"Just an *I told you so*," she said, grinning like a cat that had just broken a million-dollar vase.

"Off my picture?" She nodded. His goofy little half-grin took over his lips. "Humph. Who from — um, for — um — to?"

"Vincent."

His grin vanished. "You sent that to Vincent? Oh, no, no, no, no, no, he has Jeremy handle his texts, and he's the biggest bloody gossip, and I'll get nothing but stick from now on."

"Doubt it, honey. He lost."

"...Sorry?"

Then a text came in. Patricia grabbed the phone from him to show Casey. It was the limo.

Casey gave Adam a pat on the back as she headed for the stairs. "Baby, tell the driver I'll be right out."

Adam hiccupped, in response, and picked up his wallet and passport. Orisi grabbed at them.

"Jumpin' jeebus, son, an Orisi man don't carry no wallet!"

Adam danced away and giggled. "Well, this one does, and if you don't like it you can kiss my very UN-war-axed arse." Then he barked.

Casey scrambled upstairs to get out of Orisi's way.

Patricia ducked behind the bar.

The crew took one step back, their eyes wide with horror.

Orisi growled at Adam. Moved closer to him. Eyed him with cold deliberation. Then exploded in a monster of a laugh and grabbed him by the shoulders.

"Jumpin' jeebus, Casey gave me a sow's ear and, hot-DAMN, if I didn't make him into a silk purse. I am brilliant!" He spun around with glee. "Patricia, Stolichnaya for all, again." Then he pointed a finger at Adam and added, "But still no *Golden Globes*."

"Why not?" Adam huffed.

"You're in burgundy and blue," said Orisi. "They cry for bone and black."

His crew nodded, in unison, shocked at how gauche Adam was. Then they downed their shots, in unison. And held out their glasses...in unison.

Adam gaped at them then stumbled for the door. The sooner he was away from that madman and his maniacal minions, the better.

But he caught a glimpse of himself in a mirror just before he exited and had to stop to take a closer look. Sure enough, he was that lean, clean, Navy-blue machine staring back at himself.

To cap it off, the Amethyst tie clip and cufflinks complimented the soft glow of the mandalas on his hands (when the clay had been scraped off the second one, he had no idea, but at least they matched). In fact everything worked together so well and made him look so good, the only thing he could think to say was, "Bloody hell, Orisi *is* brilliant."

"Jumpin' jeebus, son, already agreed to! Now GO!"

Adam jolted, spun around to look at him...and couldn't stop himself before he spun around, again, then took a deep breath, regained his dignity, and strolled outside, secure in the certainty that the weirdest part of the night was over.

SIX

Adam wandered out and took in a deep breath — and felt a bit dizzy. "From hunger and fumes," he told himself, "thanks to whatever it was they polished my nails with, fingers and feet." He looked at his hands and chuckled. "But they are quite clean and do gleam nicely." He even admired how Julie's soft mandalas now matched perfectly.

Then he hiccupped, again.

And chuckled, again.

The madness of Los Angeles was obviously getting to him. He hadn't felt this odd since he'd had a fourth pint with the lads after they'd won a match against a very inferior team, the memory of which brought a smirk to his lips. Which led to him recalling how shocked everyone had been when he took up the game, not only because it was completely opposite to their view of him, but also because he was fifteen. That was late to begin. Connor and David had started pigmy football leagues the moment they could run, and Beryl had bent it like Beckham from the time she began to notice boys were something to be noticed and she wanted to be noticed by them. But Adam had never been the sports type; sitting in a chair with a cup of tea and some biscuits while reading a book was his persona.

When asked by Beryl why he had chosen to participate in such a dirty, violent game, Adam had responded, "David's fault."

But in reality it had begun with their mother. When her career had shifted from being a Sister to a physical therapist, Mum's focus had become how poorly people cared for themselves, and how too many now had to rebuild their bodies to keep from crashing deeper into illness. So she had never tired of telling him to get some form of physical activity, despite it never working. Until she noticed he'd watch ballroom dancing competitions on television, to laugh.

When she finally asked him why, he said, "They're funny."

"What's funny about them?"

"You can't tell the boys from the girls, the way they pose. And they're all so serious about it, with big fake grins."

She had dragged him to a dance class the next day and said if he would stick with the lessons for six months, she would buy him a full set of Dickens. He had already told his father how much he'd enjoyed reading *David Copperfield,* so even though he was only nine years old that was sufficient to make him agree.

He drove the instructor mad the first few months, with his silly exaggerations of the poses. But then he met Chandra, who took ballroom dancing seriously. And because she did, he did, and he stuck with it for six years. They made quite a little team, with her tawny skin against his freckles and semi-sunburn, and even won a couple of junior competitions. They would have kept on longer except she met a lad two years older than her and six inches taller than Adam. Since he liked her, as well, she changed partners and started dancing in high-heels.

Then two months later, Adam's father had died and he needed something to focus his anger and pain on, and dancing wasn't doing it. The instructor even asked Adam to take a break because his attitude had shifted back to derogatory. That was when David had suggested Adam join the school's soccer team, telling him, "It's like chess but with real lads and lots of running."

Adam had tried it, to make everyone happy, but David's comparison was nonsense. He was about to quit when he learned a classmate's brother played rugby on his college team. Adam tagged along to a game, joined him in practice, found he liked the push and pull of the scrums and stuck with it through University. Not a broken clavicle, nine staples in his head from a center's elbow, or that broken finger had deterred him. What was even better, it kept his mother silent when he'd spend other hours seated in an easy chair devouring a book...with a cuppa and biscuits.

Which is what he much preferred to be doing at the moment, cozied up in an airport lounge devouring Undset's Nobel Prize-winning work instead of what was really nothing more than a posh movie night.

He sighed...then finally noticed what looked like a two-block-long limousine waiting in the driveway. How it fit around the curve was beyond the laws of physics, but there it was, so over he jaunted to the driver's door, singing to *I'm An Englishman*:

> *It's for the Alice, don't you know?*
> *And I'm down a bloody rabbit hole.*

He tapped on the window. It whispered down and Adam told him. "Half a mo', mate. Casey's not quite — "

"Ready." The word came from by the front door.

Adam jolted up to see her exiting the house — hair brushed to perfection, a touch of rouge on her lips and cheeks and a simple dress of red silk flowing around her like delicate clouds to give her the aura of an angel come down from on high. She wore a chiffon wrap and carried a sparkling purse that was barely the size of her hand.

Before Adam could even think he popped out with, "Bloody hell. They spent more time on my big toe."

She gave him a quizzical look and asked, "Is that cool, crap or lemme out of here?"

In answer, he scurried around to open the door for her. She glided in, the scent of roses surrounding her. He followed.

Once inside he would have sworn that whoever built this car had worked out how a Tardis could have a Cadillac exterior and a sheik's mansion of an interior, with leather and polished wood and gleaming chrome and plush floor coverings.

He lowered himself into a seat, saying, "Here sits Aladdin atop his magic carpet." Whereupon the limousine began to move and he felt tickled in a spot he'd never been tickled in, so he twitched to try and make it stop.

Casey cast him a smile then opened an application on her phone. Up came an image of her paparazzi twins standing atop the motorbike, looking over the wall surrounding her home. They almost bounced with happiness as they looked at each other.

"Wait'll Lando sees Casey's new toy," popped out of the one with a camera around his neck.

"This'll bring us nothing but joy," the other chirped.

Adam gaped at the phone. "What the devil's that?"

"You'll see in a minute," she said.

They passed through the entry gate and Adam looked out the window to see them drop onto their bike, laughing, to chase after the limo.

Adam pointed back at them, saying, "You're spying on those men." Casey nodded. "Because they're spying on you."

She nodded. "Sean and Shawn, my own private paparazzi. S-E-A-N for photographs; S-H-A-W-N for video. Follow me everywhere." She showed him a bumper-level POV of the motorcycle behind them. "I've got little cameras all over the place. If one comes sneaking in, the cops come calling. Doesn't do much good against long lenses, but it's better'n nothing, and gives me the pleasure of hearing things like this."

She shifted to another window on her phone. It showed Sean and Shawn seated on their bike when Patricia drove up with Adam. He could just hear Sean say, "That's the bitch what slapped me down."

Shawn sighed and replied, "Yeah, you don't mess with her, I found."

Sean's voice was almost a whimper as he said, "We'd have made a mint with Casey's shot."

Shawn's snarky response was, "Night's still young and may be hot."

"They're Australian," said Adam, remembering Christopher Meillon was, too. "Good you're keeping a close watch on them."

Casey smiled. "Boys like that think they're smart and savvy, and never even consider that other people have access to the same spyware and machinery they do. They'd be so surprised that I'm never really surprised at what they pull."

"Seems rather elaborate and expensive."

She shrugged. "Part of the deal. One video creep needled an actor in a grocery store until the guy lost control and hit the prick, then he sued the actor for a million bucks. Settled for a hundred thousand. The actor had nothing to back up his version of events." She settled back. "Okay, first the movie then the after-party — "

Adam twitched, giggled and snapped, "Oh, bloody hell."

"What's wrong?"

"It's the glittery bits on these briefs. They tickle my...um...me."

She shrugged and said, "Orisi said you can free-ball it."

"Free-ball?"

"Take 'em off."

Adam bolted upright. "Here? Now?"

"I've seen naked men, before. But if you're still shy after Orisi's crap, I'll close my eyes." And she batted hers at him.

He glanced between her and that phone...then around the limo. There were probably a dozen cameras hidden in the car to make sure he didn't try anything, and he could see them getting an eyeful, so grew flush and much too proper. "And, um, and then have nothing between me and a ten thousand-dollar suit? I don't bloody *think* so."

She smiled. "You always like this when you're stoned?"

"Stoned? I'm not. I don't use drugs. I mean, I — " He stopped and took in a deep breath and leaned back, his mouth agape. "Oooooooooh. *Your batch, her batch,* those weren't just cookies!" He looked at Casey in a very cock-eyed way. "No wonder Julie called me a bad boy. I almost gave one to Dumpling. And that-that-that wasn't just orange juice, was it?"

Casey sighed. "Probably a Screwdriver."

"It seemed tart but sweet. I thought it's just California oranges-es. Oh, God, I can't be smashed." He leaned forward to lay his face in his hands.

Casey all but growled, "I'm gonna kill my mother."

He popped upright. "Food. I'm bloody hungry. Empty stomach makes it worse. Food. You — you mind if we stop someplace that bakes Tarclay's. Uh, takes Barclay's?" Then he glanced at his suit and added, "And maybe has a tablecloth I can use for protection?"

She gave him a tender smile and pointed to a small door under some side chairs as she said, "Check that cabinet."

Adam oozed down to sit before it, crossing his legs like Buddha before he remembered the suit. He huffed and accepted that it was too late to change direction, then he looked inside a door to find it had champagne and plates of healthy-looking nibbles. Very healthy. Extremely healthy.

He pulled them out to sniff at and asked, "Are you sure these aren't table decoration?"

She shrugged. "Low-cal, low-carb, high whatever the current food craze is. Might be good. Hold you till the party."

"Will there be real food there?"

"I'll make sure you're fed."

He huffed and handed her the tray. She popped up a small table between the back seats as he pulled out the champagne and looked back into the cooler. "No *Dom Perignon*? *Veuve Clicquot*? *Cristal*? Oh, dear, is Orisi's man allowed to drink the dregs?"

"It's just an act," Casey said. Adam snorted, making

73

Casey laugh. "Adam, don't worry about it; he likes you."

He huffed and hiccupped. And giggled thanks to the tickly bits.

"No seriously," she continued. "You didn't see him with Lando."

"Made him over as well, did he?"

"Tried to. But Lando was already set in his ways."

Adam shook his head, murmuring, "Quidam non scire canibus."

"What?"

He began working on the champagne as he said, "Hmm?"

"What did you just say? It sounded French or Italian."

It took him a moment to focus on her. "Sorry? Oh. That was Latin. Translation — *Some dogs never learn*." The champagne cork popped as the limo rounded a corner. He just managed to keep the spurt off the suit but, "I got it all over the carpet."

"Baby, that's expected. There's a cleaning fee included."

"Well, then..." He poured some into the glass, for the most part, and offered it to her. She produced a Towelette to wipe it clean.

"Thanks," she said. "I thought Latin was a dead language."

"Hmm? Oh. My specialty's incunabula, a lot of which is in Latin. Greek. German." Then he poured himself a glass...with a bit less spillage.

"How many languages do you know?"

"Those...and enough French to get by. Read it better than I speak it. But they come in handy-dandy when doing things like provenance. Articles. Blog." And the last word came out more like a burp.

"Baby, there's a nice seat up here." She pointed to the other side of the table.

"Hmm? Oh. Brilliant." He crawled his way up...and sat

74

cross-legged on there, too.

Casey looked him over and said, "Comfortable?"

He nodded. "Keeps everything in its place." Then he picked up one of the nibbles — a little white wrapper made from some kind of rice flour surrounding a questionable combination of cold vegetables. He bit into it and sighed. Not a hint of taste to any particle of it. Just squishy. "God, what I'd give for a pack of crisps...but it's for the *Alice*," he murmured.

"This is a real chore, to you."

"Sorry, it's just..." He leaned back into the seat. "Well, I'd be in bed, about now, after a nice quiet evening of reading. Cup of tea. Some biscuits. More reading done. I just have to keep reminding myself, it's for something very special," He grimaced and looked at her. "That's not to say I'm unhappy at what we're doing, but...."

"I don't get it," she said. "All this for an *Alice In Wonderland*."

Adam sat up straight. "Oh, no-no-no-no-no-no, no, no. No. This isn't any just *Alice* — just any *Alice*. It's the first impression, first bound printing — very, very, very rare. Very. One sold at auction, not so long ago. One-and-a-half million pounds."

"For a book?"

"Mm-hmm." And he hiccupped.

"Why?"

"Well...John Tenniel — he did the illustrations in it — he was displeased with their quality in the first printing, so they were disposed of. Only several had already been sold. Given away. Dodgson — um, Lewis Carroll asked for them back. To be destroyed and replaced. All but around fifty were returned. Only twenty-four are known to still exist, and most are in museums or university collections."

"Okay, so I guess that's why Grandy did it."

"Um...what — what's a Grandy?"

"My grandfather. He bought the book so I'd have

something to fall back on in case acting didn't work out."

"Hmph. Quite the insurance policy. How long did he have her?"

"Fourteen, fifteen years. Something like that."

"She's probably doubled in value from what he paid."

"Really?"

"The one that sold for one and a half million? It was bought for around four-hundred-thousand pounds back in 1997 or 98." He yawned and leaned back, and noticed the limo had a sunroof and he could see the stars through its glass, winking and nodding as the black forms of trees passed overhead...and remembered a song his mother sang to him, so whispered —

> *Watching the stars travel 'cross the sky.*
> *Watching my world go whispering by,*
> *From the day of my birth to the day that I die.*
> *Watching the stars travel 'cross the sky.*

"Mum would sing us to sleep with that song. Da read to us, all manner of books. Including *Alice*. I was five when he did. Read it meself a year later." He leaned closer to her, grinning and secretive. "I should tell you, this is not my first time handling an *Alice Sixty-five*."

"Is that what you call it?"

He nodded. "When I was fifteen, I minded the shop while Da popped out to collect one. Um, he had an antiquarian book shop and would represent clients at auction, and he'd won a copy for a gentleman up by Aberdeen." He focused on the whispering stars. Tender. Gentle.

"When he came back he had a clamshell case of green cloth. The cameo of Alice woven into it. Damask or satin, if I remember right. Lovely shape, even with burn damage on the back and the brass snaps needing a good polish. Inside was lined with the softest silk. *Color of champagne*, he said. He lifted it away like he was unwrapping a gift at Christmas to show me this worn little red book. Cloth binding. Much of the gilt rubbed off. He took her out of the case to show me the spine. Macmillan had been half washed away by a tea stain — that's the publisher's name; the edition that followed was put out by *Appleton* and is more common, though still rare. We have a copy of that at Merryton.

"Da told me not to, but while he was with a customer, I opened her to look at the title page. It was hardly faded. Minimal foxing. The only damage I could see was a small tear in the upper left corner of the frontispiece."

"Frontispiece?"

"Hmm? Oh, the page with the sketch of the Queen of Hearts holding trial, opposite the title page. I think it still had the original sheet of onion-skin between them." He looked back at the sunroof. "She was a beautiful book. Beautiful." He sighed. "I'm sure yours will be, as well. I'm so happy you sold her to us."

"Sold it?" Adam looked at her, blank, so she continued with, "Vincent doesn't tell you much, does he?"

Adam yawned and stretched, blinking. "Sorry? Um, tell me what?"

"The book never was mine. Grandy left it to Merryton."

Adam jolted upright to cry, "*Left* it to us!?" — and spilled champagne on a pants leg.

He jumped to his feet and hit his head on the sunroof glass and yelped, in German, "*Oh, shit! Shit! I've ruined a ten-thousand dollar suit! I can't believe it. Orisi'll send me to a bloody prison. I knew this would happen. I knew it!*"

Casey patted his arm and said, "Adam, Adam, Adam, coolness, baby. It's okay. It's okay. Towelettes are in that drawer." She pointed to under another seat. "And can you continue in a language we both speak?"

Adam sat back down, rubbing his head and forcing himself to take deep breaths. "Right. Right. Sorry. But this is exactly why no one should ever pay more than ten quid for trousers."

"Adam, coolness. They're just clothes."

"*Just clothes*," he snorted. "Not the categorization I'd use."

He sat on the floor, opened a bottle of water and wetted tiny paper napkins to clean the champagne, realizing this was the fourth time he was doing a wash within twelve hours. An unbelieving smirk came to his lips. And to think the family thought of Connor as being the neat freak.

Casey's cell phone rang, so she shifted the spy app to a small window and answered. "Yeah, Mom? ... Beryl Markham? Who's that?"

Without a thought, Adam murmured, "Champion horse trainer. Bush pilot. Aviatrix." Then he saw little granules of paper were sticking to the wet leg and growled, "Oh, God, now it looks like the suit's got dandruff."

Casey chuckled at him. "What was that last one? *Dominatrix*?"

Adam gave her his most confused-kitten look, then he blinked and shook his head and said, "Sorry? What did you say?"

"Beryl Markham?"

"Oh, um, yes. Female pilot. The Thirties. She was the first woman to fly from the UK to America. My sister's named for her."

"Oh, okay." She turned back to the phone. "You get that, Mom? Is that who it is? ... *She* dropped out? Don't be surprised I'm not surprised. It's not the first time she's pulled that just before production. ... Sure, if you can get the script I'll read it, but they won't consider me for it."

"Why not?" Adam asked, then he remembered Casey was on the phone so quickly added, "Sorry."

"It's okay, baby," Casey replied. "I'm known as an action bitch or scream queen, not drama. Type-casting. Hard to break out." She turned back to the phone. "Yeah, I know, our favorite paparazzi're sniffing our butts. ... Of course I've got a camera on them. I'm not stupid."

Adam looked through the back window and said, "Oh, forgot about them." Then he lowered a side window to look out...and almost tumbled through it.

Casey grabbed his coattail, to keep him in. "Adam. Baby, c'mon, use the sunroof." She hit a switch and it opened.

Adam looked up, joyous. "Oh, right. Sunroof. Right. Brilliant."

Casey kept talking on the phone. "Yeah, I'm here, I'm here, and you and I're gonna have a real talk, tonight, about — What?!"

Adam stood up through the sunroof and saw —

Sean shooting photos of him as Shawn drove the bike, video cameras mounted on both the center of its handlebars and on his helmet.

Adam laughed and called, "Hi-ho, way to go, paparazzi are the show!" Then he dropped back into the limo, laughing, a second before he heard a whoosh pass overhead. He looked out the rear window to see a low tree branch whispering away under a street lamp as two separate voices blurted from Casey's phone —

"Aw, one more moment's hesitation."

"And we'd have had decapitation."

"Damn, damn, damn."

Adam could not believe it. "Those bastards!" he snarled. "They were hoping I'd get my head smashed." He turned to Casey. "I can see why you don't like those men. They are not nice."

She just laughed, ended her call and flipped back to the spy app, joyous. "Oh, Lando. What an idiot."

"Sorry?"

She turned to him as she slipped her phone into her purse. "He's got Tito at the premier, watching for me. Pathetic."

"Oh. Of course." He focused on trying to clean the bits of paper napkin off his pants leg...then he stopped and looked at her and asked, "Um, what's a Tito?"

"Lando's bodyguard, backup, wing man. He doesn't

want to arrive before I do, so he's parked two blocks from the theater. Tito's gonna call him when we get there."

"He is not." She nodded. "This Lando sounds quite odd."

"You don't know the half of it."

Adam huffed then looked at his trouser leg. It still had dandruff. "Casey, I'm so sorry. I should probably stay in the car."

"Should've used Towelettes," she said, then she punched an intercom button. "Hi — cleanup supplies?"

The driver's voice filtered back, "Drug vomit? Drunk vomit? Food?"

"Champagne spillage, man's pants."

"Under the back-left seat."

She dropped down, opened a drawer, and removed a spritzer, a brush and a battery-powered hair dryer. "You're not the first guy to spill champagne around me," she said, in a wicked voice. Then she stretched Adam's leg out, sprayed water on it, and fired up the dryer while brushing away the lint.

All he could do was twitch and grin and say, "Careful."

SEVEN

Adam was fresh and clean by the time they pulled up to an old palace of a theater on Hollywood Boulevard. A red carpet led from the curb to massive posters on stanchions, where various Hollywood types posed and smiled as they fought the urge to spit on the scrum of paparazzi snapping photos. Hosts from entertainment shows waved them over to chat long enough to get a few five-second snippets of comments for tomorrow's broadcast while crowds of people on both sides gawked and screamed as if they were best friends with everyone there.

The moment the limo came to a halt, Adam hopped out and gave Casey his hand to help her exit, oh-so-cool and oh-so-very attentive. She smiled her thanks and buttoned his jacket.

"There you go," she said. "Nice and neat."

"Cheers," he grinned, gaping about. "My God, is it always so — ?"

"ADAM!!!"

He and Casey both jolted around to see —

"Julie! Manny!" he cried. "You're here!"

"Bloody right, mate," Manny yelled as they forged their way to the rope. "Should've told us you were coming here for this!"

"Adam, Adam, Adam," said Julie, amazed, "look at you! My God, I need a snap! You and us. Come on, Sweets."

Adam turned to Casey to ask if she minded him doing it,

but she was talking to a reporter off to one side. He shrugged and let Julie hug him to her as she said, "Hands up."

He turned his hands in a fake gangsta pose to show off the mandalas.

The people around them noticed and murmured things like —

"Who's he?"

"What's he doing with Casey Blanchard?"

"I think I've seen him in something."

Adam paid them no mind. "You really think the mandalas work with this outfit?" he asked Julie.

"Cuff-links're nice," she said. "If I'd known you were going to be in that suit I'd have added more shadow...but, Sweets, you are hot." She laid her chin in the crook of his neck and took another selfie. He chuckled.

"Oi!" Manny snapped, laughing and jostling Adam. "No flirtin' in front of the husband!" He pushed himself to Adam's other side, trying to maneuver the phone to get a good angle.

Casey noticed, said, "Talk to you later, baby," to the reporter and shifted over to take Manny's phone. "Let me."

The paparazzi scrum saw Casey snapping photos of Adam, Julie and Manny, so they snapped photos of her.

Others around them took photos, as well.

"How'd you get here so quick?" Adam asked Manny.

"Lyft," he said. "Orisi told us about this while you soaked yourself to a prune."

"And guess who's watching Dumpling?" Julie added.

Adam grimaced. "Is that wise? Your son may wind up wearing black and standing at attention."

"You've dealt with him," she shot back. "You tell me."

Adam hesitated then laughed. "*Pauvre, pauvre* Orisi."

"But good on us," Manny said.

"Going pub hopping," Julie whispered.

"Startin' with across the street," Manny also whispered.

Casey moved closer and also whispered, "Is a dozen

enough?"

Julie laughed and took the phone, saying, "Thanks."

Manny nudged her, put on a puppy dog expression and glanced between her and Casey. "Please, luv? Please?"

Julie rolled her eyes and motioned for Casey to stand next to Manny with Adam on her other side. "That's good."

Casey did as she was told, smiling as Julie shot away.

More people noticed and snapped pictures, as did the paparazzi.

Julie laughed at Manny. "I can't believe you didn't get one at the house."

Casey's smile widened. "Check your picture file."

Julie gave Manny a solid *What have you been up to?* glare. He grimaced a grin and said, "She weren't dressed like this. Nor was he!"

"I've never dressed like this," Adam said.

"I'll post it on me site," said Julie. "Snag a copy for your Mum."

"She'll not believe it."

"Come on, baby," Casey said to Adam. "Still gotta run the gauntlet." She stepped away, brushing aside other photo requests with a *Hi, I see you* point and the *Look around with a big grin* action to let everyone know she really, really cared.

"Gotta go," Adam told Manny and Julie. "I'm in attendance to the Queen." Then he followed Casey.

"Have fun, Sweets," Julie called.

He grinned back at them and saw two women nudge her, one saying, "What was that on his hands?"

"Her work," Manny replied, "and she don't do it on just anybody," then handed them Julie's card.

"So who *is* he?" asked the other one.

"You don't know?" Julie shot back, a twinkle in her eye.

"Adam Verain," Manny added, feigning shock at the woman's ignorance. Then he and Julie shook their heads at each other and muttered, "Americans," as they headed away.

Well that really got things going in the crowd.

"The guy with Casey Blanchard is Adam Verain."

"Never heard of him."

"He's English or Irish or something; I heard his accent."

"Is he the guy who's gonna be in that new Gray's movie?"

"With a suit like that he's gotta be somebody."

"He IS somebody! He's Adam Verain!"

"OH MY GOD, IT'S ADAM VERAIN!!!"

Adam cast a quick glance back at the crowd, nonplussed, then he heard Casey call, "Hi, Tito," and looked around to see she was smiling at a man near a side entrance. He was decked out in a block of a suit, and he looked Adam up and down as he pulled out his cell phone.

Adam nodded. "So that's a Tito."

Casey almost snarled, "Lando on the deck in ten...nine...eight...you get my drift." She slipped her purse into his coat pocket as she led him to a massive poster of the film. "Hold this for me, will you, baby?"

This poster was bigger than life, with a close-up of Casey's full face, looking vulnerable. Lando stood behind her, holding a pistol and posing in oh-so-deadly-serious a manner.

Adam glanced it over and his voice grew dramatic as he read, "Ah, *EVA NOTORIOUS. What he did was unforgivable. What she did was worse.* Or as Mum would say, *It's always the woman's fault. Right?*"

Casey cast him a smile. "Your mother's brilliant."

"She'd agree."

She patted him on the shoulder and said, "Wait here," then she went before the firing squad. Photographers called poses at her and asked questions and snapped pictures, and through it all Casey smiled and grinned and ignored the questions and let herself look as beautiful as she could.

Adam noticed Sean and Shawn had joined the pack. *Stubborn little men*, he thought. Then he heard an engine roar and tires squeal so turned to watch a half-million-dollar convertible spin around to skid across the street and come to a perfect halt at the red carpet. Behind the wheel was a man who was so butch, so buff, so much-better-looking-than-you, it had to be Lando Grissom. He wore a too-cool sports coat over a too-cool tee-shirt and too-cool jeans as he stood to accept cheers from the crowd. His grin was as bright as the sun, his profile sharp beyond belief and his sunglasses gleamed in the spotlights. He hopped out of the car and buttoned his coat in so sophisticated a manner, two women and a man swooned. He was perfection and demanded the full attention of one and all, and got it...

Except from a group of people who stayed focused on Adam...who didn't realize he had wandered close enough to them for one girl to grab the tail of his coat, yank him back to her and slam a huge kiss on his lips as someone else took a photo. Then another girl appeared over his shoulder for another photo as the first girl danced away, squealing, "Adam Verain kissed me!" More sets of hands grabbed him in places they should *not* have been grabbing, making Adam yelp and tear himself away as the crowd chanted, "Adam, Adam, Adam," and called to him with questions like —

"When's your next picture coming out?"

"Will you be naked, again?"

"I've seen everything you've been in!"

"I love your tush!"

Lando noticed and his grin tightened, then he spun around to open his car's passenger door...and out flowed Veronica D'Amour, barely in her twenties, barely in a dress that was barely Victoria's Secret, legs all the way down to there, face painted to L'Oréal gorgeousness, and hair coiffed and glowing to the maximum degree. She caught the entire crowd's attention and they screamed at both of them with —

"Veronica. I love you."

"Oh-my-God, Veronica! You're beautiful!"

"I want to have your children!"

"Veronica, I've got the perfect picture for you!" And on and on.

Casey heard them and called, in a tight voice, "Adam, over here."

He neatened himself, checked to make certain her purse was still in his pocket, and went to her, saying, "I have never had anyone grope or grab me in such a manner. Is this common practice?"

"When you're a sex symbol," she said as she took his arm. "Is there a video camera and somebody with a microphone up the carpet?"

He noticed she had closed her eyes. "Are you all right?"

She nodded. "Just giving my eyes a rest."

"I'm surprised you're not permanently blinded by all this."

"It's come close."

"Well...there's a woman holding a microphone next to a camera on a tripod, and she's waving us over. About thirty feet up."

"Be my guide dog?"

"Woof," he said then maneuvered her up the carpet, casting a quick glance back down it. "So that is Lando. About what I expected, though much taller."

Casey huffed and her grip on his arm tightened. "Check his shoes."

"Ah, he's in boots, as well." Adam looked closer. "With Spanish heels." And then it hit him. "Wait, wait, wait, wait, wait, are his also three inches!?"

"Puts him at six-four." Her grip began to really hurt. "He has to, because the Amazon beside him wears stilettos meant for bondage magazines, not real life."

The crowd kept roaring at Lando with love and joy and wishes as Casey's grip on Adam's arm finally reached the point of extreme pain and he had to pat her hand and say, "Casey, I'm right here. No need to take my arm off."

She hesitated...then relaxed, whispering, "Sorry, baby."

"It's all right," he said. "Just might need this hand. You never know." He looked back down the carpet. "So...the crowd seems to think the woman with him is someone, as well."

Casey jolted, opened her eyes to look at him...then look down at Lando and Veronica...then look back to Adam. "You don't recognize her?"

"She is somewhat familiar, but..."

Casey almost laughed. "She's in a medical drama on TV. Been in some movies. Covers of magazines." There was still no recognition in his eyes so she added, "She was in *Ilithium Four*."

That is when he nodded. "The seeress. Of course. Very odd take on it, I must say. Here you go." He positioned her in front of the video camera then just turned away to discreetly massage his arm.

Casey still noticed. "Oh...I really dug in, huh?"

He forced a smile. "Just...final aches from a match, on Saturday."

She gave him a slight shake of her head and put a hand to his cheek, saying, "You're sweet."

Some people in the crowd noticed and focused back on Adam and Casey to cry —

"Look at that! He's a gentleman!"

"Oh, my god, they are so in love!"

"Adam, I love you, you're perfect "

Casey heard them, grinned, and grew bright and bubbly in front of the Show Host as the woman said, "Casey Blanchard. Good to see you."

"Hi, baby, how you doing?" And they did the kiss-kiss thing.

"Big night for you, isn't it? Are you excited?"

"Couldn't be more. My first movie with sex, drugs, nudity, rock-n-roll, couture, violence, gun-fights and action out the wazoo, all in one package — so very mainstream; people're gonna have a blast."

"Sounds like it." She turned to Adam and asked, "So who's this on your arm?" in a tone of voice that was anything but professional.

Casey blinked in surprise then said, "Oh, this...is Adam."

Adam jolted around at hearing his name...and had to catch himself before he went around, twice.

"Sorry?" he said. "Um, yes. Yes. Adam Verlain."

The Host kept purring, "You made quite a hit with the crowd." He grinned and shrugged. "You sound English. Where you from?"

He gave her a cock-eyed look as he answered, "England."

"Wonderful." Spoken without irony. "And that is a class suit."

Casey maneuvered Adam closer, wrapping a gentle arm around his as she purred, "Not just anyone can look good in Orisi."

Adam brightened into a smile to say, "Oh, right, right, right. He's brilliant. Just ask him; he'll tell you."

Casey gave him a bigger grin as she said, "Just like your mother?"

He turned to her with complete seriousness to say, "Almost, but he's less militaristic."

The Host sighed and purred even lower, "Oh, Casey, if you ever decide to get rid of this one..."

"Never," said Casey. "He's unlike anyone I've ever been with, and that is so nice..."

Adam grinned at her as the crowd *ooh-ed* and *ah-ed* and said things like —

"They are the perfect couple."

"Stopped on the carpet to be with each other."

"What gorgeous children they'll have."

Adam kept facing away to keep them from seeing him fighting a laugh, then he noticed the paparazzi twins had set up next to the theater entrance, flashes and lights going...and he saw his reflection in the glass doors, on and off with each flash...and twinkly little sparkles twinkled and gleamed down around his crotch and —

Wait — his *crotch* was twinkling?!

Indeed it was, nice and bright and happy.

He froze, telling himself he must be imagining it. But more flashes got more twinkles down where Orisi's briefs were tickling him. Which made no sense...unless the sequins on the damn briefs were catching the light through his trousers whenever a flash hit him. No, it couldn't be.

Then he saw another set of sparkles.

And another!

Adam was horrified. All he could think to do was jam his hands in his trousers and hold them in front of his crotch — which actually wound up making him look amazingly casual and cool.

Of course, that is when the Host waved at Lando and Veronica. "Lando, over here. With Casey Blanchard." Then she whispered to the cameramen, "Keep both of them in the frame."

Casey seemed not to hear her, but Adam did, and he grimaced as Lando strutted up, Veronica locked on his arm. The man cast a long look at Adam before turning his sunglasses to Casey.

"Hi, Case," he said, in his deepest richest most melodious voice. "How's it goin'?" Making half the women in the crowd scream, along with more than a few men.

Casey let her fingers drift back to Adam's cheek as she said, "Peaches and cream, baby. Can't you tell?" He grinned.

"Who couldn't tell what's really going on with you?" Veronica purred, glancing her up and down with barely concealed condescension.

The Host popped in with a perky, "So, Lando, Casey, you two're doing okay since the breakup?"

Casey smiled. "It wasn't a breakup. Just a de-coupling. Like two cars on a freight train."

Lando's grin widened. "Yeah, sometimes people just

don't connect; other times they do."

Veronica shot a smug glare at Casey in a way that she was sure to notice and said, "Many times for the better."

"Depends on what you consider *connecting*," Casey said right back at her. "There's *so* many ways to do it."

Veronica straightened up to nearly Lando's height, her fingers twitching as her focus bore into Casey.

Watching them made Adam very uncomfortable, so he said, "Me Mum says the best way to connect with someone is through shared likes."

"Yeah, just be sure you find out what their likes are, first," Casey said, beaming at him. "Had I known what Lando's were...well..."

The Host's smile grew wary. "So...Casey, is this serious with you and Adam?"

Casey turned the beaming onto her. "All I can say is, he was there for me when I needed someone. Right, baby?"

"Um, yes," Adam said. "I was there, and now I'm here."

Lando turned his sunglasses to him, smiling as he said, "I'm glad, Case. I'm happy, too."

Casey grinned at Lando saying, "I'm so happy you're happy."

Lando kept his focus on Adam. "So how long you known Case?"

Adam blinked and shrugged and finally said, "Oh, um, seems like mere hours."

Casey sighed, "Time flies when I'm with Adam."

"Stands still for me," said Lando, "especially when this beauty's on my arm."

Veronica got all girly and sweet and gooey and said, "Oh, Landy."

Casey turned away to roll her eyes and mutter, "Oh God."

Veronica heard her and deliberately asked, "What did you say?"

"Just noting you're on his arm, tonight," Casey shot back. "Different position from the last time I saw you two together."

Lando tightened.

Veronica took a deep breath and fought to keep smiling.

Adam gulped, his mind a blank.

The Host gave a fake laugh and popped in with, "Uh — so — how about the movie?"

"It's great," said Lando, making himself turn to her, "turned out great. But I'm already set to start my next one."

"Yes," said Casey, her voice silky and cool as she smiled at Veronica, "he's always working on his next one."

Lando grew tighter.

Adam drew Casey back a step and whispered, "Y'know, Casey, I would dearly love some water." She seemed not to hear him, so he repeated, sharp and loud, "Casey, I would dearly love some water."

Casey gave a slight jerk. "Right, baby." Then she gave the Host a quiet smile and said, "Almost time for the movie. Lando can tell you more about it."

She casually aimed for the entrance. Adam was barely able to shoot out, "Thanks ever-so-much," before she dragged him away, with her.

"Good luck," the Host called.

Once they were in the theater's elegant lobby, Casey's face changed into something like a scowling grin as she glared back at Lando and Veronica. "The people calling for you instead of him!?" she muttered. "So perfect. Did you see his face? No wonder the son-of-a-bitch pulled his shit with Veronica. And that bitch calling them over — "

"...Casey..." She glared at him like she did not know him. He hesitated, pulled his hands from his pockets and said, "Do you really think we...we should have come to this...this event?"

Her face softened, again, and she said, "Had to, baby. It's in the contract. And it's important to let the world know I'm okay.

But thanks for getting me away from them."

"Will you be all right, then?"

"Peaches and cream."

"Then if...if you don't mind," he said, "I — these trousers're soiled and the briefs are quite the nuisance; I think I will remove them."

She nodded. "See that bar?" He looked around to find a portable service center where the bartender was handing out glasses of wine. "Get some water there, no charge."

"Thanks. Bring you something?"

"No. No, that's okay."

"Right back."

"Fine, baby, I'm in the theater." But she was back to watching Lando and paying Adam little attention.

Adam scurried to the washroom and slipped into a stall, then he hung the suit jacket on a peg and removed the trousers. Next came discarding those bloody briefs. He stared at the sequins, trying to make sense of it. What sort of idiot puts something like that up against a man's private parts? How bloody stupid can one be? And then for them to make his crotch explode in twinkling light!? It was without compare, to say the least. Were he ever to see this man, Orisi, again, he doubted he would bother to hold himself back from a serious retort.

But then he began to think about his own actions. He must have made a complete fool of himself, the way he'd been with Julie and Manny, and allowing people to think he was someone he wasn't. And there was that near fight between Casey and Lando. It escalated so quickly he couldn't think of a thing to say except he was thirsty. How stupid can one be?

His father wouldn't have allowed the situation to even begin. He'd have known what to say to defuse the anger, keep everyone on balance. He was never flustered, always even, in control, precise, calm...and happy. He'd have turned the chatter from viciousness into something positive.

Adam learned this when an older lady had entered the

shop to look for a first edition of Somerset Maugham's *Ashenden*.

"Published by Heinemann, in London," she had told him as if he knew nothing about books.

They had a copy, but he had miscataloged it as a first instead of a second. When he showed it to her, she knew it wasn't right and began to complain about him raising her hopes only to dash them.

Adam had just turned thirteen and was rather more contrary, so he'd begun to argue with her, but Da had come straight over and sent him back to the counter. *To study.* Then he led the lady to the back office for a cup of tea with the promise he would find her the exact right copy. As he worked, he soothed her and learned she was of limited circumstances so could not afford a true first edition; she merely wished to look at it.

Adam heard and muttered, "Then why raise a bloody row over it?"

"Here we go," Da said to the lady loudly enough so Adam could not help but hear him, which he understood to mean, *Be quiet.* "There are some lovely first editions at our better antiquarian book shops," he continued, "but I wonder if you might be interested in a very nice American first, in hardcover at a shop just two streets away. The only differences between that one and the one you seek are, of course, the American spelling and the dust cover. The art is less dramatic than the British one, but it may be within your price range."

The lady grew hesitant. "May I ask, what is the price?"

"You may. Eighty-five pounds."

"Oh," she said, a bit more perked up. "Would — would they be willing to put it aside for a day or two? I would so love to have a nice copy, even if it is in American."

"I'm sure they would," said Da. "But let me ring them."

Which he did, and they did, and she left quite pleased.

But Adam huffed, "All that work for nothing."

"Hardly," Da said, not looking at him. "This lady's father passed away a few days ago, and it wasn't till he was on his last breath he told her of what his father had done, and how Maugham had known him and used his exploits for one of the stories. She had always thought of her grandfather as a suit of clothes, nothing more. Now she must re-evaluate everything. But what's important is, she left happy and when she returns," whereupon he cast Adam a look, "and she will return, then she will buy something. Because she will remember us as the shop that helped her."

True to Da's belief, at Christmas she bought a dozen books for Boxing Day. They only totaled up to a hundred pounds but his father was happy. He liked people...liked matching books with people...and for the first time Adam had thought that might be why he and Mum got along so well.

She had been a brisk no-nonsense Sister till they were married, then she became a brisk no-nonsense physical therapist. All *best-for-you* kind of certainty in her actions, touched with a gentle humor. David and Beryl took after her while Connor was an exaggeration of her less delicate qualities. Adam was the only one of the family on his father's wavelength. The only one who loved the shop as much as he. And as Da ran it, the shop did well enough, and would probably still be going had he not died.

But he had...and what was done was done.

Adam sighed. Remembering his father's steadiness brought a sense of calm back to him along with the understanding that it was not the end of the world. Any foolishness he might have committed here would quickly be forgotten, and he would soon be back in his own little cubicle, safe and protected. Casey and Lando were all people really cared about and, to his credit, he had pulled her away from a situation that threatened to degenerate into an embarrassing public fight.

So Adam pulled back on his trousers — which felt odd, not having the briefs to hold everything in place. Then he took the coat to slip on — and Casey's purse clattered to the floor and popped open to reveal folded money, comb, keys, lipstick, phone, compact...and three gleaming neon prophylactics.

He burst out with, "Bloody hell — what're those for?"

"Buddy, if you gotta ask..."

To say Adam jumped five feet into the air would not be an exaggeration. The voice came from the stall next to his. He'd had no idea anyone else was even in the room.

"Sorry," he said. "I just meant — nothing."

He scooped everything back into the purse. Naturally, his knee found the one sticky spot on the floor. From what he had no intention of hazarding a guess, still he burst out with, "This thing's a bloody magnet for filth."

"Ain't we all?" said the voice.

Adam bolted from the stall, almost back to being flustered. He used a paper towel to wipe at the dirt on his knee then just sighed, stuffed the briefs into a trousers pocket and held Casey's purse as he exited the washroom —

To find the lobby deserted. He could hear the movie had begun.

"Bloody hell," he muttered. "How long was I in there?

He scurried to the theater doors, but an usher blocked his path and asked, "You on the guest list?"

"I...I'm with Casey Blanchard," he said.

The usher checked a sheet of paper and shook his head. "She's not a plus one."

"A what?"

"No guest. She didn't list a guest."

"She must not have had time; she invited me only this afternoon."

"Got proof?"

"Go ask her."

"Can't. Movie's started." He motioned to the purse. "That hers?"

Adam looked down at it. "Yes, I'm holding it for her."

"Any ID in there? Phone? Camera? Something?"

He started to open it — then stopped. In no way did he want anyone to see what it contained. He said, "I — I — no, I can't go into this; it — it's not mine."

"Yeah. Sure." And the look on his face said, *Get lost*.

There was no need to argue. Besides, he hated watching a film after it had begun. So he backed to the bar, saying, "When she comes looking for me, I'll be right over there, and you'll wish I wasn't."

The guy seemed not to believe him.

The bartender was almost packed away when Adam came up and said, "Excuse me, I'd just like some water, please."

He didn't even look around to say, "Closed."

"Just a bottle of water."

"Closed."

Adam huffed and went to the concession stand. A pretty girl who was probably in high school greeted him with, "Yeah?"

"Excuse me," he said, "do you accept cash cards? All I have on me is Sterling."

"Input what you want, over there. Pay. I'll have it ready."

She pointed to something that resembled a cash machine. Standing alone. By a column. Like a bandit.

He went to it, wary, saw it had a massive screen with very bright graphics on it, and for once was glad the instructions were simple and basic. He input his order...and it came up asking for payment of sixteen dollars.

"For popcorn and a bottle of water!?" he huffed. "Maybe you are a bandit."

But he accepted the charge, slipped the chip into the reader, and input his passcode. It was declined. Twice.

He called over to the girl, "It's not working."

She shrugged and said, "Try another card."

"This is all I have. It should be fine. I've plenty in my account."

"Try that one." She pointed to another machine.

He went to it and did, but the same thing happened. He finally decided it might be because he was in Los Angeles and hadn't informed his bank, so he asked, "Is there a phone about that I could use?"

"Phone?"

"A public phone. I don't have an American SIM card for my mobile — and besides, I don't have it with me."

"Used to be one outside, around the corner."

Adam headed out...and noticed the usher was watching him as if he were a terrorist. He shook his head. Americans could be very odd.

He looked around to find there did used to be a phone, outside, but now the apparatus to hold it was empty. He glanced about the entire building. No more stanchions. No more posters. No more crowd. Just cars whipping past on a very busy street and rock music blasting from somewhere. No sign of the limo they had come in. No phone anywhere. Adam huffed and returned to the theater's entrance...only to be stopped by the same usher.

"Got a ticket?" he asked.

"You just saw me come out here," Adam said.

"No ticket, no entry," he said, his eyes filled with false concern.

"I know I can't go into the film," I said. "I just want to wait inside."

"No invitation, no entry," he said.

"All right...fine...but how much longer is the film going?"

The guy shrugged, his eyes still *so-very-concerned.*

Adam huffed and stormed over to a bench, only to find it covered in more bird shit than the pier in Brighton and —

"ADAM!"

He spun around and saw nothing but passing cars and blank buildings — and then Manny across the street, cigarette in hand, jumping up and down and waving at him as he cried, "What you doin' outside!?"

"Long story," Adam called back.

"Come over! Tell us 'bout it!"

Adam decided the movie would be going for at least another hour so headed for the corner. He reached it just as the traffic light turned in his favor and started across, causing a car that intended to turn right to hit its brakes, causing the car behind it to slam into its rear, almost knocking it into him.

The driver burst out of the rear-ended car, screaming, "What the fuck's wrong with you?!"

"I had the signal," Adam shot back.

"You should've fuckin' seen I was turnin' here, you son-of-a-bitch!" The man was getting ready to hit him. In response Adam growled and got ready for the idiot to try and —

Manny appeared and shoved him towards the other side of the street, saying, "Go on, mate. Julie's waitin'."

The driver snarled up to Manny, "Who the fuck're you?"

To which Manny bellowed, "I'm his fookin' bodyguard, ya fookin' git. Ya don't wanna mess wit' Adam Verain, ya fookin' arsehole, 'cause if ya'd hit him, ya'd have been in the shite for centuries. What ya *do* wanna do is watch the arsehole what smacked ya, 'cause he's about to make off an' leave ya to handle th' fixin' of ya car, ya'self!"

The driver spun around, saw the other car backing up and bolted over to it. "Hey, where the hell you goin'?"

Then Manny shoved Adam the rest of the way across the street and down the sidewalk, laughing all the way.

"I can handle meself," Adam protested.

"Oh, you don't want trouble in America," Manny said. "They're the arseholes of the world when it comes to prison."

He pushed Adam into the noisy California version of an English Pub and called, "Julie, look what I brought home! Can I keep him?"

Adam saw her at the other end of the bar, talking to a man in a blinding white suit. They both spun around and waved as Julie screamed, "It's Adam!"

And what did the man in white say? "Jumpin' jeebus!"

It was Orisi.

EIGHT

"Sweets, why're you over here?" Julie cried as she pushed her way through the crowd to Adam, Orisi right behind her.

"Too bloody full of himself to bother with his own girl's movie," Manny laughed then called around the bar, "Oi, this man's dating Casey Blanchard!"

Adam huffed. "We're not dating!"

"Yeah, right, escorts her to a premier but they're *not dating.*"

Adam huffed. "Manny — "

Julie grabbed Adam's tie, yanked him around to her, and said, "Go with it, Sweets. I know men who'd gladly die to be in your place."

"Damn right," Orisi laughed. "So what — she banish you for bein' you?"

"No!" Adam gasped. "We got separated when I went to remove those bloody briefs of yours."

"What'd you do that for?"

"They sparkle through my trousers!"

"Bullshit! This is brushed wool."

"Tell it to the glittery bits you put on my bits," Adam retorted. "Then they wouldn't let me into the theater because I'm not her *plus one*, whatever that means, and — well, my mobile is — um, I can't find a — I need to call my bank and can't find a phone."

"Here," Julie said, pulling hers from her purse and handing it to him. "Now what's your poison?"

"Thanks, I'll pay the charges. Front me a Guinness? Pint?"

"A man after me own heart," said Manny. "Oi, barkeep, my famous friend, Adam Verain, will have a pint of Guinness!"

Adam almost corrected him then decided it might be better if no one knew his real name. He dialed the number on the back of his cash card, then as it rang he motioned to Orisi, who was now talking to a group of Japanese tourists, and murmured to Julie, "Wasn't he watching Dumpling?"

She carefully lifted the back of Orisi's coat. Underneath it was the little beast in a baby snuggler, sound asleep.

Adam grimaced and whispered. "Is this legal?"

Julie put a finger to her lips. "Bartender hasn't noticed."

Adam just sighed. Then he saw some of the Japanese people were watching him and pointing at him and smiling at him so smiled back, sort of, and turned his full attention to the phone. He was still on it when his Guinness was set before him. And when his second was, thanks to a Mr. Bunko, who *wanted to buy a celebrity a drink*. He was close to giving up when the bank's customer service accepted he was who he claimed to be and unlocked his card. Just in time to buy his own round.

"Perfect," he chuckled, then jolted and asked the bartender. "Do you serve food?" The man held up a bag of Cheetos. Adam nearly cried with happiness. "Brilliant. I'll take ten — and if you have a bowl..."

A clear basin was put before him. He opened all the bags into it, then jolted to a halt and looked around to see —

Orisi was off in a corner miming to Los Lobos' *Kiko and the Lavender Moon*, several Japanese women watching him, enraptured.

Adam tapped Julie on the shoulder and asked, "Does he still have Dumpling?"

She nodded. "Little beggar's knackered."

"Oh, God," said Adam, "did Patricia feed him — ?"

"Not like what you had, Sweets. *She* had brains enough."

"You — you knew what she was feeding me?"

Julie's grin went ear to ear. "Oh...you didn't?"

"I did," Adam huffed then admitted, "eventually."

Julie laughed and grabbed Manny. "You gotta hear this."

Adam sighed and dove into the Cheetos and the brew. Julie and Manny joined him as did a number of other bar patrons, who bought their own bags to add in.

Orisi finally appeared beside them to gobble down a fistful with as much gusto as anyone else...until he realized what he was eating, saw the orange dust on Adam's lips and fingers, and grabbed a cloth from the bartender to wipe Adam's mouth as he howled, "Jumpin' Jeebus, son, you're gonna cellulite right out of them pants! Work them carbs off! GO!" He pushed him into the center of the room, crying, "Barkeep, somethin' fast and furious!"

Adam pulled away from the man, asking, "What're you taking about? What do you want me to do?"

"Bust a move!" Orisi said as Ricky Martin's *Livin' la Vida Loca* began blasting over the speakers. "Found a video on *YouTube* of you 'n that girl, junior competition..." He did a quick circle around Adam, clapping.

"Orisi, you'll wake Dumpling!" Adam growled, soft and low.

"Then better get to it, son."

"Here, Sweets," Julie screamed, "show us what you got!"

Adam looked around. Others were clapping and whistling along with Orisi. It took him a moment, but he finally decided, "Bugger it. Just like with Chandra but without her."

He whipped off his coat, slung it to Julie, took a dramatic pose and spun into an old-style *Flamenco* with a healthy dose of *Paso Doble*.

The floor was wood.

His heels were hard.

His hips swiveled but his posture was exact.

Everything about him radiated perfection.

Patrons clapped and pounded on tables and women screamed at him like he was a Chippendale's stripper.

He fed off it to become more and more intense, taking sharper poses and faster turns and making more elaborate moves.

Manny grabbed Adam's coat and held it like a cape.

Adam snarled, made like a balletic bull to whisk after it, then stomped around and posed and did it, again. Even Orisi seemed impressed.

When the song ended, Adam froze in an elegant finish...then broke into laughter as patrons crowded around to tell him he was great and lovely and talented and amazing. He fought to catch his breath, but he didn't have a chance to collapse against the bar for another ten minutes.

Then he downed half of his third Guinness.

Julie appeared on his right, grinning. "Living up to your image, Sweets."

Adam laughed. "I haven't done that in fifteen years."

Orisi appeared by Adam's left to say, "Damn, son, first it's rugby, then it's ballroom?"

Adam took another deep breath, accepted a towel offered by the bartender, wiped off his face, and ran his hand through his hair then said, "Five years lessons — no, six." Julie cast him a *You're kidding* glance. Adam chuckled. "Helped in rugby."

"So you really are a rugger bugger," Orisi cooed, his hand now on Adam's shoulder. "Thought you was just foolin' me."

"No, no," Adam said. "I mean, yeah, it's a pub league and we play for fun and have pints after, but I'm not a thick-headed arse — am I?"

"Oh, calm down, son," Orisi said, casting him a sly look. "It's just — thinkin' about all that body contact. Pressin' hard against each other. Hands everywhere, gettin' all worked up for *more fun*, after the match."

"What're you on about? By that point, all I'm ready for is a hot shower, a good book, and some sleeps."

Orisi gazed at Adam, for a long moment, then sighed and said, "Of course," and swatted his butt and wandered away.

Adam froze...then blinked...then turned to Julie to whisper, "Wait, was Orisi making a pass at me?"

She barely kept from laughing. "You couldn't tell?"

"Didn't even think about it. Why would he do that?"

"Why wouldn't he? You're his creation."

Adam huffed. "Hardly on the scale of *Pygmalion*. Besides, I'm not the sort gets passes made. By men or women. They want Tolkien's orcs or elves, not...not hobbits."

"You call yourself a hobbit?"

"My brother does. Connor. Named me. Rightfully..."

She brushed a hand across his shoulders, smiling. "You don't think much of yourself, do you?"

Adam wiped Cheetos dust off his lips and hands before answering, "What...what's to think about?"

"Hopes. Dreams. Possibilities."

"Those can go from bad to worse. World has a way of doing that, you know."

"Could go better."

Adam grew very still. "Not in my experience."

Manny broke in to nudge Adam. "Cinema's lettin' out."

"Time to get back to your girl," said Julie.

"She's not *my girl*," Adam said. "And my Mum would give you the stick if she heard you refer to another woman that way."

Julie winked. "If your Mum'd seen you two together, she'd agree."

Adam huffed then said, "Let me know how much I owe you, right? Including the charges on your phone."

"No, Sweets," she laughed.

"Julie, I pay my own fare — "

"I got five jobs off people seeing your hands, two of

them movie stars, at triple rate. This is now a very profitable holiday, so shut up."

He hesitated. "You sure about this?" She just smiled at him. He looked at her for a moment longer...then smiled back. "Cheers."

The bar patrons crowded around to call farewells, and clap him on the back, and swat him on the rear, and everything else you can imagine. Fortunately, he had already given out a dozen autographs and the Japanese group had long since moved on, so he was able to escape fairly quickly.

He headed back across the street, this time jaywalking because traffic was snarled. Naturally a maniac waiting on the inside lane of a cross street at a red light decided to turn right in front of two lines of cars, barrel down the center lane of the road and very nearly run him over.

He exploded with, "Oi, watch where you're bloody going!" For all the good something like that does to quickly receding rear lights.

He made it to the other curb just in time to see Casey appear in the theater lobby. She was smiling and people were thronging around her, but her face was tight, her pleasant expression more a mask than honest. Then she tightened more.

Adam followed her gaze to see Lando at a different door, just as thronged, Veronica molded to him and beaming even brighter. The man looked back at Adam, his smile widened...and he slipped the usher some money.

Adam scowled. Had he actually paid the little creep to keep him out of the theater?

"Why you out here?" Adam jumped around to find Casey beside him, her mask gone and irritation in her eyes. "The movie was half over before I gave up on you."

"I had no money for food," he said, "and needed to use the phone and couldn't get back in."

Casey blinked then looked at that usher. Her irritation vanished into weariness. "He the one who stopped you?" Adam nodded. She sighed, "You should've just waited in the limo. Plenty of food and water in there."

"Where is it?"

She looked around to find a dozen limos on the street. Others had parked in a nearby lot with more on standby in front of a higher-end hotel.

"I'll send him a text," she said. "He'll be right up." She took back her purse and pulled out her phone, then frowned. "Adam, there's money in here, and my phone; why didn't you just use this?"

"It's not mine, and you weren't here to ask."

She looked at him as if seeing him for the first time. "Lando would've taken a fifty and kept the change."

"Your Lando is definitely quite odd," Adam said, glaring at the man as he continued to hold court in the lobby. "You sure you want to leave? Seems the patrons are not done patronizing."

"I just spent two hours in a freezing theater watching a man I used to love pretend he loved me. I need a double-dose of Midol. Triple." The tight face-mask was back on.

"Head?" Adam asked. She gave a soft nod. He slipped behind her and set his fingers on her shoulders, with his thumbs pressing against her spine. "Here." He ran his thumbs up her neck.

She tried to pull away, saying, "Baby, no — "

"Please, just give me a chance," he said as he pushed on. He could feel the tension in her. "Good God, you are tight." He started massaging, soft and easy.

A moment later, Casey sighed and said, "Oh, Adam. Baby. Magic fingers."

He had to chuckle at that. "Told you, Mum's a physical therapist. She knows how to make pain vanish. And she would give you the stick for letting yourself become so tense." He let his voice grow close to wistful. "But your skin — the, um, the result of Orisi's cleansing products?"

"If I don't use that crap, I'll never get styled in this town, again."

"Something I needn't worry about," he chuckled. "Was...was reaction good for the film?"

"Who knows? Sorry you didn't see it."

"I will when it's at the local cinema."

"Thanks." She hesitated then murmured, "Adam, those cookies and juice — Mom never should've slipped that crap in on you."

"No worries. Effects are now in the past."

"You're sweet," she sighed. "My mother — she thinks that's how everybody should handle life. Like she does. More and more, lately." Adam just kept rubbing. "She focused her whole self on my career. Now? I've got agents and a manager and — and I — I think she's lonely."

"Surely she has friends."

Casey chuckled. "You know what a friend is in this town? Someone you see twice a year. Maybe three times. More than that and you're in a relationship. Not like your world. I bet you have lots of friends."

"I don't know about lots," he said, still rubbing. "People from university. Mates on the team. Neighbors. The spouses and families of David and Beryl. Connor's, not so much; they're all in France."

She almost turned to look at him. "You keep inventory?"

He laughed. "No, these are just people I've been around forever. People who know me...understand me. Let me be."

"Sounds so nice. People say they understand me, but only when they're after something. Nobody really knows me. Not even me."

"Doesn't everyone feel that way?"

"I guess." A moment later, the limo arrived and she asked, "Feel like more table decorations?"

"Um, no, don't mix with Guinness." He gave her shoulders one last squeeze, sending tingles into his heart. "All better?"

"Baby, I feel beautiful."

"You? How is that possible?"

She swatted him, laughing, and got in the limo and —

"There he goes! There's our Adam!"

He popped up to look across the limo and see the entire bar outside watching him, Orisi in the center of it all, holding Dumpling. Adam waved at them, got in and appeared through its sunroof, arms spread wide, laughing. Casey joined him.

"Is that where you were?" she asked, motioning to the patrons.

"I couldn't exactly wait on those bloody benches; they were covered in bird feces."

Casey laughed, pulled him close and waved to the group as they started to drive away.

The group cheered and chanted, "Casey! Adam! Casey! Adam!"

Lando, still thronged with people just outside the theater, heard them and looked around.

Casey saw him, laughed and flipped him off as the limo eased into traffic.

Adam took on Vincent's headmaster tone as he said, "Casey! How positively horrid of you."

Still laughing, she opened the video app on her phone to show the paparazzi twins were back on their motorbike. He could just make out that were telling each other —

"Blow up should be happening soon."

"Then it's gonna be *High Noon*."

"How much you wanna bet they got a good shot of it?" Casey chuckled.

Adam looked at her. "Are we planning something to fulfill this dream of theirs?"

She gave him a wide grin as she said, "No, baby. It'd be stupid, doing something like that. I'm tired of being stupid." She rubbed her arms, so he removed his coat and put it over her shoulders, to her surprise. "Adam, you don't have to — "

"I'm from London," he said. "This is like a fine

summer's night there. I'm quite comfortable."

She pulled it tight. "Thanks. Y'know, I still need to make a quick appearance at Lando's, then we'll head back to my place. Light a fire. Order in Chinese or Indian. Get you a good night's sleep. That okay?"

He let a long sigh out. "Sounds like heaven."

She kept her eyes on him for a moment longer, nodding. "Yes, it does."

— NINE —

Lando's place was a huge two-story rectangle of black glass, silver metal and blank white sides that was set fifty feet back from the street and had a dozen thick trees and shrubs in two groupings in front. To its left, a neighbor's compound was encompassed by a massive brick wall dripping with ivy; to its right, the grounds were lined with a fence of wrought-iron spikes sticking up from thick bushes. The only sound came from traffic down on Santa Monica Boulevard, which was a bit too close for the area to be considered high-end...but the photographers prowling across from the house were still properly silent in their fake respectfulness.

Adam was taken aback at the sizes of the three estates. "I thought land was premium price, in Southern California," he murmured.

Casey laughed. "You should see my property taxes."

The limo whispered past security guards and up a wide curved driveway to a valet, then Adam and Casey hopped out. Photos flashed.

He chuckled. "Can they see anything from the street?"

"Look at how the trees are arranged," said Casey. Adam realized they were spaced just wide enough to allow the photographers a good view of the front entrance. Casey continued with, "This is all they get; in *Lando's* back yard, the level of security is insane. C'mon."

"Hey, Case."

Adam turned to find Tito blocking the door, tablet in hand.

"Tito!" she said, happy as could be. "How'd you beat us?"

"Private screening last night. Came back to handle the early crowd. Why you here, anyway? Lando's squeeze'll toss a fit."

Casey gave him the sweetest smile she could. "Just answered your own question."

He fought a grin, nodded and stood aside. Adam followed her in, pulling his suit coat on with a cockeyed smile as he said, "I'm her plus one. I really am."

Tito just shook his head.

Inside was nothing but gleaming bronze and glass furnishings that reeked more of IKEA than Rodeo Drive, all atop a sleek Teak floor. The foyer was open like a courtyard, with stairs to the right, while a dining room, living room and office were to the left, all feeling private yet unenclosed.

Casey stopped and checked her phone. Adam looked over her shoulder and saw the limo was pulling back onto the street, its camera showing the paparazzi twins arriving to join the other reporters.

Adam shook his head. "They're like shadows, aren't they?"

"Lando hates those two," she said, smiling. "They caught him making out with a co-star behind a club on Ventura and sold it to half a dozen tabloids. Got her divorced and him almost married. Let's go."

She led him into a long room that was as tall as it was wide, with hundreds of colorful Japanese lanterns filling the ceiling. Dozens of people in exotic masks of gold and chrome and white plastic danced as they drank neon-colored liquids through straws that lit up; some also vaped on neon-lit cigarette pipes. A DJ worked flashy turntables by a wall of windows looking out on a yard and pool that were landscaped to seem like the South

African veldt. All relatively normal except for one thing.

The silence.

There was no music. No voices. Barely even the sound of shuffling feet. It was spooky quiet as the dancers texted on their phones and read each other's phones and silently laughed at each other's phones and argued via each other's phones and blew fake smoke into the air and lit up their straws as they sipped. It was so bizarre, Adam had to check his chin to make sure his mouth was shut.

Someone slipped up behind him to place an elegant mask over his face and hook it behind his ears and —

MUSIC POUNDED INTO HIM, SHARP AND THUMPING, VIBRATING TO THE VERY TIPS OF HIS WELL-PEDICURED TOES.

He jerked it off to find ear-buds built into the ear-rests, and a girl who couldn't have been legal age was casting him a bewildered look.

"You hear the music with these," she said.

"Why?" popped out of him.

"Beverly Hills noise ordinance." She smiled and wandered away.

"Dear God, Casey, is this how — ?" But she was not next to him. "Casey?" He looked around. She had vanished. Then he felt the weight of her purse in his coat pocket and huffed, "I'm bloody Gunga Din, to her."

A woman of indeterminate age, dressed in near-nothing couture with a streak of gleaming silver in her blacker-than-black hair, oozed up to ask, "Did you say you were somebody?"

"What do you mean?" was all he could think of as a response.

"I heard you say you're somebody," her voice like a whisper trying to sound loud.

"I...I was merely referencing a literary character and — " Adam replied.

She shook her head. "If you're not somebody, now,

111

you're nobody, unless you were somebody, yesterday, or might be, tomorrow."

Adam blinked. "I don't know who I could be but me, today."

"Then why are you wasting my time?" And she oozed back into a shadow.

He blinked, shook his head and leaned against the window frame to watch the silent dancing increase in frenzy and —

Incense appeared before him, sharp and smoky. He jerked back to bump against the glass. "Careful," he said.

An Earth Mother dressed in a flowing Sari with a multitude of beads dripping around her neck, hair frizzed into half a halo secured by headbands, held the stick straight up and rolled it between her fingers. She nearly caught his nose with it.

"Please...stop!" Adam growled.

"Your aura needs serious cleansing," the Earth Mother said. She spun about and swirled the incense smoke around them both.

He coughed and tried to wave the smoke away. "Orisi did quite enough of that, thank you."

She gasped and grasped Adam's hands to look closer at the henna designs. "What exquisite work," she whispered, awe-struck. "The depth and lacey intricacy, and so fresh."

Adam took his hands back and held them behind him as he said, "Thank you."

The Earth Mother pressed closer to Adam, her eyes bright with joy and fire, the scent of cinnamon wafting about her. "They look like Julie Marshe-Croton's work. She's renowned for her Mendhi, and she's English. Like you." She threw her hands in front of his face to show him elegant designs were laced around her fingers and colored her nails. "My daughter did these. She worships Julie Marshe-Croton. And you say she's here? In L-A?"

"I, uh, I-I-I-I said nothing — "

"She is! Look how the incense curls around your nose!"

Adam went cross-eyed to look. It was!

Before he could think of a thing to say in response, the Earth Mother slipped two sticks of incense crisscross through his mask's eye-sockets, singing, "Keep them together and all will be well." She hugged him nearly to death then pulled out her cell phone and bounded away, saying, "Serena has to know!"

Adam removed the sticks from the mask and shoved them into a potted plant, growling, "I. Am. Down. The bloody rabbit hole."

"Hi, baby," screeched into his head. He jolted up to find Casey beside him, mask on her face. She removed it to say, "Sorry, little girl's room called. You not having fun?"

What could he say but, "It...it's all very odd."

"Wanna go?" He nodded. "C'mon. I'm done here."

They headed for the front door, opened it and were about to pass through when —

Lando's car zoomed up the driveway.

Casey spun around and said, "But just one dance. Okay? Just one."

"Casey, I — " was all he got out before she put the mask on his head and jerked him into the middle of the dancers.

Paula Frazer's *What Is and Was* drifted through the ear-buds. Casey started moving as if the gentle melody were flowing from her.

Adam huffed and called out, "Casey," but she just motioned for him to dance with her. She was beautiful, elegant, sexy, not a care in the world...still he put up his hands and cried, "STOP!"

She did, confused.

"If you really want to dance," he said, "let's do this."

He took her left hand with his right, set his other hand on her hip, drew her tight to him...and led her into a whispery Rumba that fit the music as if it were meant to be, telling her, "Slow, quick, quick, slow, turn, slow, quick, quick, slow, turn."

Casey was startled and stumbled a bit, then laughed and let him take the lead. Dancers stood aside to watch them; some even joined in.

Adam saw Lando and Veronica enter the foyer followed by crowds of people from the theater — who kept coming and coming and coming like the never-ending scarves from a magician's sleeve. They continued to fawn over their king and queen, the girl putting a mask on every one of them.

A wicked grin crossed Adam's lips and he whispered to Casey, "Let's do a bigger turn." Then he swung her into a glorious swooping dip, elegant and smooth and sure.

As she rose, she saw Lando watching them, a cold grin on his face, and laughed, "Again."

So Adam did. Some of the dancers clapped for joy.

That is when Lando pushed over to them, the forced grin still on his face, followed by Tito and his tablet. He offered Adam his hand, forcing him to stop. "We didn't get introduced. Lando Grissom."

Adam removed his mask to take it. "Adam Verlain." Casey continued dancing, seemingly oblivious.

"Ver-LAIN," Lando said. "Oh, that makes sense, now." Tito nodded and turned away.

Adam was taken aback so said, "Sorry?"

"Nothin'." Lando motioned to Casey as he continued, "Glad to see Casey's finally gettin' over me. We were worried about her, hidin' herself off, like she did."

"Hiding herself?"

"Holed up at her house. No word for weeks. Breakup hit her, hard."

"...I'm sorry to hear that."

Veronica appeared at his side, eyeing Adam. "What're you boys talking about?" she asked.

"Just introducin' myself, gorgeous," said Lando. "And wonderin' why he ain't got a mask."

"I have," Adam said as he held his up. "You saw me take it off."

Veronica took it and set it over his face, seductive to the

max. "Gotta wear it," she said. "My party, my rules."

The music had shifted to hip-hop or gangsta or something so he removed it, saying, "In a moment."

Veronica saw the mandalas and took Adam's hands, purring like a street cat about to pounce. "Lovely work. This a tattoo?"

Adam shook his head. "Mendhi...um, henna. Not permanent."

"Too bad. Looks just right on you." She glanced at Lando. "Didn't the cleansing lady say something about a henna artist being in town?"

"The what?" Lando asked.

Adam jumped in with, "The woman with the incense." Then he focused on Veronica. "Um, you were in *Ilithium-Four*. The Seeress. A very unusual take on it."

"Oh, you're not gonna bitch me out for going topless, are you? She was, in the book."

Adam blinked. "She was five, in the book."

"So?"

"There's a bit of a difference, anatomically."

"What do you mean?"

Lando gave her a squeeze and said, "I think Andrew's joking, gorgeous. He's English. Their sense of humor's off-beat."

"It's Adam — and what does my — ?"

"Andrew Adam," Veronica said, pressing closer to him and making him back up to a window, her fingers caressing his blond highlights and her breasts about to poke his eyes out as she cooed, "Don't cuddles just ooze from his name? And he's so cute; just like a teddy bear."

Adam huffed.

A real grin filled Lando's face as he chuckled, soft and low and endless, "Oh, Ronnie..."

"And I love this suit," she purred as she toyed with Adam's lapels. "Landy, do you think it would look as good on a tall man, like you?"

Now Adam snarled, "I beg your pardon."

Casey heard him, stopped dancing and hopped over to slip an arm around his, her eyes locked on Veronica as she said, "Oh, baby, is this greedy bitch trying to steal you, too? Don't be surprised I'm not surprised."

Veronica curled back over to Lando, but her eyes stayed focused on Casey. "Can't steal what's been abandoned."

"Can't abandon someone who's left you," Casey said, pulling her purse from Adam's pocket. She took out her lipstick and compact, making sure two neon condoms were easily visible as she purred, "I doubt *you'll* need these, *Landy*, considering her talents."

Veronica tightened. Lando edged between the two women, taut and angry. "Casey, c'mon, I told you I was sorry."

"Yes, you did," Casey responded as she used the compact mirror to touch up her lips.

"Aw, Jesus, why'd you come to the party, anyway?"

She locked her eyes on Veronica. "Had to, baby. Show we're peaches and cream. And we are. Just needed somebody to prove it's easy to move on." She put the lipstick and compact back in the purse.

"Coming from a girl who makes a habit of it," Veronica sneered back. She toyed with Adam's lapel. "Don't get too attached, Andrew."

"It, um, it's Adam." And he was wishing they had left when they had the chance. Then a waiter in a mask offered them a tray of tarts, so he grabbed it from him and said, "Oh, here. Thank you! I am ravenous and these look quite...interesting."

He bit into one — and froze. The best comparison he could think of was when he was three and thought chewing on his mother's dishcloth immediately after it had been used to wipe down the sink was a good idea. He could barely hide his dislike of it.

Lando, however, dug in. "Oh, yeah. Ronnie's recipe."

It took Adam a moment to regain control of his gag

reflex. "Yes, they're...they're quite different."

Lando pulled Veronica close and said, "She's a little health nut. Makin' sure I eat right, keep fit, all that crap."

She beamed at him. "It's only 'cause I love my Landy and want the best for him."

Casey's grip tightened around Adam's arm as she said, "Then what's he doing with you?"

"Living again," Veronica said, looking straight back at Casey. "It's what happens when you find someone who cares."

Casey's grip grew tighter. Adam knew this was not going to end well, so he pointed to a far corner.

"Dear God, did I see Angelina Jolie over there?"

Lando and Veronica whipped around and Lando said, "I told you she'd show. C'mon, gorgeous."

As they walked away, Veronica shot over her shoulder, "Nice to meet *you*, Andrew."

Andrew? What the devil? "Really, it's just Adam!" Casey's grip was now at the point of extreme pain, so he added, "Casey — Casey! As noted before, I like my arm attached."

She jolted, then looked at him and let go. "Sorry, baby." She glanced around, lost, finally focusing on the tray. "What — uh — what's the real story on those?"

He eyed her, for a moment, then followed her gaze and said, "Even the rats in our library would turn up their noses, and if they did partake, Henry Fourteen would refuse to eat them." She looked at him, confused. He smiled. "Our office cat."

She nodded, absently. "You really hungry?"

"Oh, God, show me a dust bin, and I'll forage in it."

"That means garbage, right?"

"Yes, but one man's garbage is another man's feast. Unlike these." A waiter was passing so he handed the tray off to him. "Here you go, m'lad. Wretched refuse for undiscerning rats."

The waiter gave him an understanding sigh and tried to offer them around. No one partook.

"C'mon, baby," Casey said, then she guided Adam

117

through a dining room where more of the questionable edibles were stacked high on a black and silver table.

The next room was a state of the art kitchen of chrome and brass, gleaming bright and obviously used only by the caterers, who were wrapping up more of the *delectables*. Casey and Adam wove their way past them to a corner area that sported a massive refrigerator, eclectic electric range and a microwave.

"Good God," Adam said, looking around in awe, "this room's bigger than my flat in Ruislip."

"That where you live?" Casey asked, paying him no real attention as she pulled two cartons of Mac & Cheese from the freezer.

"Nora and I. Till we parted. Couldn't afford it on my own."

Casey said nothing, just popped both cartons into the microwave.

He watched her, uncertain, the noise of the catering staff offering them a cocoon of separation from it all. "Is this all right?" he asked, motioning to the microwave.

"I bought these," she said with a bare smile, "Lando thinks Mac & Cheese is beneath him, and Veronica — she just sucks the life out of people. At least, that's what I caught her doing with him, last week."

Adam jolted. "Just last week?"

She shrugged. "Eleven days — no, twelve, but who's counting? That was four helpings of Lasagna. Meat lovers."

"Casey," he said, "may I say, your Lando is a fool."

She handed him a spoon, smiling. "You may."

He saw the distant expression return to her face, the tight mask with it, and whispered, "We should have gone elsewhere."

She did not look at him, just pulled more utensils out to put onto napkins as she said, "Had to come back. Make everyone think all is well and good. That's so important in this town. Always land on your feet."

"Even after hiding away?"

She cast him a wary glance then shrugged. "Don't you love gossip? Especially when it's rooted in reality?"

"Well...you've been here, so let's leave. Now. Find somewhere else to feed. My treat."

She looked at him, warmth hinted in her eyes. "In a minute. I don't want to leave anything behind; it'll just rot. There's water in the fridge."

The microwave dinged and Casey pulled the steaming boxes out. She set them on a counter and peeled off the plastic film covers as Adam found a couple bottles of sparkling water and opened them, then handed her one. He noticed a couple of the catering staff casting them looks of quiet horror when she pushed one of the cartons to him.

"Chow down, baby," she said.

He smiled, then felt the aroma dance up and around and through him. "God, cheesy pasta. Mum calls this *nourishment for heart attacks*, but..." He took a careful bite, let it simmer on his tongue then growled, "Starting to feel large, again." And he dove in.

Casey watched him eat. Manners radiated from him even as he seemed to wolf his food down. She toyed with hers, looking around as she said, "Y'know, I helped Lando find this house. Spent months looking for it. Fixing it up. Connected him with my decorator. I was here more than I was at home. And now? Now I don't know why he and I ever got together; we're too much alike."

"I'd argue that point," Adam said after a sip of water.

"You don't know me." She finally took a small bite of her Mac & Cheese. "Mom thinks she matched us, but I'd already seen him around. Parties. Awards ceremonies. He was up for a daytime Emmy back when I was dating an actor from one of the Soaps. Vinny. A nice guy who couldn't decide if he was gay, straight or bi." She smiled, adding, "But being with me gave him good press in the gossip rags."

Adam sipped more water. "They always been at you?"

She nodded. "I have a reputation for being a difficult out-of-control bitch, and they keep trying to find ways of backing it up. Filling pages in...oh, in England it's like *The Telegraph, The Daily Mail*, *OK, Hello*; I mean, you must've noticed how they can be."

"I've never paid them any mind."

She watched him take another bite. "You're unusual." He gave her a smiling shrug then she continued with, "It's all bullshit, you know. Vinny's the perfect example. His then boyfriend saw me in Neiman's and warned me, *He's using you, so don't be surprised about me.* I wasn't; I can add two and two. That's what I told him, and he smiled and walked away.

"The *Star Inquirer* turned it into a screaming match in the middle of cosmetics, photos arranged to look like we were about to get into a knife fight." Her voice grew overly dramatic as she said, "*I was disparaged as the other woman in a gay man's life.*"

"Bad Casey," Adam said, chuckling. "Bad, bad Casey."

"That's when I started recording everything. Court order lets me go on the talk shows, play the video and shut down the lies. It sucks up the money, but it's spared me so much grief."

She was silent for a moment then continued, "After that, I saw Lando at some more parties, but I was with a writer...who suddenly decided he loved his wife." She looked at Adam. "I didn't know he was married."

Adam was still as he said, "You needn't explain yourself to me."

"I want to tell somebody. Just get it out. Look at it. Try to understand."

He took in a deep breath...and had another bite.

"Anyway, one day my limo vanished, so Lando gave me a ride home, and we talked, and Mom said he was just right for me. And we started seeing each other. We were tabloid fodder by the third date, but this spin was positive. He was kind. Attentive. Loving, even though I was a bigger name than him. Had a dozen movies to my resume. Two series. I liked that. Wanted him with me...so got him onto *I-Four*."

She didn't notice Adam had stopped eating.

"Then a week into shooting we were at a beach resort near Cape Town and had an off day. I'd finished my PPK — " Adam gave her a blank look. She smiled. "Publicity Press Kit. Lando'd done his, too, and it was getting dark, so we took the cable car up to Table Mountain. It was the last car so we couldn't stay up long...but the ride." She leaned back, sighing with remembrance, her food forgotten. "Clear skies filled with red. City lights glowing around the bay as we whispered up and up. Every pin-prick of light down there representing people whose lives were as distinct and meaningful as ours. Hundreds of thousands of them glittering under the late evening's shadows. The beauty of it — such overwhelming beauty — I could barely breathe. I started to weep.

"Lando slipped up behind me. Wrapped his arms around my waist. Laid his chin in the crook of my neck. And then he whispered, *So fucking cool.*"

A laugh burst from Adam. He tried to cover it with a cough and bite of the Mac & Cheese, but Casey wasn't fooled.

"Yeah," she said. "Shakespeare couldn't have put it better. But I didn't care. We gave the tabloids a lot of niceness to fill their front pages for the next three years. Helped my reputation as well as his career."

"I find it difficult to believe anyone could believe anything negative about you."

She chuckled. "You're sweet. But my first series...word got around that I was demanding. A little diva. It's followed me, no matter how perfect I am. Keeps getting brought up when something goes wrong. Like it did two weeks ago. And now look where I am; in a kitchen, comfort-eating and spilling my guts to a man who never wanted to be here. Cut. Print. Next scene."

"Casey," Adam whispered, "I'm glad I accompanied you."

She smiled. "You're not at all what I thought you'd be."

"Is that good, bad or let me out of here?"

She laughed as she said, "Good. Very good."

"Thank you. Nor are you what I expected, really."

"Adam, let's be honest — you hadn't even heard of me till you came on this trip, had you?"

What could he do but shrug and smile? "The rest of my family would know of you. They watch the telly. Follow social media, online, phones, tablets, whatever. But for me, if it's not a volume that goes onto a shelf nothing else matters. Which can be problematic; I have this habit of losing myself in my books and research to the point of forgetting things like meet-ups and anniversaries and such. Nora was often quite aggrieved."

"C'mon, baby, you really that bad?"

"She wanted me tested for autism. Said I'm too easily distracted by minutia. Then one day we met for tea and she told me to get on with my life. So I moved back with Mum." He noticed a slip of paper on the refrigerator with *Meat-flies; water-vaYter; come-comb; house-wees; go-gone* written on it and asked, "Is Lando learning German?"

Casey shrugged. "He was in Berlin doing publicity, a few days ago. He's off on the Pacific tour, tomorrow. Shanghai, Sydney, Hong Kong, Tokyo, you name it they loves their Lando Grissom."

Adam cast her a careful glance. "Don't they love their Casey Blanchard, too?"

It took her a moment to answer. "Not like they used to."

"I'm sure this film will change all of that."

She shrugged and sipped some water.

He turned back to the list. "Y'know, the pronunciation's off on these," he said.

Casey sighed. "Everything's off on him."

"Then let's go," he said as he used a pencil on a string to make some quick notes beside the words — *Meat - Fly-ish; water - Vahser; come - come in; house - Hows; go - gay-an.* "The pasta was a lovely appetizer but I could murder some Chicken Tikka with Saffron rice, Sag Aloo, Raita, Samosas in plum sauce and — "

"Casey, what the fuck?"

Adam jolted around to find Lando standing behind him as Tito herded the catering crew out of the kitchen. Lando held Tito's tablet; on it, Adam saw his university profile...showing the awkward photo of him working on Blake's *Albion.*

Lando showed it to her. "He's just some book geek, but you let people think he's some new actor you're with? That you left me for him? Are you out of your mind?"

Casey all but purred, "Oh, Adam, my ex-boyfwiend had his widdle feewings hurted at me being with somebody else."

Lando huffed. "A *nobody* else. You really think people're gonna believe you went from a guy like me to a midget like him?"

"Hang on!" Adam snapped.

"I never said he was anyone," said Casey.

Lando all but spit, "Bullshit. The only reason he's here is you and Orisi made him up like he's somebody; just the latest asshole of yours. All nobodies you signed up with. At least I had a career 'fore we hooked up."

"Right, third lead on a daytime soap, close to being canceled."

Lando started for Casey but Adam stepped between them and said, "Both of you, please! Can — can we talk like adults?"

Lando looked around him to snarl at Casey, "That's the problem, ain't it? You didn't get to make me up from nothin'. I didn't have to beg you to be with me. I already had a followin'. I didn't have to always come to your place to see you; I got a cool joint of my own. I didn't have to work on just the projects you liked; I could get my own goin'. I even got the sequel to *I-Four* set up on my own."

"And got me passed over on it."

Lando howled a laugh. "Aw, is that really why you're crappin' all over me? Professional jealousy. I'm on the rise and you're goin' nowhere."

"Let's see how long you last without me," Casey shot back.

"I thought you were pissed 'cause of me and Ronnie, but you know what this whole little act of yours proves? You still want me in your life."

"Bullshit," Casey snapped.

"Bullshit, right back at you!"

"This says you're the one full of shit!" She slung her Mac & Cheese on him. Adam barely avoided getting some on himself.

Lando roared and grabbed at her, but Adam pushed him back.

"Lando, LANDO, stop! Stop it! Casey, we should leave. Now!"

"You're right, baby, we — "

"No," Lando snarled, "I still got questions for you!" He lunged for her again.

Adam grabbed him, swung him around, and they wound up on top of a kitchen counter. Bottles of water and utensils crashed everywhere. Adam danced back up on his feet, crying, "Lando, this is completely inappropriate!"

Lando rose to his full height and cast him a glare that would have killed a raging elephant then screamed, "Tito!"

Tito appeared in the doorway, saying, "Yeah?"

"He's not invited!"

Tito roared in to yank Adam from the room.

"Hang on, I'm leaving!" Adam yelled. "Casey's leaving with me."

"Like hell!" Lando grabbed Casey and pulled her down a side hall. "We need privacy! I wanna know what the fuck you're really up to!"

"Lando," Casey snarled, "tell Tito to stand down or I'll scream about how big you ain't."

"After this dumbassed stunt? Who's gonna listen?"

And he was right. The party-goers' ear buds were in, so they neither heard nor paid attention to the commotion.

Adam used a rugby twist to break free from Tito and bounce back to the kitchen, but another pair of guards appeared and stopped him. Then Tito's arms wrapped around his chest and neck, and the guards took his legs, and despite his struggles they carried him out the door.

"Wait," he choked. "Casey! Bloody hell, leave me alone! This is assault! It's kidnapping! Casey! Lando!"

He saw the Earth Mother was near by, closing her phone, so tried to reach for her, gasping, "Help. Please."

She just shook her head and said, "I told you, keep the incense with you."

Then she lit another stick and twirled it around.

TEN

Tito and friends carried Adam down to the street with as much ceremony as a cat being put out for the night. The entire way he fought and howled, "*You can't do this! It's an outrage! Casey wants to leave with me! I'll call the police!*" It being in German, they paid no attention.

Of course the photographers fired their flashes like mad as the men dumped Adam on the sidewalk. Tito motioned to the outside guards and the valets, saying, "He gets back in? You get no tip." Then he and the inside guards headed back to the house.

Adam scrambled to his feet, but the outside guards held him back.

"*Listen to me, Tito*," Adam cried, still in German. "*Casey wanted to leave with me! This is kidnapping!*"

Tito flipped a hand in Adam's direction and said, "Scat, 'fore I call the cops."

"Ring them!" Adam yelled. "Explain your actions to them!"

"Who's gonna listen to a nobody like you?" Tito shouted as he slammed the door shut.

Adam almost made a run for it, anyway, but the guards and valets had grouped together in defense mode and were daring him to try. So he stormed over to the photographers, who were still snapping shots of him and howling —

"Hey, buddy, what's your name?"

"Who are you? What's goin' on?"

"Is there a fight in there?"

"Did Casey pull some shit, again?"

"Please," Adam said, "I need to ring the police and I haven't my mobile with me; may I use someone's — ?"

They all offered him a phone as they growled —

"You callin' in a SWAT Team?"

"This a drug raid?"

"Arrest everybody?"

"Did I see Angelina in there?"

"WOW! This is gonna be great!!!"

Their howling startled Adam. "SWAT Team? Drugs? No, I just — it was a disagreement and..."

But the camera-hounds were convinced Casey had a gun and Lando was snorting coke and everyone was having underage sex in the pool, sounding more and more like rabid dogs. Adam backed away, muttering, "Never mind. It was just a disagreement. Over the — the hors d'oeuvres being served."

"Hors d'oeuvres?" snarled one of the photographers.

That's when Sean pushed through the middle of them and said, "Y'know what's happening here?"

Shawn followed him, adding, "What it is, is perfectly clear."

"Casey hired this lad for the night."

"For Lando to see, just for spite."

"But the rent boy then tried to cash in."

"Without talent — and that is a sin."

"In this town. So out he was thrown."

"And told that he'd better go home."

"So spending your time on this lad."

"Would just be a waste, and so sad."

The flashes stopped flashing and the photographers turned away, some snarling —

"I used half my storage on nothing?"

"Food fight? Really?"

"What a shit-burger."

Adam backed down the sidewalk, half-perturbed at his dismissal by the paparazzi twins yet half-relieved he hadn't added to Casey's woes with the gossip rags. He stopped by the neighbor's brick wall to try and work out what he could do, if anything, while glancing between the growling photographers, Lando's front door and the guards and valets. While he doubted Lando was stupid enough to actually hurt Casey, he needed to get back inside to be there for her, just in case.

Then a Bentley convertible zoomed past and up to the valet, a silver-haired man driving, a super-stylized woman whose hair did not move in the wind seated beside him. The couple got out, the man snapping, "Keep it close," as he tossed the valet the keys. On cue, they posed at the door to let the photographers' flashes bombard them. They were somebodies.

The valet drove the Bentley back down to the street, nearly hitting Adam, then zoomed down to turn onto a side road.

Adam watched him go, the beginning of a smile on his face. "The back yard," he murmured. "Could I slip in?"

He saw the photographers were still focused on the couple at the door, while the guards were focused on the photographers, so he snuck down to the side street and around the corner.

That brick wall dripping with ivy led him another two hundred feet to an alley that gently wound to behind Lando's house. A line of cars was parked along one side and he saw —

The valet was headed back for him!

Adam ducked between two cars before the man could see him, waited till he passed, then kept close to the wall as he slipped down the alley to find —

A guard was seated by a door in Lando's back wall, walkie-talkie in hand.

Adam looked the brick wall over. It was taller, here, and the ivy thicker. Lando's wall had no ivy, just a blank stucco exterior and wire fencing arcing from the top to high over the back yard, like a zoo enclosure. Trees lined the neighbor's wall, but there were only a few deep inside Lando's yard.

"Casey's right," Adam murmured to himself. "No one gets in here." Still, it took Adam two seconds to decide, "Don't know till you try," and climb onto the back of a car to grip a thick strand of ivy and —

The car's alarm sounded.

He spat a quick, "*Scheisse!*" and scrambled up on top of the wall to hide in the thick trees, barely able to pull some strands of ivy around him before the guard came down to check the area. The alarm finally stopped, so the man returned to his chair.

Adam heaved a sigh of relief then slowly and quietly crawled through a hundred feet of tangled vines to close in on Lando's yard. Dogs barked from the neighbor's house as birds rustled on their perches and the wind whispered through the leaves. He slipped and almost fell, a couple of times; apparently, Italian boots were not meant for climbing walls. He only hoped they weren't also worth a thousand dollars, a pair.

Then he reached the fence...and saw how Lando's back yard was laid-out. An Olympic pool with the appearance of an open pond took up a quarter of the space while massive boulders were carved to look like a cave, with thick shrubs placed about to make it seem like nature had put them there. Bramble-bushes lined the walls and a pair of tall thick green trees sat in the center of it all, well-away from the wire fencing. The rest was waving brown grass.

Adam looked along the fence; it was tight and arced out from the tops of the walls all the way around, making it too tall to climb over and leaving him no space to crawl through...until he noticed one thick tree trunk in the neighbor's yard had pushed partway through a section link. It was above the pool, close to Lando's house, and it looked like the opening might be just large enough for him to make use of, so he worked his way to it.

Once he was there, he found the wires were still a bit too tight against the tree. He fiddled with them then removed his coat, folded it inside out, hung it over a branch inside Lando's yard, and pulled Orisi's briefs from his pocket. He used them to carefully twist the fencing farther away from the tree. Once the space was wide enough, he turned the briefs into a cushion against the wire prongs. He began to push through...and he was making it...making it —

Then a wire snapped loose and dug into his left shoulder. He yelped — and froze.

A beam of light cut through the shadows and into the trees, for a few moments, then went away. He relaxed and bent the wire away from him. The cut was bleeding and the shirt was ruined. With a sigh, he surrendered to the probability that it cost more than his mother's Peugeot, dabbed at it with the briefs and pushed the rest of the way through to crouch atop a branch.

Inside, the arced fence felt even more like it was meant to keep someone in rather than anyone out. Then something struck him — no one was in the back yard.

"*With a party like this? On a beautiful night like this?*" whispered from him. In German.

"Somebody up there?" It was the guard speaking...on top off an odd low growl that whispered through the trees.

Adam grimaced and berated himself for not being more like James Bond instead of Tarzan. That beam of light danced through the leaves, again, so he meowed like a cat.

Sort of.

The guard chuckled and said, "Hey, kitty cat, you don't wanna be near that yard, trust me."

Which caused Adam to meow a question mark. What could the man mean? He looked around at the big beautiful pool, that was too close for comfort...and the thickness of bushes around the rocks...and the massive trees in their center, their branches trimmed away from the fencing...and the arced wire along the rooftop and — wait, even on *top* of the house there was a fence? What — did the paparazzi climb onto the roof and rappel down to take photos through a window or peer into an office?

Like he was doing? Looking at two people in one, right now, on the ground floor?

Two people named Casey and Lando.

Holding each other and kissing.

Hands everywhere kissing!

Adam couldn't breathe. Casey wasn't in trouble; she was back in Lando's arms! Just like she wanted. The whole night's events fell into place, and "Bloody hell," popped out before he could even think to censor it.

He heard the guard cry, "Okay, that wasn't no cat. Tito, we got an intruder in the back yard."

Then he heard Tito's voice laugh on a walkie-talkie as he said, "Don't worry, he'll come out soon as he meets Gertrude."

Gertrude?

"Don't we want him alive?" the guard asked.

Alive? What the devil were they talking about?

Then he heard a whispery growl. Deep. Rumbling. Stronger than any dog or cat he'd ever known. More like a motorcycle revving. He looked around. Searched the bushes. Searched the yard. Searched the trees and found nothing —

Except a pair of cool yellow eyes in the shadows of the leaves. He looked harder and finally saw the form of a big beautiful black panther lounging on a branch. Watching him. Curious. Almost sad.

Until it hissed and howled at him!

He jolted back against the fence and that damned wire jabbed him in the rear. He jumped forward, crying, *"SCHEISSE! Nein! Nein!"* He grabbed at the branch but lost his grip and fell onto another branch that bounced him onto a diving board that bounced him off into the deep end of the massive pool.

Where he promptly sank.

He thrashed, swallowed water and choked, barely able to kick himself back to the surface to cry, "Help!" before sinking, again, and fighting his way up to gasp a more feeble "Help..."

He heard Casey's voice cry, "Adam?" then he sank,

again, and —

Something bumped against him and grabbed him by the collar to drag him into the shallow end so he could stand and cough and wipe water off his face, as best he could.

"Adam? Adam, are you all right?" It was Casey's voice.

His eyes burned like fire and he was retching, but he was finally able to look around and see her at the edge of the pool, watching him, fear in her eyes.

Lando sat in an open window, drink in hand, chuckling, "See? All he had to do was stand up."

"He was in the deep end, idiot," Casey snapped. "Gertrude pulled him over."

"What? From five foot to three foot?"

Veronica joined Lando, saying, "What's Gertrude up to?"

"She went fishin'," said Lando. "Caught a minnow."

A sudden rain cascaded onto Adam. He looked noticed the panther shaking the water off herself. She then stretched out on the grass near the pool to watch him. Beyond her, the partygoers had noticed the commotion in the back yard and were pressed against the windows, fascinated, masks still on.

"Gertrude, have you been a good little guard cat?" Veronica asked, slipping an arm around Lando.

"She earned her Kibble, tonight," he responded.

Adam realized his trousers were around his hips, his shirt clung to him in ways most uncomfortable and he was missing a boot. And a sock. He wiped his face with the glittery briefs to clear away the last of the water.

That's when he heard Veronica say, "Oh, cute, his hankie got sparkles."

"They're — briefs," Adam choked out.

Lando burst into laughter. "Damn, Case, you got him out of his pants, already? I had more control, than that."

To which Veronica said, "You better, or it's off with your head."

132

Casey snarled, "Which one, bitch?"

Adam looked around, asking, in German, "*Where are my glasses?*" He found half the frame caught in his trousers, snapped at the nose. He put it on to see the panther, whom he supposed was Gertrude, playing with the other half, and, "*Oh, this isn't good,*" burst from him. Still in German.

Gertrude looked at him and gave a soft purr.

Casey walked over to the pool's steps, saying, "Adam, come on out; she won't hurt you."

"Naw, better not, Andrew," Lando laughed. "Gertrude don't like gay undies."

Adam headed for Casey, finally beyond caring as he snapped back, "Tell me, Lando, were you born to be such an arse? Or is it just because your Mum and Da named you after a secondary character in a derivative science fiction film?"

Lando climbed through the window, snarling, "Hey, book-boy, Lando Calrissian was the coolest guy in the whole series."

"Who doesn't appear until chapter five," Adam snarled back. "Hardly in the same caliber as Luke or Han."

"It's not how much you do; it's what you do with it."

"Spoken like a man who knows the true limits of his capacities."

"Yeah, come on out of my pool. Maybe I'll tell Gertrude your ass is steak."

Adam hesitated. He had just noticed Gertrude was pacing him, her eyes locked on him, the other half of his glasses over her nose. But then he remembered it was this panther who had saved him so continued on to the steps, one hand gripping his trousers so they would remain around his waist and not his ankles.

"Dammit, Lando, send her away," Casey snapped. "Adam, are you all right?"

"Brilliant," Adam said. "But I seriously doubt Orisi will want his outfit back."

Lando laughed. "Those're *his* briefs? Dude, no wonder

133

you took 'em off."

That's when Tito appeared at Lando's side, saying, "Want me to call the cops?"

"Naw, I'm gonna have Gertrude chase him around. She needs the exercise." Then he said, in sing-song, "*Gertrude, jag de fleiss.*"

The panther let out a soft growl.

"You know how to run, Andrew?" Veronica asked, too happy.

"My name is ADAM," he snarled.

Casey was almost beside herself. "Oh, for god's sake — Gertrude. House. HOUSE."

The panther looked at her but did nothing.

Lando did his sing-song, again, calling, "*Gertrude, hou de vater.*"

This was too much for Adam to bear. "It's *wasser, dumkopf,* and you're making no bloody sense!"

Then he saw Gertrude lose the broken glasses and slide into the pool with a happy little growl. He bolted up the steps, startled, barely able to keep his pants from falling. The cut over his eye was bleeding, again, as were the jabs to his arm and derriere. That is when he saw the missing boot at the bottom of the deep end, his sock next to it. Now he understood the need for a pedicure; one never knew when one's toes might be exposed.

Casey brought a towel over to him, asking, "What're you doing out here? Nobody comes in the back yard."

He pushed the towel away. He dared not look at her, he was quivering with such anger. "You knew about Gertrude," he said, his voice cracking.

"He's had her a couple years. Why didn't you just wait in the limo?"

"Like a good dog?" he snapped. "I — I thought I forgot something. My mistake."

He pushed away from her. His head pounded. The bottom of his stomach churned. He grabbed up the mangled half of his glasses to put on with the other lens — which made him look very cock-eyed — then he stormed for the house, limping thanks to the boot still on his foot. He saw Tito standing between him and the door and was contemplating the best tackle to use on the lumbering ox when he realized, "Oh, no, something *was* forgotten," spun around, and headed for the wall.

"What was?" Veronica called.

"His brain," said Lando, "just like that tin-man guy."

Adam shook his head in awe. "Dear God, Lando, you should never speak without a script. You reveal not only your inadequate knowledge of English literature, but also her language." He leapt up to grab a branch of the tree then climbed the wall to retrieve the coat. As he hopped down, he saw Gertrude watching from the pool.

"Wow," said Lando. "Who knew you could climb so good? Beef up a little, add six inches to your height, I could use you as a double."

Adam limped back to the house, saying, "Thanks, but I've no wish to play the arse, in your stead."

Lando blinked and said, "Huh? That didn't make sense."

Veronica chimed in with, "What'd you just say?"

Adam cast them a harsh laugh. "Oh, dear God, a bite of cabbage has more intelligence than the two of you, combined!" Tito was about to jump him but got a glare of fury and a hurling snarl of, "Keep away from the mad dog!"

He kept.

Adam limped inside, slammed past the partygoers and, in a fit of rage, ripped the boot off his foot and slung it aside before grabbing a stick of burning incense from the Earth mother. "You're right," he snarled, "I need cleansing."

Then he bolted out the front door.

****

Adam had no idea why he'd taken the incense, how he could use it, or even where he was going with it. The stick just gave him something to do to keep from thinking and he needed to not think, not be around anyone, give himself time to calm the turmoil in his pounding brain before he careened into madness...and the incense forcing its aroma into his mind would not let him focus too completely on what had just happened.

He had never felt so brutalized. Not when Chandra had dumped him for a boy she could wear heels with. Not when Nora had dismissed him from her life. Not when Connor had nicknamed him hobbit. Even his father's death and the chaos that followed had at least been rooted in a sense of reality and consistency because quietness had whispered around them all to let the truth of their new world settle in. That had been soul-wrenching, but he had been able to understand it and face it and live with it once given the silence and space he needed, to adjust.

This, however — this confusion in his heart and head, it twisted him in its grip. Refused to let him step back and view it with a calm rational mind but surrounded him with loss and hurt and confusion to where he was on the verge of losing what little control he still had, and his one instinct was to leave. To go. Just go. GO!

Of course, the photographers saw him slam outside and started taking more shots, calling their usual —

"What's your name?"

"Who are you?"

"Why're you all soaked?"

"Is that blood on your face?"

"On your shirt?"

"Hey, you're that guy!"

"Was there a fight?"

"Did you and Lando get into it?"

"Any broken bones?"

"C'mon, tell us who you are."

As if they hadn't dismissed him only minutes before.

He was barely able to growl, "Nobody, I'm nobody," over and over as he tried to walk around them.

But then Shawn grabbed him and forced him to stop, demanding, "So what you doin' with Casey Blanchard?"

Adam glared at him and spat, "Bloody proving it!"

The photographers swirled around him like a pack of hyenas. He tried to push them away but their cameras' flashes exploded in his face and their voices howled as they snapped and snarled their questions, refusing to give him a moment to even think, and he grew lost and confused.

He was about to spin into an wild version of a Rugger Devil when Casey raced up, crying, "Guys, guys, Lando and Veronica're fighting."

Half of them called back, "Bullshit," as the whole pack shifted to get both her and Adam in the same shot.

"No, it's true," Casey said. "She's pissed-off 'cause he kissed me, and she slapped him and knocked my buddy in the pool."

"Buddy? Like hell!" Sean laughed. "More the rent boy!"

Casey laughed and held up her phone. "I got that on video, bitch! Now if Adam wants to, he can sue you for slander 'cause you're too stupid to see what's going on. Veronica went after me and he...he came between us and — " A soft quiver entered her voice as she continued, " — and now he's leaving so he doesn't go nuts on her. That's why I got out. She thinks I want Lando back, so she's throwing dishes and glasses and — "

It was the promise of broken crystal that got them to cry, "Holeeee shit," spin around, and race back to the house, en masse, to overwhelm the guards and valets.

All except Shawn; he ran half way to meet with Sean, who had just returned from the side street, then they slipped into a shadow to huddle.

Adam stumbled around, finally realized he was no longer surrounded and staggered down the street, still holding the stick of incense in one hand and his coat in the other, one sock on, one sock gone, his mind still screaming left and right and up and down and back and forth.

Casey backed away from the house then turned and quick-walked after him, calling, "Adam, wait. Wait. Adam, please."

Adam just shook his head and growled, "You used me."

"No, I — "

He did not look at her. Could not. "No, I understand, now, I do understand. This entire evening was meant to make that stupid arse jealous and bring him back together with you — "

"That's not true."

"Oh? OH!? Your comments with Veronica? You wanting to dance with me when Lando arrived? You nearly taking my arm off when you're around him? Dressing me up like a bloody doll? Your mother making book on me? And don't deny it; I finally understand — she lay a wager with Vincent over whether or not I'd turn out presentable enough to matter to that bloody bastard, back there, and she won. Meaning he was against me. Vincent was against me. He didn't think I would, meaning he knew what you were planning, but he sent me here, anyway, knowing what all of this meant to me and — and I — I thought you were in trouble, in there! I was trying to get back to help you and instead I find you bloody kissing him!"

"I had to," she said, grabbing at him. "It's the only way I could think to keep him from figuring out I was after my book."

Adam shook her off. "Kissing like you were on fine terms and in love and — wait, wait, wait, wait, wait, wait, wait, wait, wait, wait." He jolted to a halt and spun around to look at her. "Don't you have the book?"

She hesitated then said, "I...I told you, it's in a safe deposit box..."

Adam felt the world go white and silent and cold. Control of his voice was at a minimum as he whispered, "Please. Please, it's not Lando's box, please tell me it's not..."

"Okay, it's his," Casey said, not looking at him. "Somebody tried to break into my house, and other people've been after me to sell the book to 'em, and when I told him how much it's worth, he said I should put it there to keep it safe. But then I caught him with that bitch, and for some stupid reason smearing his Ferrari with dog-shit pissed him off even though I'm the one who was being cheated on and — "

A freezing sense of calm settled over Adam, just like it had when he learned his father was dead. He staggered back from Casey, feeling far more light-headed than could be considered good, then turned and continued towards Santa Monica Boulevard, muttering, "No, no, I can't believe it. I can't. I can't. Lando has the book. Bloody Lando! He'll never give it to me, now."

Casey caught up to him. Tried to make him stop walking. "Adam, c'mon, baby, stop — it'll be okay."

He knew he'd crash into oblivion and never come out of it if he didn't keep walking so continued on, snarling, "Casey! An *Alice Sixty-five* is in the hands of a bloody Neanderthal, who probably considers it nothing more than scrap paper, if he even knows how to bloody write, and you can say that?"

Casey grabbed him and spun him around, her voice filled with both anger and confusion. "Why're *you* so upset? It's my book."

Adam's heart pounded and his head was close to exploding as he screamed, "No, it was your grandfather's book, and I thought you were smart about it! At least, smart enough to know it was worth more than just the paper and binding, but you don't even understand what's just happened here! I will be blamed for losing the *Alice Sixty-five*. Me! And I will be sacked from a job that I love. Because of this." He picked at his glasses then his trousers. "And this. I was trusted to come here and collect her and bring her to safety, and instead I've destroyed everything by alienating the one man who could give me what I came for. I'll be lucky if they let me work in a WH Smith, after this!"

Casey's anger vanished and she shifted into being soothing and motherly. "Adam, baby, c'mon, I'll explain. I'll make it right."

He could have strangled her. His stomach twisted at realizing she honestly thought a few soft words would salve everyone's concerns. He backed away, barely able to whisper, "How? How? My father was killed whilst carrying a copy of this book. He was killed, and it disappeared. He was a decent man. He liked people. But his name is only remembered in connection with losing an *Alice Sixty-five.* And now here I am, faced with the same bloody situation whilst standing in the middle of a bloody street, dripping wet after nearly drowning, having lost an even rarer copy, all thanks to a girl I trusted who couldn't be! You cannot! Make that! Right!"

He spun away from her to see a bus was about to leave a nearby stop so bolted over and slammed on the door. "No, wait, wait, please. Please." The bus opened its door and he got in. "Thanks, ever-so much."

Casey almost followed him inside, crying, "Adam, come on, I've got the limo right here; I'll take you home and we'll — "

"No," shot out of him. "No, you stay away from me. I'll make my own way back, thank you." Then he turned to the bus driver and asked, "Excuse me, which way am I going?"

He gave Adam a wary look and said, "You don't know?"

A laugh burst out of Adam. "I haven't since I arrived."

Passengers on the bus pointed to Casey and used their phones to snap photos and record her as she grabbed at Adam. "Come on. Please. You're bleeding. Let me take care of this."

"No," snarled from Adam as he pulled away and shoved his arm into a sleeve of his coat.

The bus driver glanced between them and said, "We're headed for Santa Monica."

Adam forced a smile. "Can I get to the airport from there?"

Casey tugged at the coat's other arm, nearly yanking him

off-balance, saying, "Please, I'll fix you up and get you back in your old clothes."

"No," he snarled as he ripped the arm away from her.

Whereupon the bus driver said, "Yes."

"Brilliant," whispered from Adam.

Casey kept on with, "Baby, c'mon, I'll even buy you new ones. I know where there's a twenty-four hour Target, and you're the only person I'd ever admit that to."

Passengers took more photos of Adam pulling out his wallet, water dribbling from it as he removed a very wet bill that was close in size to an American dollar. He managed to say, "Do you take cold, wet cash?"

The driver chuckled. "If it'll go in."

"Adam, please." Casey was almost begging. "Why won't you let me help you?"

He glared back at her and howled, "BECAUSE, CASEY, I WOULD REALLY RATHER *NOT* MURDER YOU, TONIGHT!" Then he turned back to the driver and said, "Can we go, now?"

The bus doors closed as Casey said, "But I got Lando's key!"

Adam was about to shove a five-pound note into the money receptor, hoping it would work, when *KEY* slammed into his brain.

Key?

Lando's *KEY*?

He stopped.

He couldn't go back. No not possible. It was a mistake.

But still...key? Why *Lando's key*? Why?

Before he could stop himself, he said, "Wait. Wait. Sorry, but this — this won't work. Would you please let me off?"

The driver looked at him, wary. "You sure?"

He shook his head, "No. But I...I forgot — all I have on me is sterling, and it won't work. It...it won't work."

The bus stopped at the next station. Adam hesitated then

forced himself to get off. As it drove away, the limo pulled up next to him. Apparently, Casey was going to follow the bus all the way to Santa Monica. He was close to kicking himself for not making her do so, but then she jumped out of the car, her face wracked with concern, and now he had to know.

"Lando's key?"

She pulled her compact from her purse, opened it and showed him one of the neon rubbers had been unwrapped and wrapped around an odd-shaped key, and was now dusted with makeup.

Adam looked at her. His head pounded. His heart throbbed. He could barely formulate the words, "For the safe deposit box?"

She nodded. "I got it when I went to pee. That's why I had us dance and...and I kissed him. He was getting suspicious, so I wanted...I wanted him to think I...I wanted him back. That I was doing this just to make him jealous. It worked." She hesitated then forced a smile. "Damn, it worked."

Adam's stomach began to grow calm and the world stopped shifting, a little. But one question still needed answering. "Do you have access to the box?"

"Yeah, I'm authorized. I made sure about that. But, c'mon, baby, he could've changed it with a phone call, so..."

It wasn't a huge ray of hope, but it was enough to let him regain control and pull his coat the rest of the way on as he said, "I — I don't — I won't need new clothes. Not if mine are washed."

"Adam, the maid's not in till Thursday."

He let her lead him back to the limo, nodding. "Right. Right. May I use your washer and dryer? Please?"

She all but beamed, saying, "C'mon, baby, you gotta ask?" She motioned for him to enter.

The door was open so Adam started to get in...and that is when he noticed Casey's phone on the table between the seats...showing Sean and Shawn were watching them from down the street, near some bushes, camera and recorder at full throttle. Their voices were the barest of whispers.

"So what's all this about a key?"
"I dunno, you sure got me."
"And he's her buddy. Right. Like hell."
"I told you tonight would go well."
And in unison they sang,

We got the cover of People.
We got the cover of People.
We got the cover of People.
We're gonna make a mint."

At that particular moment, Adam would happily have set the both of them on fire.

ELEVEN

An hour later, Adam's clothes were into the rinse cycle of their second wash, and *Raindrops Keep Fallin' On My Head* had serenaded him as he showered. Ravaged cartons of Chicken Vindaloo and Sag Paneer were scattered atop the bar, and an elegant fire of real cedar wood was happily popping and snapping in the hearth. He was lying face down on the couch, wrapped in a bathrobe and finishing his plate as Casey tended to the puncture on his derriere. Before this evening's events, he would never have let himself be semi-naked with anyone he had just met, let alone a young woman, but it seemed childish modesty was rather absurd, by this point.

She had changed into a light shift and was taking an inordinate amount of time on this injury in comparison to how quickly she'd mended the gash to his arm.

"This looks deep," she said. "Have you had a tetanus shot?"

He nodded. "My foot caught a nail during a match, last year. Got one then."

"I just can't picture you playing rugby. You're so neat." Then she dribbled something on the wound that stung like madness.

He yelped. "What is that?"

"Alcohol. Gotta make sure it's clean."

"I think you succeeded," he muttered.

"You should be glad Gertrude didn't go after you. That would've meant the ER. Or morgue."

"She wasn't dangerous around you."

"She knows me. That's probably why you were okay. Anybody else? They stay out of the yard."

"How *did* Lando wind up owning a panther, anyway? They're quite rare, black ones."

"He bought her from this guy, outside Cape Town."

"And just carried her into America?"

"Baby, Lando was on a daytime soap. All he had to do was show up to some wife's birthday party and give her a kiss to get a waiver. Same for B-Hills. The bastard does know how to know who to know to get what he wants."

"He's still an arse." She smiled her thanks. Then he asked, "Did you actually smear his car with dog feces?"

"A passing Doberman's. Just the seats and steering wheel...but that mutt really needed a better diet."

"Nothing more need be said," he croaked. "Is that why he wouldn't return the *Alice*, to you?"

She hesitated. "He stopped taking my calls and wouldn't answer my messages..."

"So you thought slipping into the party and stealing his key was a good idea?"

"Opportunity knocked; I answered."

"But why did you need me for your larceny?"

"If I'd shown up by myself, he'd have known. He still got suspicious. But you did a great job as wing man."

"Considering I hadn't a clue as to what you were doing."

"Worked better that way. Genuine reactions and no history of acting."

"Neither has he, for my opinion."

"Doesn't need to; he's a name, now." She sighed as she said, "Big enough to get me dumped from *I-Four-point-Two*."

"But how can he do that? *Ilithium Four* is Mar-lee's story; Creggan is secondary, in the first two volumes, and dead in the third."

"The people financing it want to focus on him."

"And desecrate a classic book! I like him less and less."

She laughed. "He doesn't like you, either, so... " She shook her head. "So you really can't swim?"

He sighed. "Tried to learn. For years. Then Connor pushed me in a lake. Said that would force me to work it out. I damn near drowned before David got to me. Now it's a pathological fear of water that's too deep."

She taped a bandage over his wound. "What an ass." He looked at her, his expression cockeyed. She huffed. "Your brother."

He grinned and nodded. "He lives in Paris, now. Thinks we're all beneath him."

She patted his rear and said, "All done."

"Brilliant." He stood up, pulled the bathrobe tight and threw his empty paper plate into the fire. His posterior was not yet ready to allow being sat upon, so he took a sip of tea and put it on the mantle. "I understand you were on *The Family Saint*?"

"Just Season One," she said as she gathered the medical supplies together. "Next door neighbor's obnoxious brat."

"Mum and Beryl used to watch it. I only saw bits, but I remembered it being with a black family, next door."

She rose to take the first aid kit behind the bar. "From second season. After they got renewed, producers decided to go that way."

"That's unfortunate."

"That's the biz." She leaned against the counter to examine him as if he were some specimen under a microscope. He felt more than a little discomfited so checked to see if his bathrobe was fully closed. Which made her smile. "Y'know, I dated an actor from England. You and he are nothing alike."

"I'm hardly a prime example of Her Majesty's people."

"I meant that in a good way. He was a shit. Or should I say," and her voice took an *Eastender* tone, "a *bloody fookin'*

146

shite, since that was his favorite phrase?"

He had to chuckle. "Thank you for making the comparison positive, on my part. That so rarely happens for me. Even Nora, the woman I was with, would try to make me different. Point out things in lads she saw that I should try. Hair. Clothing. Attitude."

"Like what Orisi and I did?"

"Yours was not meant to be permanent," then he gave her a wary glance and added, "Was it?" She shook her head. He smiled. "With Nora, she even suggested I take up smoking. Might loosen me up. When I pointed out how addictive it was, she said I could then quit and she would help me. Rather Munchausen of her. It got to be quite maddening. I think she wanted me to be a bastard and was disappointed I never took any of it to heart."

"What happened to her?"

"She married a lorry driver out of Liverpool and is about to have her first. Twins, if rumors are to be believed, though I can't imagine her accepting that as a possibility."

"She may not have any choice in the matter."

"You don't know Nora. She wouldn't even let me bring Albacore around."

"She didn't like tuna?"

"My father's dog. He became mine after Da died. But he was rather old by the time I was with her. Change of household would have been bad for him." He was silent for a moment. Sipped some more tea. "I've kept contact with her. In part to keep an eye on her future children, in case she does go Munchausen."

"God, you should be glad she broke up with you. She's a controlling bitch." Then she straightened up, looked him square in the eye and added, "Just like me."

"You and she are nothing alike," he murmured without a moment's hesitation.

"You can say that after tonight?"

He grimaced. "Well — you could have told me what you were planning."

"I didn't know you." She came around the bar to sit on the arm of a couch. "The first guys I dated, I met in acting class. On set. At parties. It's not smart to be with a self-centered brat when you're one, yourself. So I stopped with actors...and hooked up with that writer — this man who rewrote *Sky Knights*. He was kind and steady. Gave it good dialogue. Built up the characters. And got no credit. That was so wrong. I felt for him. Introduced him to my agency. They took him on, and he sold a script for over a million. He's the asshole who went back to his wife."

"Bloody hell."

"Yeah. What's even better? She knew what he was doing and pushed it. Didn't keep me from being tabloid fodder for a month, as a home-wrecker. And you know about Vinny...and Lando."

"I told you, you needn't explain yourself — "

"I know. It's just...I did ask Orisi to make you look extra good. Prove to the world I could land on my feet. That he made you into a guy to drive Lando crazy with jealousy — oh, did mama have fun playing with that. But you're right, I did use you, and I'm sorry. Sorry I didn't trust you."

He blushed, said, "No worries," and sipped some tea.

"See? I treat you like shit and you're still nice and polite." She grew soft as she continued with, "You even came back for me. I've never had anyone watch out for me, before — except for Mom and Grandy."

"I should have figured you wouldn't need my assistance."

"We all need a little help, sometimes. Don't you?"

He chuckled. "After all I've been through, this evening, I think what help I do need is psychological." Without thinking, he sat on the hearth...and stood right back up, grimacing. "Oh, God, that hurt."

She laughed. "The couch is softer."

"...In a moment." He finished his tea and gave a long sigh, then he gathered up the suit's pants, which had shrunk by about two sizes. Brushed wool. Of course. "Ten thousand dollars. Well...I've some savings. With the exchange rate it might be enough to repay Orisi..."

She bolted over and grabbed the pants from him, growling, "It's fifty bucks worth of material. The rest of the value is Orisi's attitude." Then she tossed them in the fire. He was so shocked, he couldn't move. She continued with, "He got fifty-thousand in free advertising by you wearing that suit and being with me at the premier. So shut up about it."

He had to fight chuckling as he said, "Yes, miss. But I'm keeping those briefs as a memento," then added under his breath, "you controlling bitch." And he winked.

She laughed and swatted at him. And he yawned.

"What time does the bank open?" he asked.

"Boxes're available after ten. You want some dream-time? I've got five bedrooms in this crib."

"A bit of sleeps does sound lovely, but I still have to put my things in the dryer. I think I'll just sit here, a little." He carefully settled on the couch, before the fire.

She flopped beside him, saying, "Y'know, Lando's leaving on that publicity tour, tomorrow. Why don't we wait till he's gone to pick up the book?"

Which jolted him into shifting around...and his rear let him know it was not happy about that. After he was done holding back a few choice words, he said, "Please tell me you have legal authorization to the box. We're not about to try something sneaky, again? Banks tend not to appreciate that."

"Yes, I do. It's just — well — aren't you having fun?"

"Please," he said as he settled into a somewhat comfortable position, "I lead a very simple life. Rise. Breakfast with Mum. Tube. Work. Dinner. Work." His voice grew softer...his words slower. "Tube. Supper with Mum. Read. Bed. Saturdays is rugby. Sundays, *The Sunday Times,* oddly enough." He said nothing for a moment then continued, "It's the only way I can keep any sense of myself. Been like that since Da died...God, nearly fifteen years ago."

He gazed at the fire. "Da and I, we...we understood each other. Were comfortable together. His shop was near Leicester Square. Got it from his father, who got it from his father and so on. That shop — it was his life, and I loved helping him with it. Mum said I'd have lived there, if I could." He took in a deep breath. "To her, it was just an income. She's nothing if not pragmatic. Direct. Focused. No patience for fiddle-faddle, while I'm her prime fiddle-faddler. After Da died, I said I'd take it on but..." His voice trailed off.

"But...?"

It took him a moment to continue. "It had to be liquidated. To pay off the loss of the book."

"What're you talking about?"

He looked at her. "Sorry? Oh. That copy of the *Alice Sixty-five* Da won at auction. I told you about her, earlier."

Her voice became a whisper. "You said he was killed, and the book disappeared..."

He nodded. "He was en route to his client. Was robbed. In Glasgow. Pushed down some stairs. His neck..." It took him a moment to continue. "Wallet taken. Briefcase, too. Everything except his return ticket. For the train. Police tracked him, through that. Nothing was ever found. Nobody charged. The book never appeared, again. Everyone thinks the thieves didn't know what a treasure they had and tossed it aside. Our insurance covered three-hundred-thousand. The shop was sold to make up the rest."

"...I'm so sorry."

He gave her a vague smile of thanks, his voice a whisper. "I hated them doing it. That's why I started rugby — needed something to focus my anger on. And hurt. Help me feel in control, again. Kept at it...though not as much since I got on at Merryton. Been there since university. Nice. Safe. Careful. Stationary."

He sighed and stretched, slow and easy, then leaned back to rest his head. "Like Albacore. He used to wait at the door for

Da to return. And wait. Not understanding why he didn't. It's like he was afraid to move for fear he'd miss him — or have to face the reality that he never would come home. So he sat. And waited. And waited. Till I put him on my lap, one day, as I was about to read. After that, he would come lie on me whenever I sat down with a book. Did until the day he was gone. Poor old Albacore never did understand."

He sighed and closed his eyes.

"It's just as well I didn't take on Da's shop. I'd have lost it, anyway. That world is dying off, with smaller places like his going the fastest. And more's the pity. More's the pity."

Then he drifted into a deep sleep.

— TWELVE —

As Adam drifted awake, he felt Nora snuggled next to him and sighed a smile. Every morning they lived together, when the alarm went off she would be on the other side of the bed, curled up tight, her back to him. He asked her about it, once, and all she said was, "That's how I sleep." The discussion ended there. But now? Feeling her next to him was nice...so nice. No need to even open his eyes...maybe catch a bit more sleeps.

Adam couldn't remember why he and Nora chose to live together. They hardly made the perfect couple. She was pretty in a round perky way. Decisive. Sure. No nonsense. Just like Mum. He had noticed her when he started at Merryton, but it was two years before he asked her out. Then by the third date she was deciding where they were going and what they were doing, and he had gone along because that was how his mother approached life, so he was used to it. Just like his father had been.

That had worked well for his parents — Da being quiet and supportive, lost in his books; Mum being the one who got things done. But they also held completely different views of the world, something Adam never thought about until he got her reaction to a book they had both read.

It had arrived via the Post, wrapped twice around in what was once a *Weetabix* carton and held closed with a lot of cello-tape. Da was at that auction, so Adam had the shop to himself. He carefully opened the package to find a copy of the Pantheon paperback edition of Simone de Beauvoir's *The Blood of Others*. It was trade size with soft gray-brown covers, edges worn, spine cracked straight down the middle and a small tear where OD and O had been in the title. It was over twenty years old, so the condition was not unexpected...but it had not been cared-for.

He carefully opened the book to find pages yellowed with age, almost brittle. The top still held hints of the dust that had accumulated, there was a small stain of some sort over an area near the spine and some margins had writing in them. In ink! He murmured a sharp, "Philistines," in response. Hardly the good condition promised by the seller — more like acceptable, at best — but he still cradled the book like the finest of the fine.

The shop was quiet so he cleaned his glasses, set aside the papers he had planned to sort and researched her on ABEBooks. Not much showed up.

When Da returned, Adam showed the book to him. He looked her over and sighed, "I asked him to send us a sample of the best ones, and this is all that came?"

Adam nodded. "ABE believes she's worth about two or three pounds, but that's in good condition."

Da gave him a look, as if he thought it curious Adam would have researched the book, then he asked, "What do you think?"

"Whoever owned it, they weren't book people. University student, maybe? Reading for a course? I've never read de Beauvoir but this copy — she makes me want to read her."

"How so?"

"The way bits are missing from the spine as if to hide what she truly is. Makes me curious. And the cover with the young woman in modern clothes, hair cut short; the man dressed from a hundred years ago; the poster in the background reading 1941. None of it matches, so is quite intriguing."

"Would you buy this one for the shop?"

"Dunno. I might. We don't have any de Beauvoir."

Da smiled and handed the book back to him. "Remind

me — did he mention the number of books he had?"

"His list carries eighty-eight titles, Twentieth Century, all, but some are multiple volume, so I'd say the total number is more like ninety-five to a hundred."

"I doubt we'd sell this for more than a quid, but write him back and let him know we'll take the lot for sixty pounds if he'll ship them to us. May not be worth it."

"Don't you think they'll bring a price, Da?"

"Some might. A book's worth what you're willing to pay for it."

Adam huffed. "That's not how I see it."

Da smiled. "You know what I mean."

Adam nodded. "If I remember right, one of his e-mails said he'd be in London, next week. He could drop them off then."

"That would be best. Perhaps something else in his library will intrigue you."

"You mind if I read this one?"

"Of course not. Ask your mother about it."

Adam couldn't believe what he said. "Mum's read it?"

Da's eyes twinkled as he nodded. "Yes, your mother has been known to open a volume or two. Her answer might surprise you."

Adam brought the book home to show her as they sat around their tight dinner table. She took it and nodded. "A strong, caring man and the woman who loves him, as written by a woman. Be interesting to hear what you think of it."

"Didn't you like the book, Mum?"

"I'll not tell you till you're done."

Adam was back in the shop on Saturday to cover the register while his father handled the customers. It wasn't a particularly busy or difficult day, and the upstairs shelves were in good order, for a change, so he had little to distract him. Still it took till closing for him to finish the book. Normally, once he began to read a story all else fell by the wayside, and for a slim volume such as this he expected to be done by noon. After all, he'd read *Le Corbeau* in three hours. On a busier day. In French.

But Jean was tiresome in his incessant questioning and indecisiveness, which led to nothing; Marie was clingy and obsessive and weak, someone who felt incomplete without a man at her side, even if she had to force him to be there; and all around them the world raced to war, but they paid little attention. It kept changing from first to third person, sometimes in the middle of a sentence, and the ending was a cheat. No serious reason for why she changed her mind about helping Jean, and no explanation as to how she'd been mortally wounded. As if it didn't matter.

But that clued him in to thinking perhaps the point of the story was that there were no heroes, only weak people lost in their own little worlds until their lives were torn away from them, and they either stopped thinking and started doing...or they didn't.

He told this to his mother over dinner, that night, ending with, "This might be a poor translation. Perhaps I should try her in the French."

Connor laughed. "I've heard your French."

"I can tell you where to stick it," Adam snapped back.

"Boys," Mum said, the tone in her voice saying, *Stop it.*

"Connor's a language snob," said Beryl. "He wants to live in Paris."

"*Who wouldn't?*" Connor replied, in French, smiling at her.

"I like London just fine," said Da, a twinkle in his eye.

Mum smiled and turned to Adam. "You're much too kind about the book," she said. "I found there was so much focus on the weaknesses and selfishness of the characters, I lost any sense of them being human in any way."

"Well, yes, they were tiresome," Adam replied, "but so are most people." Then he glanced at Connor.

"Adam, compare this to when you read *Anna Karenina*, last year. Remember how you'd rush up to tell me about passages you found exceptional?"

Connor laughed. "*Levin reaping wheat with the peasants.*

It's poetry, POETRY, I say!"

Adam glared at him. Beryl laughed and swatted Connor, then cast a look at Adam as if to say, *See? I'm telling him to be nice.*

Their mother gave them all a warning smile. "You will behave or you will see no dessert."

"Can't have that," said Da. "Angel Delight. Butterscotch. And I wonder whose favorite that is?"

Connor put on a very serious face.

Adam tossed Connor his best condescending sneer and said, "Actually, the best part was when Levin and Kitty reconciled by using single letters traced into a felt table covering, working out words and phrases to reveal their true feelings about each other. Most intriguing." Then he turned to his mother and asked, "So you didn't like *The Blood of Others*?"

"I felt it a story about a selfish, indecisive man, who was involved in his own thoughts to the exclusion of others, and a weak clinging woman who forced him to love her. All for naught."

"But it falls under the Absurdist banner, doesn't it?"

She looked at Da, a knowing gleam in her eye. "Did you tell him to say that?"

"I've made no comment about the story," said Da, rising from the table, smiling. "I'll get the dessert."

She turned back to Adam. "Well I think it falls under me wanting to kick Jean down the stairs and slap Marie for being a twaddling idiot."

Adam huffed. "Really, Mum, you said the same thing about Anna and Vronsky, who gave up everything for each other — family, position, wealth — only to have it fall apart."

"At least they did it for love. Or lust, if you prefer. That was understandable."

"Which made Kitty and Levin a nice romantic contrast," said Da as he returned from the kitchen with a tray of bowls.

"Is that what you're going to do, Adam?" Beryl said in a

voice dripping with honey. "Ruin yourself for a great passion?"

Connor cast Adam a cold sneer as he said, "Only if it's a lad in the same dance studio. He's the poof of the family."

"*You're an idiot*," Adam shot back, in French.

"Would that matter?" Mum asked, her face letting Connor know what his answer had better be.

"Mum, I am not interested in other lads," Adam growled. "But why do I get the feeling you'd be upset if I wasn't?"

"I just want you to know it's unimportant," she replied.

"Adam will love someone from afar," Beryl sighed, "and hope someday she'll notice, and love him back."

"And wank him in the toilet," laughed Connor, "since that's all he'll ever get."

Adam snarled and splashed the last of his milk onto Connor's face. Connor jumped to his feet only to have Adam's dessert flung at him, too.

Before Connor could react, their mother stood, her voice an angry bark as she said, "Adam, your father's office! Connor, clean yourself and then your room! Lose yourselves in them."

Connor drew himself ramrod straight and smirked. "Fine. Listening to hobbits chatter on books is boring." Then he sauntered upstairs.

Beryl shook her head after him. David merely shrugged and dug into his dessert.

Adam rose, wiped himself off, and stormed into his father's office, a tight room filled with stacks of books, a world where he felt safe. A few minutes later, Da joined him.

"Come to lecture me?" Adam snapped.

"No," said Da. "It's just that I've noticed things are growing more difficult between you two. It might help if you understood — Connor may have been born after David, but by less than a year and has always felt like he should have been first. He's a bit like your mother, that way. He likes to take control. No patience for things deemed unimportant. To him. I suggest you learn how to ignore his comments before you both wind up with pistols at twenty paces."

Adam huffed a laugh. "I'd choose swords."

"Even with him being taller?"

"Da!" Then Adam saw his father chuckling so shrugged and said, "Yes. Dance lessons makes me better at it. Footwork, you know." He rose and looked his father straight in the eye to say, "I've been thinking. I'll be sixteen, next summer. Is your shop good for an apprenticeship?"

Da sat at his desk and eyed Adam. "I can look into it...but your mother and I would much prefer you take your A-Levels and continue on to University. My alma mater would be nice, and Vincent St. George is there."

Adam took on an overdone headmaster tone as he replied, "If one does not attend Oxford or Cambridge, one has not attended University." Then he added in a still-angry voice, "Just ask Connor."

"Then he'd best focus on his A-2s if he wants acceptance to the LSE."

"He'll get in. He knows what to do, for that." He looked at his father. "So Mum's talking to him, eh?"

Da nodded. "As I said, she *was* a lot like him when she was younger. Did well for her as a Sister. But she's mellowed, so..."

"Thanks to you, is my thought."

Da smiled. "We fit well together. Love each other. I can't imagine a life without her. I believe she feels the same."

"You were lucky, Da."

His father looked at him, for a moment, then said, "You'll find someone who opens up your world like she did mine. Who fits you as perfectly. Just between ourselves, Connor won't."

Adam was taken aback. "Da..."

"Because you read, Adam. That takes you outside of yourself, and opens a window into the beauty of life. Helps you like and accept people. Connor — he cannot see beyond the material things he wants, no matter how hard we try to show him how limiting that is. Rather tragic, isn't it?"

"I — I hadn't thought about it, like that."

His father rose. "Perhaps you should set him a good example. Show him how the printed word can lead you to the humanity in us all." He ruffled Adam's hair. "Did a good job with that de Beauvoir."

"You've read it?"

Da nodded. "I agree with your assessment." Then he leaned in to whisper, "Now come on; Angel Delight."

Adam tried to follow Da's advice, over the next few weeks, talking about the elegance of and lessons learned from the books he read, but Connor just increased his needling until it was impossible to ignore.

Then Da died.

That brought about a soft truce between them as his mother went quiet and still and seemed unable to make any decision. More than once during this time, when Adam looked at her he wondered if she were even breathing. Which scared him. But things had to get done, so he wound up arranging for Da's body to be returned to London as David and Beryl made preparations for the service and internment in a small cemetery near Epping.

While Connor remained silent. Just like Mum.

Through it all, Adam read nothing. Tried not to think. He felt he'd shatter into millions of pieces if he allowed himself to even contemplate what his new world truly meant.

It wasn't until their solicitor told them the situation with the insurance coverage, and the client's refusal to accept the loss, that Mum took charge, again, still very quietly. Over Adam's objections, the shop was put up for auction, and it brought in just enough to cover their *legal entanglements*. After that, she got back to work and never discussed Da's death, again.

Then Adam joined rugby. When Connor saw he could take down lads half a foot taller than himself, he shifted his taunts to Beryl. In response, she grew nails and, after a nasty argument, dug them into Connor's neck deep enough to draw blood, making him back away from her, as well. It didn't hurt that the scars remained for weeks, as a warning.

David, being taller and stronger and still in his punk phase, was never a target, so Connor shifted his subtle digs back to Adam, just to anger him. It continued until he began the LSE; after that, he was too busy to bother anyone. Then he met a woman named Catherine during a semester at The Sorbonne, decided it made legal and financial sense for them to be together, to which she agreed, so he married into one of France's *better families*. They now lived in a tower overlooking The Seine, and Adam hadn't seen them since Christmas, last. An arrangement all parties were happy with.

Adam sighed. This was hardly the outcome his father had hoped for, from him. But lead by example only works if others pay attention.

Some of Nora's hair tickled his nose so he shifted to get away from it, opened his eyes and came to realize he wasn't in a bed; he was on a couch. In a strange place. Covered with an afghan. His rear and arm very sore. That's when he looked to see who was sleeping next to him.

It was Casey.

The whole night flooded back over him. Memories of how she had used him. How she had begun to seem like the worst part of his mother and brother. His anger at the realization. But now he could see she was reacting to the pain of a cruel breakup, so she couldn't be blamed, really. People who hurt are always difficult.

He had seen that in his mother, crystalized when she had suggested he work in a local bookshop part time, after school.

"It will help with some of the expenses," she had said, in her sharpest no-nonsense manner.

Adam had agreed without argument. "I want to pay my share, Mum."

She had stiffened, snapped, "Don't say things just to

make me happy," and gone off to be quiet. again.

Adam had checked on her, an hour later, to find her sitting at the kitchen table, sipping tea, so sat next to her and helped himself to a cup.

She did not look at him. Said nothing for a couple of minutes. Then she murmured, "I'd rather you not have to work. Prefer you focus on your studies."

"I'll do all right."

"I know that!" she'd snapped. "Wouldn't ask it, otherwise." Then her eyes had shifted to his to say she was sorry for snapping at him, and he had given her a soft nod and no more was said.

Adam thought nothing of it, then, but now he could see she hated being in control, even though someone in the family had to be. Now his father's loving support seemed a bit more like simple acquiescence, because all of the difficult choices had been left up to her. And wouldn't even the most decisive person hate being in that position all of the time?

Perhaps that was what sent Nora away — not boredom or his refusal to change, for her, but the non-stop reality that she would always be the one making the decisions, and Adam had given her no indication he wanted things to be different. Now her life was about to be taken over by twin girls, if gossip was to be believed, and her decisiveness would be needed non-stop. He hoped her husband would be as supportive of her as Da was of Mum.

Casey shifted, beside him. Grew even lovelier, if that were possible. He liked being next to her. Liked the protectiveness he felt towards her. He could see she needed a bit of relief from always having to be on her guard. Always careful. He wished he could give her space to relax, be someone she could trust and lean on instead of having to wonder if he was just another manipulative cretin. He wanted to always be there for her, and he would have been happy to stay right where he was till she awoke except for one very intense problem.

He desperately needed to pee.

Well...when reality had to be faced, it had to be faced. So he carefully extricated himself and gently maneuvered over her to stagger to his feet, then took a few moments to work the kinks out of his back and rub his sore rear. He noticed a clock over the mantelpiece read 9:42 then saw his clothes were slopped over on the bar.

Before he could wonder how that had happened, Patricia poked her head around the foyer door, put a finger to her lips and held up a bag of coffee and box of tea. He all but begged for the latter. She pointed to a new toothbrush and little tube of toothpaste, beside the clothes. Obviously, she came prepared. He fought back a chuckle of joy and took his clothes into Casey's office bathroom.

Within minutes, he felt like a new man, with his own briefs and trousers and shirt and socks and everything that was his back on. In fact, he all but strutted with pleasure. He even used Orisi's brand of deodorant and a touch of the man's signature cologne. Then he hung the robe from the darts on the bathroom door, hiding Lando's brutalized image, got his rucksack and stuffed Orisi's sequined briefs into it along with his extra pair and socks. As he was doing so, he noticed the photos on Casey's desk were still turned away and a post-it on a monitor read — *BA 0288 1:40 Wednesday*. That seemed odd, but he shrugged it off, loaded the toothbrush, hopped into the bathroom, began brushing and felt even better until —

0288 1:40 Wednesday?

He was on the night flight, not the afternoon. Wasn't he? If not, they needed to get going, now, now, now. He scrambled to the computer, toothbrush still in his mouth, took the post-it and rushed into the kitchen.

Patricia was pouring a steaming cup of tea as he entered and showed her the note. She gave a half-laugh.

"No, you're on the nine-oh-five," she whispered. "That was the only other flight with first class seats available. I kept the info in case Vincent was a problem."

"Vincent?" Adam mumbled back, adding a sweet smile. "Whatever could you mean?" Then he remembered to take the toothbrush out and rinse it.

She handed him the tea. He smiled his thanks and started fixing it his way as she said, "So, Adam...got in late...slept on the couch instead of a bed...and this mornin' I find you in nothin' but a robe..."

He nearly dropped a carton of milk, in shock. "How'd you know?"

"I checked."

He pulled his shirttail a bit lower, asking, "Why did you do that?"

"You were sleepin' by my daughter. And she's got two condoms in her purse, when there were three, yesterday. And I worry 'bout her gettin' involved with somebody new when she's so vulnerable and hurt and, well, I thought you were a nice guy. Now I'm wonderin' if you're just another male animal usin' her emotional distress to fulfill his own basic needs." The look on her face gave him clear warning.

"Sorry?" he said, then he realized what she was thinking and burst out with, "Oh! No! No. I — I just — I fell asleep."

She looked at him, wary, then said, "You know, I think you're tellin' the truth. And for the first time I'm almost sorry." Then she added with a glare, "Just *almost*."

"I'm not sure how to take such a comment."

"Oh, just...just ignore it, honey, 'cause at least you bein' here got her out of the house. And she's sleepin'. And I know you didn't eat all that Indian food by yourself. Real happy to see that."

"I thought — she mentioned having lots of lasagna."

"Makin' it ain't eatin' it." She touched his arm, tender and motherly. "Adam, couldn't you stay a couple more days? Help her come more out of her shell?"

Adam chuckled. "Oh, I think we did a great deal of that, last night."

"Okay, honey, you'll start at the beginnin' and keep goin' till the end, all over breakfast. Or can you call it brunch on a Wednesday?"

"Call it whatever you like; I'm ravenous, and it's my tea time."

"Tea time? What time's tea time?"

Adam turned to see Casey entering, still sleepy, still lovely. "Any time of the day you want it to be," he said, "but right now it's almost ten. Good morning."

"Hi. Sleep okay?"

"That is a surprisingly comfortable couch. Are they all like that? I've never laid out on one, before."

She smiled. "I have...way too many times."

Patricia cut in with, "So — eggs? Bacon? Hash browns? Pancakes? Toast? The works?"

"Yeah, lay it on," said Casey. "I can always throw it up, later." Which jolted Adam. She laughed. "Baby, c'mon, I'm not that stupid."

"You...you never know, the stories one hears in Hollywood." And he chased the comment with his most lopsided grin. Casey smiled her glorious smile. He continued with, "So, have you an iron I might use? I'm rather rumpled. Cotton shirt, you know."

"You sure are," she said, brushing her hands over his sleeve. It was all Adam could do to keep from purring. "Sean and Shawn will make sure everyone gets the wrong idea, off this. Mom, *do* we have an iron?"

Patricia was pulling ingredients from the refrigerator so she did not look at them as she said, "No, we got dry-cleaners."

"Then how did my clothes get done?" Adam asked. "You said you couldn't work the drier."

"But I can use a phone to call tech support and have them walk me through it," said Patricia. "Wasn't as hard as I thought."

"Brilliant," Adam said, "so if you don't mind, I'll get to

ironing."

He filled a mid-size pot with half water and set it on the stove, got a towel from the bathroom and spread it over the counter, then removed his shirt and laid it neatly over the towel. He checked the water to find it was already hot enough, so took the pot and slowly drew it down the shirt's front panel, smoothing out the worst of the wrinkles.

Patricia set everything by the stove and stopped to watch. "Wow, who showed you this?"

"Me Da," Adam said. "Our iron broke and we couldn't afford to replace it, for a bit."

"They're that expensive in England?" Casey asked.

"We just had to wait till some money cleared the bank to purchase a new one; Mum does not approve of debt. And Da — he liked to touch an iron to our shirts and trousers in winter." His voice grew soft and his gaze was distant. "Made you feel cozy and warm against the chill."

"You miss him," Casey whispered.

It took Adam a moment to answer "Yes. Might not have been so bad if he'd made it home, I suppose. Been with us a bit longer...instead of just...just being gone..." His voice trailed off and he looked at Casey. Her eyes were locked on him. He offered her a bit of a smile. "Don't you miss yours?"

"Miss the son-of-a-bitch who robbed us?" popped out of Patricia.

Casey flinched and turned to the table, saying, "C'mon, Mom, let's get breakfast going. Gotta get to the bank."

Adam almost reached over to touch her and say something absurd like, "I understand," but hesitated...then focused on finishing the shirt, hung it up to keep it neat, and helped set the table for breakfast.

Patricia worked up a perfect brunch, right down to toasted English Muffins. Except Adam noticed her slathering the muffins with butter and a yellow jam and had to ask, "None of that has anything extra in it, does it?"

"Adam," she said, "you think I'd get you stoned, again?"

He eyed the muffins.

Casey eyed her mother.

Patricia smiled and said, "These are mine." Then she tossed more into the toaster. "There's some strawberry in the fridge."

Adam chuckled. "I prefer honey, if you don't mind."

"The strawberry's for me," said Casey. "Mom's allergic."

He smiled, shrugged, pulled out the jam and sat at the table, shirtless and feeling very Bohemian. Then they told Patricia of the previous night's events, finally laughing at how huffy Adam had become after his encounter with Gertrude. Patricia took special pleasure in how Casey had tricked Lando. Adam felt as if a smile was on his face the entire meal, while Casey cleaned her plate...something Patricia took quiet notice of. Then as Casey showered, he and Patricia cleared the table.

He was bringing the last of the plates to load into the dishwasher when she said, "Y'know, I probably shouldn't tell you this, but Casey does miss her father. It's just...that little shit, the way he used her, he was his father's son. And he spent her money like you would not believe." She closed the washer and looked at him. "She tell you about her first series?"

"*The Family Saint*," said Adam, nodding.

"Ten years old. Bringin' in more in a month than her shit of a father, in a year. He used it to start a hedge fund. Said that was how he's protectin' it, accordin' to law. Wanted it to keep goin', forever. And it might have. She had a seven-year contract and the show was hittin' good numbers. It's just — this one producer had free-roamin' hands, if you know what I mean."

Adam jolted and gasped, "With a child!?" Patricia smiled. "*Scheisse*."

"Her father wouldn't even talk to the bastard to back him off. So I did. And he banned me from the set."

Adam frowned. "Can he do that? She was under-age."

"So long as one parent's there," said Patricia. "Casey was miserable, so she and I decided to make 'em want to get rid of her." She closed the washer as Adam pulled on his shirt. "It was easy. Just tell the writers their words don't sound right for an eleven year-old, ask non-stop questions about motivation, act like you're doin' it because you *want the part to be real and not like somethin' written by middle-aged men.* Hollywood types hate that kind of shit, even as they praise it.

"Her father warned her that if she kept messin' around like she was, they'd kill her character off. She got more intense. He threatened, ordered, begged, pointed out how good the money was...but at the end of the season, they released her from the contract. The producer blamed me. So did her father. Called me a stage mother. I let 'em 'cause that took the heat off her. But I also set some stories goin' about that producer. Last I heard, he's doin' seven to ten for kiddie porn."

Adam's only response was to shiver.

"Problem is, the actors playin' her parents lost their jobs, too. One went on to bigger and better things; the other vanished into obscurity. When Casey realized that, she cried for a week. And that son-of-a-bitch rubbed it in. That's when I kicked his ass to the curb. We were in the process of gettin' divorced when he vanished."

"Vanished?"

Patricia looked at him. "With that hedge fund. Hundred million bucks. Casey was fourteen. Haven't seen him since.

"Up to that point, his father took his side," she said as she led him back to the fireplace. "But the little bastard even took Casey's money. The big bastard offered to replenish it if I'd agree to him havin' control of her trust, but I told him to fuck off. So he tried to take custody. Claimed what happened on the sitcom was evidence I was unfit. He backed away when I told him 'bout that producer and how his son's inaction would come out in court. That's when he got that book and said he'd hold it for her, just in case, 'cause it'd increase in value. When he saw how Casey was doin', he changed his will. A bit of control on his part. Thank God it wasn't needed."

They sat on the couch, her with a cup of coffee, him with another cup of tea — and sitting very carefully — as she continued, "You know what's funny? Now I think the old bastard bought it 'cause he felt guilty for what his son had pulled. His form of an apology, I guess. Don't expect remorse from sociopaths, do you?"

Adam thought of how Connor never apologized for anything, and shrugged.

Patricia smiled. "I'm not a good judge of men. I thought Lando — well, since he already had a good career, he'd be different from the other guys she'd seen. Wouldn't use her to help himself. Now? He's another piece of shit I'm glad is gone." She was silent for a moment, then said, "But you — I really do wish you would stay."

Adam smiled and without thinking said, "I could return, once I've delivered the book. I have the weekend. I'm not sure what a flight would cost but — well, I'd just need to tell Barclay's I'll be here, this time."

Patricia smiled. "We got five bedrooms, includin' a pool house..."

"What you talking about, Mom?"

They looked up to see Casey descending the stairs, fresh and ready to go in jeans and a comfortable shirt.

"I think I convinced Adam to come back," said Patricia.

Casey looked at him. "Yes. Do."

Adam could barely breathe. "Someone wanting to see me, again. Unbelievable."

Patricia drew a finger along his chin. "Don't beat up on yourself, honey."

"Ready?" asked Casey.

Adam nodded and grabbed his rucksack and jacket. "Thanks for everything, Patricia," he said. "Breakfast was brilliant."

"And slow," said Casey. "The bank expected us two hours ago."

"That's on time for Hollywood royalty," said Patricia.

"Yeah, right, Mom. Later."

"Cheers," said Adam, chuckling as he slung his rucksack over one shoulder. Then he and Casey headed out to the convertible, looking like a happy couple off on holiday.

Patricia waved bye-bye till they were gone...her face an unreadable mask, throughout.

THIRTEEN

Casey drove them to a black glass and steel building in the center of Beverly Hills, left her car with the valet and led Adam through a massive lobby reeking of wealth to a low-key office. Ten minutes later, he was watching her and a clerk use their respective keys to pull a metal container from its slot, all under the harsh eye of two CCTV cameras. The clerk set it on a table in a private room and left, then Casey pulled out a slim Solander box covered in deep green cloth, nothing but a gilt border as decoration. She looked at it with a frown, shrugged and handed it to Adam, all so very casual.

He accepted it with every ounce of tenderness he could muster and checked the box for weak hinging. He could barely breathe.

Casey watched him, fascinated. "You handle it like it's a baby," she said.

"Books are my life," said Adam. "They're so much more than just the binding and pages and words within. Ideas and histories accompany them, as do all the people who've touched or been touched by them. An antiquarian volume is a universe unto herself, if you're willing to let her become one with you, each one of them unique." He caressed the box. "But this one — she deserves so much better than a standard Solander for protection."

"What do you mean?"

"This box — it's rather ordinary, but the book is

anything but. We keep empty cases, like this, in The Dark Chamber to use when we receive a book that needs one or should have one."

He carefully opened the box to find a soft blue silk lining bunched around a recessed space where a faded hardback book bound in red cloth and gilt trim rested. A gilt cameo of Alice was in its center, half worn away. He removed the book from its bed, still with the utmost care as he said, "Lovely. And consider — before this, there was no Mad Hatter. No Cheshire Cat or Queen of Hearts. No Alice." He inspected the spine to see how well it was holding. "After — well, she's not something you'd want to, as your mother put it..." and his voice grew softer and absent as he said, "...flip through on the crapper..." and a frown came to his eyes. Then he continued with, "This is not an *Alice Sixty-five*."

"Baby, that's the book I got from Grandy."

"No, no, no, no, this is the *Appleton* edition," Adam said. "See? *MacMillan* should be on the base of the spine, and the copyright page — " He opened the book to the title page and saw 1866 at its base. "It should be 1865." Then he jolted and flipped back to the front end paper. It took him a moment to believe what he saw — a soft graphite *EB* had been partially erased from the upper left corner in a way he had seen and corrected far too often in far too many books. "That's Elizabeth's mark!" he finally said. He glared at Casey. "This is the university's *Appleton*. What's going on?"

Casey's confusion was absolute. "Adam, this is the book I got. I sent pictures of it to Vincent."

"No, no, no, no, no, no, that's not possible; he'd know."

"But it's got a note from Grandy! Something like it's just in case things don't work out, and I know it's from him because it's handwritten."

Adam hesitated then carefully looked through the pages. No note was enclosed. He felt a cold anger begin to build within him and he could barely whisper, "Oh, dear God...Casey, who else knew about this?"

She almost laughed. "Mom. Lando. Vincent. You. The dozen assholes trying to buy it. Some Australian who wouldn't take no for an answer. That's all."

Adam had to close his eyes to fight the anger. "Bloody hell. The one-forty." He finally looked at Casey. "How far is it to the airport?"

"This time of day? About an hour. Well, forty-five minutes, the way I drive. Why?"

"I think I know where your book is."

Casey made the trip in thirty minutes, flat, ignoring every law there was and making up a few of her own. Adam said nothing the whole trip, because if he had opened his mouth he knew he'd have screamed like a child, more than once, at Casey's maneuvers.

Five minutes after she dropped him at the international terminal, he entered the cool, calm, elegant first class lounge of his airline and dropped into a plush leather seat, still a bit shaken.

Though not as shaken as Patricia.

"Unbelievable," he said, glaring at her.

It took her more than a moment to finally growl, "Adam, how'd you get in here?"

He held up his ticket. "Premier Class. Remember? Gets you caviar with your crackers instead of crap. Hopefully, with no vomit. But straight through security." Then he pulled the Solander box from his inside jacket pocket and continued with, "You must've known I'd look at the book."

"I thought I'd be gone, first," she said. "How the hell'd you get here so fast?"

"Wasn't it you who taught Casey how to drive?"

She gave out a long, long sigh. "Damn."

"So, why all this subterfuge?"

She huffed and puffed but finally said, "Word was gettin' 'round. Casey got calls from people wantin' to buy it. One jerk from Australia was a real hard-ass, and we almost got broke into, twice. When I told Vincent about it, he said he didn't want a repeat of what happened with — um, I mean..."

Adam froze. "He...he told you what happened to my father?" Patricia grimaced and bit a lip. "Vincent doesn't — he doesn't believe Da was targeted for the book, does he? That it wasn't just a random robbery?"

"Honey, I — I think he just felt this'd be safer."

He nodded. It took him a moment to continue. "So I was meant to be nothing more than a decoy." Then his voice took a harsh edge. "And if I did happen to be robbed, beaten and killed? All that mattered was you'd have had the correct book. Right?"

She had no answer.

Adam didn't trust himself to say anything more, about it; the turmoil and fury in his heart was too great. He just took a deep breath, released it, and murmured, "May I at least see her?"

Patricia hesitated, then she pulled an item wrapped in felt from her purse as she told him, "Vincent didn't really think there'd be trouble. Swappin' 'em out was just a precaution."

Adam took the bundle from her and unwrapped the felt to reveal a green cloth clamshell case...

And an ice-cold blade slipped into his heart and the world vanished around him as his head began to pound and his breath went soft and slow. He could barely control his shaking as he gazed upon the case.

It was covered in soft Damask, with the book's cameo of Alice woven into the cloth and some burn damage to its back. A light decorative border was also woven in. The spine had recessed hinges, and the cover was held closed by two brass latches on the fore-edge.

"These latches could use a good polish," croaked out of him, then he forced himself to press them open.

The inside was layered with champagne-colored silk and had a recessed area where the book was lying. More silk was folded gently across it, like a protective blanket. He lifted it away to reveal a fine copy of *Alice's Adventures in Wonderland,* bound in red cloth and gilt trim...and the world crashed back in on him.

"You exchanged copies more than two weeks ago," he said in the barest whisper. "Before everything was decided."

Patricia sensed his turmoil. Her voice became soft and tender. "Actually, it was decided last month, honey. We just had to finalize the paperwork and set up customs. I was barely able to swap 'em 'fore Lando got Casey to put it in his box. I had to wait till I got the one Vincent sent, and he had to find a green box that's sort-of like this one so she wouldn't notice the cases're different, 'cause there's somethin' about this case bein' important, too, but it was all so rushed and — "

"She didn't know," he said, nodding. "I'm glad for that." He rose and wandered to a nearby sconce to examine the book under a bright light. "Did you look at the *Alice*?"

The announcement that her flight was now boarding filtered over the speakers. Patricia rose. "Honey, that line about readin' it on the crapper — I was only jokin'."

He nodded. Tenderly closed the book, brought it back to lay it in the case, folded the champagne silk over it, closed it, and handed it to her.

"Who's meeting you at Heathrow?" he asked, his voice still the barest of whispers.

"Import broker's bringin' armed guards."

He nodded. Took another deep breath. Forced himself to say, "Tell Vincent I may change the ticket and stay here, like you wanted." He cast her a harsh glare as he all growled, "No need for me to rush home, is there?"

He started for the exit.

Patricia stopped him. Concern covered her face as she said, "Adam, I know we've hurt you...but soon as I was on the plane, Vincent was gonna call you and — "

"Don't." He backed away from her, his hands raised. "Please. There is nothing you can say to make this right."

"But I am sorry."

He had no words. Vincent had used him, knowing full well what this meant to him, and Patricia had worked with the man to deceive him even further. What could he do but walk away?

Even as his world spun out of control.

****

When he exited the cave-like lower level of the massive international terminal, Adam saw Casey maneuvering through the thick traffic of the outer lane. He waved to her. She saw him, whipped in front of two taxis, a bus and three cars, ignoring the horns and curses, and stopped as close as she could to him. He got in.

"Finally," she said. "I had to circle ten times. Airport security was giving me a weird eye. Did Mom have the book?"

"No," was all he could say, his voice still soft. "She had this one," he said as he opened the Solander box.

She glanced at it. "Same book, isn't it?"

"No. This is a newer facsimile. I swapped the *Appleton* for her."

"I don't understand," she said.

"I have a horrible feeling I do," Adam said. "Can we return to your home?"

She nodded and wove through the traffic as he pulled his mobile phone from his rucksack.

She noticed and asked, "What're you doing?"

"I bought a SIM card for my mobile so I could make a call."

"You could've used mine."

"Casey, I've been paying my own fare since I was sixteen. I even give Mum bed-sit money. I've no intention of changing now."

As he waited for the phone to set itself up, he noticed the monitor on Casey's dashboard showed Sean and Shawn were hot

175

on their tail. He pointed to them. "Don't they even take a toilet break?"

She glanced at them as they headed down Century Boulevard, and said, "Naw, they use *Depends*."

Something told Adam he did not want to know what she meant.

When he was finally able to dial a number on his phone, the call was picked up on the first ring.

"Patricia?" It was Vincent's voice.

"Do you think my father was targeted?" Adam asked, his voice barely in control.

He heard years wheeze out of Vincent. "Oh, God."

"Do you think he was robbed for the book he was carrying!?"

"No, Adam — "

"Then why did you do it!? Knowing what this meant. Why?"

"Please understand — it's a valuable item. If word were to get around that you were carrying it on your own — "

"You could have sent a guard with me!"

"That would have added nine-thousand pounds to the cost!"

Adam had to laugh. "Now I know my value, to you. And if I'd wound up dead, like Da, well..."

"Adam, I do not believe his death was intended. And you? You're so placid, you couldn't possibly get into trouble..."

"Couldn't — ?!" Adam sputtered, for a moment. "Vincent, I was almost run down, twice, manhandled by bodyguards, hounded by paparazzi, and damn near drowned, thanks to a bloody black panther!"

"Black Panther? The comics superhero?"

"A cat! Bloody Lando's got a bloody panther as a bloody guard cat in the middle of bloody Beverly Hills."

"What the devil is a Lando?"

"Somebody who thinks he's somebody, but no one will

tell him he's not."

Casey gave him a tight nod of agreement.

Vincent, however, was completely nonplussed. "Adam, that made absolutely no sense."

"Nothing here does!" he shouted. "And you sent me into the bloody middle of it!" He had to take a breath to calm himself. "Tell me, did — did Jeremy see the photographs you were sent?"

"Are you mad? We were trying to keep this journey quiet and he's the biggest gossip in the department."

"For all the good that did," he muttered. Then he took another breath and asked, "Can you have him look at them, now?"

"Do you know what time it is?"

"Please. I — I need to be sure. He's probably still in the photography room. He uses it, after hours."

"He does not!?"

"Well, don't be surprised if you find him there."

"That cheeky little bugger. We'll see if that continues." Then his voice grew wary. "One moment. Why should I do this?"

Adam glanced at Casey, then he looked at the facsimile book and forced himself to say, "I don't think it was a real *Alice Sixty-five*. In fact, I'm hoping it was not."

Casey shot him a startled look...and nearly rear-ended a mini-van.

"Hoping?" said Vincent.

"Yes," was all Adam could reply.

It took Vincent a moment to answer, "I'll see what I can do. Cheers."

Adam ended the call, hesitated, then looked at Casey. "You have the original photographs of the book, right?"

"On my desktop," she said, her voice wary.

"May I see them?"

"Adam, you think Grandy was taken? Sold a fake?"

He looked away, his mind swirling in turmoil, then he made himself smile and say, "That's what I'm trying to ascertain."

She nodded, whipped under the 405 and turned to head for La Cienega, the paparazzi twins still hot on their tail.

Adam shook his head at the monitor, knowing full well that if he was right they'd be getting better than the cover of *People*.

FOURTEEN

Adam told Casey what Patricia and Vincent were up to as they drove, finishing just as they screeched to a halt at her front door. He heard her grind her teeth a few times, in anger.

"So my mother's a sneak, too?" she snarled.

"*Mata Hari, she makes love for the papers.*" Adam shrugged, in answer.

"German, again?"

"Sorry," he said, stopping by the front door and —

A soft growl whispered from the bushes. Adam jolted around to find a shadow hiding under a bush.

"Oh, bloody hell," he yelped, "it's Lando's panther."

Casey scrambled around the car. "Gertrude?! How'd you get out?"

Adam had an idea...but felt no need to mention how he'd snuck into Lando's back yard.

Casey was close to panicking. "Oh my God, Adam we have to get her out of here. She's probably set off the alarms. If the cops see her, they'll shoot her."

"I don't hear sirens. Have you been called?"

Casey checked her phone, shifting away from watching Sean and Shawn, and found three texts from a security company.

"Oh, crap," she said. "I forgot I had it on mute."

"So it's not just me does that," Adam said.

She checked the texts as Gertrude slipped out of the

bushes to rub against Adam. Purring. Chittering. Anything but threatening.

A soft smile crossed Casey's lips. "She likes you."

"How'd she know to come here?"

"She stayed with me while Lando's house was getting redone. Took weeks. Okay...they sent somebody out three times but found nothing."

"So she made it without being seen? *Wer sind Sie*, Gertrude? Are you a Cheshire cat?" She bumped him with her head.

"They think something's wrong with the system, so they've shut it down to run a diagnostic. Should be done in — " Casey checked the time. "Four minutes! We gotta get her inside."

"She's probably hungry," said Adam. "Have you any salmon available? Prime rib? Wildebeest?"

"I'll order some," said Casey, distracted. "Salmon, not wildebeest; I don't think you can get that in LA." She opened the front door. "Gertrude, c'mon. Inside. Gertrude. House."

The big cat looked at Casey then sat next to Adam. He ran a careful hand over her ears and she leaned up to it.

"She likes water," he said. "Your pool?"

Casey lit up and said, "The bathtub by my office. She loved it. C'mon, water. Water. Gertrude, c'mon."

Gertrude chirped in that leopard kind of way.

Adam hesitated. "Wait. *Haus. Vater. Fleis.* Oh, bloody hell, that list on Lando's fridge. Gertrude, *do you speak Afrikaans, my little kitten?*"

She rubbed his leg, almost purring.

Casey glanced between and asked, "What?"

"She's from South Africa," he said. "I don't know much about Afrikaans, but I think it has a cadence similar to German. Well...sort of. In a way." He scratched her ears. "Gertrude, *do you want to go swimming?*" She gave a near meow. Adam nodded. "Fill the tub."

"But how'll we get her inside?"

"Lando did a bit of a sing-song to get her attention. Gertrude, *would you like me to sing to you?*"

Gertrude chirped, again.

What could he do but sing, in German, to the same melody as *What Is and Was* —

> *I now see before me...a kitten who is lovely.*
> *But do I dare inform her that she is all that I could love?*
> *No, for that would be wrong.*
> *Still she makes my heart strong.*
> *How can I not want her when she is all that I could love?*

Gertrude hopped her front paws onto Adam's shoulders to rub her head against his. He quickly said, "Casey, keep the door open."

She did as he back-walked Gertrude into the house, singing.

> *I must forget her. She's not right for me.*
> *And yet to see her, brings joy straight to me.*
> *I long to be there when she awakens*
> *From her deep slumber. My love she's taken.*

Once inside, Gertrude dropped to all fours to walk next to him, her eyes locked on his as he guided her into the bathroom, repeating what he had sung.

Then he heard an odd sound like laughing seals. "What the devil's that noise?" he asked.

Casey showed him her phone. On it, Sean and Shawn were looking over the wall and dancing on their bike, crying, "Screenplay. All the way."

"Now you know why I put it on mute," she said. She picked up a colorful bottle. "You think she'd like bubbles?"

"Doubtful," he said. "Gertrude, *vater. Vater.*"

She slipped into the tub with a happy chirp.

Casey shook her head and said, "Wow."

They started for the door, but Gertrude got out of the tub, sloshing water everywhere.

"Bloody hell," Adam said, "she doesn't want us out of her sight."

"She's lonely," Casey whispered. "Why am I surprised I'm surprised?"

Adam removed his shirt, shoes, socks, and trousers as he said, "You get the food; I'll keep her here. Gertrude, *vater*." Gertrude slid back into the tub. He stepped in with her, casting a glance at Casey as he asked, "Put the photos on my laptop? Connectors are in my rucksack."

She nodded. "Soon as I make a call." Then she left the room.

Adam watched her go then scratched the panther's breastplate and said, in German, *"Gertrude — you came to Casey's because you like her, don't you?"* She purred and touched noses with him; he chuckled. *"I don't blame you."*

****

Fifteen minutes later, Casey entered holding Adam's laptop. It was open and she was focused on the screen as she said, "Fifty cans of salmon, fresh on board."

"That was quick."

She looked at him, saying, "You should see the rush charge for delivery — " Then she stopped.

Adam and Gertrude looked at her, sloshing in the tub, both up to their chins in the water. He had set some candles burning, and Gertrude seemed to enjoy the light and shadows dancing on the walls.

He rose and asked, "Hand me a towel, please?"

She did. He dried his torso off, knelt at the side of the

tub, set the laptop on the stool and opened the images in the file. Gertrude slipped up to look at them, with him.

There were a dozen photos of the book's cover, back and spine, including close-ups of the worn areas and where the gilt had almost been rubbed off, with a few shots of the first inside pages.

Adam shook his head. It couldn't be...it couldn't be...

Then one photo showed a stain had washed away some of Macmillan at the base of the spine.

He grew very still, barely able to breathe. His hands shook. He wanted to give himself time to think, but he had to be absolutely certain. "Do — do you have Photoshop?" he asked. "Any program to manipulate an image?"

"No, I don't think so."

"Oh, God. Oh, God..."

"Adam, those are the pictures we took," Casey said. "With my phone. Mom loaded them in. I watched her. And we sent them straight to Vincent."

Of course they were. Of course.

He made himself look though the rest of the images. Found one of the frontispiece showing a slight tear in the upper left corner. His shaking increased.

Casey noticed. "What is it? What's wrong with the book? Is it a forgery? Was it changed or something?"

He could not speak. He just clicked back to the file holding the jpegs and looked at the dates of the images. They were all made three months earlier...

Except for one titled *AV,* at the very top of them all; that was only two weeks old.

"Adam, what is it? Adam?"

It was a larger file — more than six megs. He clicked on it and an image came up of two photographs, side by side. One was of Adam at his desk, working on Blake's *Albion*...the same photo as used on the university's website.

The other was of Bill, holding his cup of soup.

The chaos in Adam's head screeched to a halt as he choked out, "What the devil's this?"

"What?" Casey looked at the photo then gasped, "Oh, shit."

Adam went ice cold. If only she had said something like, *I don't know what that is* or *I don't know why that's there.* But for her to say that? To cast an embarrassed glance at him? To stammer? He sloshed over the edge of the tub to grab his trousers and pull his mobile phone from a pocket and dial Vincent's number and set it on face time.

Vincent appeared on the screen, at his desk. Jeremy was behind him, lipstick smeared over half his face and his hair more of a mess than usual. Obviously he had not been alone in his photography room.

"Adam," Vincent said, "I was about to ring."

Adam pointed the phone at the laptop's screen.

He heard Vincent cry, "Where the devil'd you get that?"

Adam had to fight to keep his voice even. "You wanted to send Bill, but you still choose me. Knowing what this meant. Why?"

"I — I explained why," said Vincent, "and I — "

"It was Grandy," Casey sighed, sitting on the edge of the tub.

Adam glared at her, almost growling, "What?"

"My grandfather said — in his will — that you, and only you, could come get the book."

He gulped in a deep breath. "Me?"

"Yeah."

"Why?"

"I don't know!" Casey cried. "But if you came to get it, the university could have it, for free. If you didn't, I...was supposed to burn it."

Quiet descended over Adam. No shivering. No choked voice. Just a simple, straightforward calmness that was terrifying, because now it was all too terribly clear.

He managed to say, "That...that doesn't explain...the photographs of me and Bill..."

"Vincent didn't want you to come," Casey said. "He wanted me to use the other guy. Said he'd do whatever I wanted, that he'd even pretend to be you, but my lawyer said it was a bad idea and too easy to find out and..."

Adam looked away from her. "Vincent...did you know she planned for me to accompany her to that premier?"

Vincent sighed. "Yes."

Of course he did.

"Don't blame him," Casey said. "He tried to talk me out of it, 'cause he knew you wouldn't come if you knew about it, and I really did think about ignoring Grandy's requirement, but I showed your picture to Orisi and he said he could fix you up, just right, and it'd make Lando crazy seeing you with me, especially if I was to act like you were better than he was and I was all happy about it while you were really just...just...well..."

"Nobody," whispered from Adam.

"Come on, mate," chirped Jeremy. "What else could you be? You're not even remotely snoggable."

Adam gave a soft, hollow laugh, barely moving as he asked, "I never kissed you, so how would you know?"

"Took a poll, and Elizabeth capped it off."

"Jeremy!" came over the phone, in Elizabeth's voice.

Jeremy laughed and mimicked her as he said, "*I'd never kiss a hobbit, not even if I were drunk, there's no other man around and it's dead-on midnight on bloody New Year's.*"

"Shut up!" She entered the phone's frame, behind Vincent, also unkempt, and said to the phone, "Adam, I was joking."

Adam felt nothing about her comments or Jeremy's claims. All he could whisper was, "Of course."

Vincent shifted the phone to himself, saying, "Adam, ignore them, because the other girls did say they'd give you a snog at Christmas and your birthday."

Jeremy's face filled the screen as he laughed and said, "But never St. Valentine's."

Elizabeth grabbed a pierced ear and yanked him away, snarling, "Jeremy!" He yelped, in pain.

Vincent flapped a hand at them, snarling, "Will you two be quiet?"

Adam let himself slip back into the tub. Gertrude nudged him; he scratched her ears, paying no real attention. He still could not look at Casey.

She watched him, shredded.

Vincent said, "Adam, tricking you into making the journey was my decision. I knew you wouldn't go, otherwise. You see, I began to think...and because there was so much interest in the book, the possibility of a theft was far too great. So I...after I agreed to the terms in the will...I conspired with Patricia to use you as a decoy to provide us with the secrecy needed to bring the book safely here. I had no doubt you would instantly know of the deception once you saw the *Appleton*, but I thought you would understand how important this is and how it would minimize the chance of a repeat of happened with your...with..."

"My father," Adam murmured. "So you *do* think he was targeted."

"...The idea was put forth, back then," Vincent said, "but no one knew of any collector who would do something so extreme. No, I can assure you, our actions were merely precautionary. I...I'm sorry you found out, in this manner; it was, in all truth and honesty, an action taken solely to protect the book and — "

"Jere," Adam cut him off with, "have you seen the photographs?"

"Yeah," he chuckled. "No alterations, and I'd notice because I'm not just snoggable; I'm fluent in image manipulation."

And there was the final slap from reality.

"She's gone, again," Adam murmured.

"Nonsense!" Vincent snapped. "Patricia has the book! We took the greatest care to make certain everyone believed the true *Alice Sixty-five* was still in Miss Blanchard's possession, and you were being sent to get it. How could it *not* be so? Why would anyone believe otherwise? You're a book person and the only logical choice to send — "

"Well...I hate to tell you this, Vincent," Adam almost chuckled, "but despite all your precautions, Lando Grissom has the book and is en route out of the country. You put me through all of this for naught." He ended the call, turned off his phone and set it by the laptop.

Casey sat on the toilet. "I don't get it," she said. "Why would Lando want it? He thinks books're just paper. He actually tore the back page out of one I had because he needed to make a note."

Adam still could not look at Casey. "I hardly think he's going to read it, even on the crapper. It has more words than pictures."

"But how could he have gotten it?" She rose and began to pace. "If the one I put in the safe deposit box is the one Mom swapped out, then how could he get hold of the...the right...one?" Her voice trailed to a whisper. "Oh. Oh, no..."

Adam was as quiet as death as he said, "I think, *Yes*. You and he were involved, so one night he substituted a cheap *Alice* for your copy then convinced you to put what you think is your book in his safe deposit box. After which, he let you catch him cheating on you. Now you have no access to the book, and he's off on a long publicity tour. Which includes Sydney, Australia."

Casey sat back on the toilet, shaken. "Lando stole it for that Australian son-of-a-bitch. He was just screwin' me around."

Gertrude growled at Casey. Adam scratched her ears to calm her. "*It's all right, little kitten; it's okay.*"

"But why not just do that when it was locked away in his box?"

"That would leave a paper trail, once the book was found

to be missing. CCTV. No deniability." He chuckled. "Bastard's smarter than I thought."

Casey looked at Adam, her expression lost, the enormity of what happened now catching up to her. Finally, she said, "Adam, I am so sorry. But Grandy *did* want you to come get the book." She knelt by the tub, her face tender and hurt. "I'll show you the will."

He shifted away. He could not handle her being near him.

She kept on with, "Vincent really did try to talk me out of it. That's why I've got that picture. I don't know why, but it was in the will and — and then Orisi saw you had possibilities, and I thought it'd just be fun and nobody'd get hurt and — and if Vincent had told me about your dad, I'd never've had you do it. I'd have told the lawyers to break the will. But, baby, you chucked it back at us. You were never a dork or nerd or fool; you were even more than I wanted you to be when you came out looking so good, because you were polite and nice and caring and better than all of us and it was a stupid, childish idea and I'm so, so sorry."

Tears streaked her face. Adam felt it would have been nice to believe they were for him and not her own sense of betrayal, but he wasn't able to do that, right then. Maybe in a few years, but not right then.

Then the intercom rang. Gertrude whispered a growl.

"Shit," said Casey. "That's the zoo."

He still could not look at her as he asked, "Zoo?"

"I'm not giving Gertrude back to Lando," she said, rising. "He doesn't deserve her."

"Don't bring them in here," he said. "She's nervous, as it is."

"You gonna sing her out to their truck?"

Adam sighed. "If they have a sedative, mix it into the salmon and bring it to me. I'll let you know when she's ready."

"Okay," she murmured, then moved closer to say,

"Adam, you need to understand — "

"The salmon!" he snapped, then whispered, "Please."

She hesitated then made herself head out.

And still he felt nothing but silence.

Gertrude nudged him.

"I know, kitten," he said with a soft huff. "I'm an idiot for even thinking the outcome would have been different. What has this hobbit to offer you but boredom and *Purina Cat Chow*? With you used to The Veldt and wildebeest, every day? I'd have given us two weeks."

Then he heard whispers of —

"Think that truck's for Casey's guy?"

"Let's stick around and find out why."

Adam looked at the door and saw Casey's reflection in one of the computer monitors as she headed out of the office.

So she had heard him. Now she knew he'd been stupid enough to think they might have wound up together. At this, he had to smile.

And wish he could crawl into a corner to hide.

— FIFTEEN —

It took most of the next hour, but Adam stayed with Gertrude as she ate...and drank water from the tub...and drifted to sleep, him stroking her head and murmuring, in German, *"It's better this way, kitten. You'll find a new world to live in, one where you can be happy. So it's better this way..."* He didn't dress until it was time to bring in the zoo's people.

Fifteen minutes later, he and Casey watched the zoo van pull away. His rucksack sat beside him, on the ground. She had pulled on a jacket against the chill air.

"They'll take good care of her, won't they?" he whispered.

Casey was resigned as she said, "The supervisor told me they know where there's a lonely boy panther."

Adam nodded. "I wish her very happy."

"So you still gonna head home?" She edged closer to him. "You could change the ticket and..."

He stepped away, shaking his head. "No."

She moved back, nodding. "Okay...but your flight's not for hours; we could have dinner..."

"I'm not hungry. I'm just going to head on to the airport."

"I'll take you."

"I think a taxi is a better idea."

"Baby, c'mon. That'll cost you a hundred bucks

and...and you know I'll follow you all the way there, anyway, so why waste the money and the time?"

"Casey...I need to prepare what I'll say to Australian customs — "

"What d'you mean?"

"Your grandfather's book is an official donation to my university and has, effectively, been stolen. Lando may even try to sneak her into the country, to avoid duty and VAT. So they'll seize her, giving us time to present documents to prove our ownership. May take six months. A year. But we'll get her back. To be safe, I'll report it to IFAR, as well — uh, the Art Loss Register and the ARG, though I doubt she'll be for sale, again."

"Why don't you think he FedEx'd it?"

"Paper trail, Casey. Also, I think his ego would require him to present it in person, to receive the acclaim."

"Okay...but you still gotta know which airport he's hittin'."

"Doesn't matter. He has to be cleared into the country."

"If he's off an airline, sure, but he snagged the studio jet. You get there faster without the TSA anal probes, and really sweet customs guys when you arrive. Guys who don't mind being, oh, not so thorough if you give 'em a kiss or selfie."

That made Adam look at her. "You can do a private jet to Australia?"

Casey pulled out her phone and opened an app, saying, "Baby, you can do private jet to space, c'mon."

That was another kick to the groin. He could barely keep standing. "Then she's gone," he whispered. "Once he hands her over, I'll never see her, again."

"Depends."

He looked at her, wary. "What do you mean?"

"Here we go...his plane hasn't left, yet."

Adam eyed her, wary. "Casey?"

She looked at him in complete innocence. "What? I know where they park it. It's set to leave in an hour."

Overwhelming joy exploded through Adam and he cried, "Oh, my God — brilliant, you are. So-so-so-so it's forty-five minutes to the airport, as you drive?"

"Not LAX; Van Nuys. Less intense paparazzi."

"Do we have time to get there and still make my flight?"

She hesitated then grinned, ear to ear, said, "Baby — don't be surprised if I get us there five minutes ago," and pulled out her keys.

He dropped his rucksack behind the passenger seat and jumped into the convertible as Casey locked up, then she slipped behind the wheel, fired up the engine, said, "Fasten your seat belt; we're gonna fly," and slammed the car into gear. As they zoomed through the gate, Adam saw Sean and Shawn scrambling onto their bike to chase them. Of course.

When they turned off Sunset to head up Benedict Canyon, Adam looked at the car's monitor to see more paparazzi had begun following them. In fact, every time he looked at the twins, the pack seemed to be a bit larger. He was amazed they were able to keep up, because Casey was breaking every traffic law you could think of while screaming up a road barely wide enough for one car, let alone anyone coming in the opposite direction. After his fourth near death experience, Adam decided if he made it, he made it. And if he didn't? Well, then he'd be tomorrow's headlines.

But little more than twenty minutes later, Casey was roaring down a wide avenue that ran parallel to a runway flanked by nothing but hangars and private aircraft, all of which were surrounded by heavy-duty wire fencing. Then Adam noticed a long sleek jet on the tarmac near a squat concrete building, its engines whispering, a door open, with portable stairs leading up to it.

"That can't be it," Adam said.

Casey glanced at it and said, "Yeah, I think so."

"But it's practically an airliner!"

Casey shrugged. "They have a couple."

She rounded a corner on two wheels and, for the twenty-fifth time, Adam crushed his teeth together to keep his heart from escaping. Then they screamed to a halt in a red zone. He glanced around as he got out. "What? No valet?"

"Oh, stop," Casey said as she bolted from the car.

Adam realized the same two security guards who helped Tito, last night, manned the doors. They recognized him the moment they saw him. He smiled at them and stuck by Casey — until she froze and he bumped into her.

"What?" he asked.

"It's Lando's handlers and the publicity crowd," she said. "They should already be on the plane."

He looked through the glass doors and windows behind the guards to see a dozen people milling about. "Is that a problem?"

"I can deal with the guards, but those leeches won't let me past. I'm banned."

"Is there another way around?"

"No. Dammit."

Then Adam recognized the woman with the streak of silver in her black hair, now dressed in casual travel couture. He nudged Casey and said, "Get us past the hounds from hell and I'll keep them busy till you're on the tarmac."

She glanced at him, almost said something, then shifted to a hard smile, nodded and aimed straight for the guards.

"Hi, guys," she said. "I need to see Lando."

"Sorry, Miss Blanchard, but — "

"He's not answering his phone and his service is ignoring me, and this is important."

"You're restricted," said a second guard.

"And you guys screwed up," she shot right back. "Gertrude got out, thanks to you, and B-Hills is not happy, so if you don't want me to get your asses fired and your company banned for life, you'll back down."

"Bullshit," said the first guard.

Casey shrugged. "Call his housekeeper. She'll give you the back-story."

Adam watched the first guard hesitate then pull out his cell phone and cast a look at the side of the building. Adam followed his gaze to see a few paparazzi waiting on the other side of the fence, taking a few lazy photos of Casey at the door. They were joined by the ones who had followed Casey but, surprisingly, not the twins. He turned back to the guards to find the first one had frozen, in shock.

Casey's smile widened. "Now I can, oh, *sneak in* and make sure this is handled nice and easy and quiet, so there's no chance of blow-back to your company. Or I can leave. Choice is yours, baby."

The first guard looked at the second one. "I think those paparazzi are plannin' to give us trouble."

The second guard nodded. "Yeah. Yeah. You're right."

"We should go talk to 'em. Just for a second."

"Yeah. Yeah. You're right."

And they headed over.

Casey turned to Adam. "Your cue, baby."

"Wait just a moment," Adam said. Then he took a deep breath, said, "It's for the *Alice*," and entered the building.

The lobby had chairs from a 1960s airport lounge with plain tables between them. Travel posters hung from the walls, lush corn plants framed a table piled high with all manner of cut fruit and cheeses, and a huge water jug of champagne galumphed in a nearby corner. Soft voices and gentle Muzak whispered about.

The silver-streak woman was filling a fluted glass via the jug's spigot, so Adam grabbed some brochures from a display and went straight to her, leafing through them as he said, "Hello. Remember me?"

She looked him over. "Are you somebody?"

"I was, yesterday, Sweets, and I'll be somebody else, tomorrow, but not today. Maybe you'd like to change that."

"Why?"

"'Cause I just came up the rabbit hole, snogging away."

She brightened and offered him her hand. "Imelda Carlito Canasius Verdugo Marquez, of Pipson, Pike, Perriman and Pugg."

He shoved the brochures in his pocket, took her hand and gave it a Euro kiss. "Adam Verane, of Meryton."

"That's a British agency, isn't it?"

He put a finger to his lips. "I'm not supposed to tell."

She called around, "Brewer, Wendell, Ronson, Kikuchio — come meet Adam Verane, the next hot thing! He's interested in us, and I brought him on!"

A tall man wearing extremely stylish casual wear jumped up and nodded. "I heard them at the premier! You got the crowd really going!"

"A near riot," another similar man said.

The full crowd turned their focus to Adam as he laughed and led their eyes away from the entrance, saying, "Unbelievable, isn't it?"

"Dude, were you in the movie?" asked a fifty-year-old man who dressed like he was thirty-five and acted like he was twenty.

"I? Work with the likes of Lando Grissom? Please. I tore myself away from my main project to offer support on behalf of Casey Blanchard, the fairest of them all."

By this point, the entire group was focused on Adam. Casey barely kept from laughing as she quietly slipped behind them for the door to the tarmac.

Adam surreptitiously watched her as he said, "Oh, please don't misunderstand — there is no animosity between Lando and myself over our respective careers. Mine is that of...Shakespeare, Moliere, Marlowe, Aristophanes, while he's good with action."

"What's your latest project?" asked Imelda.

"The...glorious world of *Kristin Lavransdatter*," Adam said as he saw Casey grimace and hide behind some plants by the door to the tarmac. She mouthed the word *Tito* to him.

Through the crowd, he could just see out the door...and there was Tito heading for the building.

He continued with, "It's about a woman in the Middle Ages who fights for herself against the limits of her time, and has one true love to maintain her in her struggles. Me."

He began to work around the crowd, keeping them between him and the door as they said things like —

"Wow, that kind of shit's hot, right now."

"I'll bet there be dragons."

"Has it got lots of Vikings and swords and battles and stuff?"

"Absolutely," Adam murmured to each comment.

He saw the door open and Tito enter, saying, "Boardin' in fifteen minutes." Then he hit the food and champagne bar.

Adam saw Casey slip out, unnoticed, so he curled around the crowd to aim for the door as he continued in a whisper, "And it's written by a Nobel Prize winner."

"Is that good?" asked Imelda, also whispering.

Adam grinned. "Somewhat. But enough about my plans. I've come only to see Lando off on his journey, and since you're about to leave I must run. It was a pleasure to meet you all."

"No, we're all banned from the plane," said Imelda. "Nobody can get on board, yet."

"But I *am* nobody, today, remember?" Adam said as he danced out the doors, then he raced to catch up to Casey to say, "Better hurry."

She reached the base of the steps...and hesitated. "Still working on a plan," she muttered.

"What if the book's fake?" asked Adam.

Casey looked at him and grinned. "Okay, baby. Follow my lead. Momma's gonna play."

They zipped up the steps, the vague sound of cameras firing in their ears, and entered the jet —

To be stopped by a flight attendant whose poise and

attitude were so sharp, Adam felt she could cut them with it.

"Excuse me, but — " she began.

Casey stopped her with a pat on the cheek, saying, "It's okay, baby, he and I used to fuck."

She pushed on into a cabin that was spacious leather and polished luxury. The lights were soft. Gentle Zen music played. Candles burned in deep dishes. Incense drifted. But what made it perfect? Orisi and his crew surrounded a massage table in the center of it all, manicuring the nails, caressing lotion into the skin, and peeling wax off the ass of a man lying face down on it, heated stones on his back. He was, of course —

"Lando!" Casey chirped, full of sweetness and light. "Scored the palace for your junket. Trés cool."

Lando jolted around, sending the stones flying. He pulled a cooling pack off his eyes as he bolted to his feet. A violent red exfoliate covered his face, in just the right shade to compliment the wax.

"Casey," he roared back. "Why're you here?"

"She forced her way in, sir," said the flight attendant.

"Just came to wish you off, baby," Casey said. "Bon voyage and all that. Oh, and I need to get my book."

Adam glanced into the cockpit to see both pilots at the controls, doing their checks, then quietly looked around the cabin, hoping he'd notice a bundle that was the right size for an *Alice Sixty-five*.

"It'll have to wait," said Lando as he wrapped a towel around himself and the remaining wax on his rear. He glanced out a window to find more paparazzi had gathered on the other side of the fence, like hungry pigeons. "Aw, shit, the papa-bastards followed you."

"Of course," Casey laughed. "Who do you think I am?"

Veronica popped her head around a partition halfway down the cabin, saying, "You won't like *my* answer to that."

Casey dismissed Veronica with a flip of her hand. "You can keep your opinion to yourself."

"Here, careful, Sweets, you'll smudge it!" And who should also pop her head around the partition but —

"Julie?!" Adam cried. "Aren't you on the *Hollywood Death Tour?*"

"Missing it, thanks to you," she shot back at him, then held up one of Veronica's hands. "But told you — clients." Then she yanked Veronica back, her voice charming as she said, "Let it dry, first, *then* the cat-fight. If I have to start over, it won't look half as good and will cost twice as much."

Lando checked a window on the other side of the jet and saw, "Those two little shits."

Adam glanced out to find Sean and Shawn hovering next to a hanger, both with cameras ready and waiting.

Lando spun around, grabbed a pair of Orisi-briefs and started to pull them on. "Casey, get out. Orisi, get this crap off. We're leavin'. We'll set down in Long Beach to let you out."

Orisi almost exploded with indignation. "Crap? Orisi's crap ain't crap, and that crap ain't done, yet. And you don't wear briefs over this." He ripped off the last of the butt-wax. Lando howled in pain.

Julie shook her head. "Don't mess with Orisi, Sweets."

"Got that bloody right," Adam muttered, back to scouring the cabin for anything that might be the size of the *Alice*.

Veronica yanked herself away from Julie and stormed past several overstuffed chairs to go nose to nose with Casey, holding her hands up to keep the henna from being smudged as she snarled, "Get outta here; this ain't your turf, no more."

Casey laughed at her. "*Turf?* Seriously? What century do you live in? Lando, are you sure she's not really ninety with an excellent plastic surgeon?"

"Not with skin like that, Sweets," called Julie, putting her things away.

Lando shoved past Adam to the cockpit. "Get this puppy ready," he said. "We're outta here, now, now, now."

"Get your people loaded," the man said.

"Lando," said Casey, "I know what's going on here, and you can have the book."

Lando wasn't paying her any attention when he said, "I don't know what you're talkin' about."

"My copy of *Alice in Wonderland*. You can have it. Turns out Grandy got took when he bought it, so all I want is his last note to me."

That made Lando look at her.

So did Veronica, saying, "What do you mean?"

"You said it's worth a couple million bucks," Lando said.

That made Julie and Orisi look at them, along with Orisi's crew. In unison, of course.

"Nope, Adam saw the pictures," said Casey, casting him a smile.

"Yes," Adam said.

Veronica cast him a vicious glare and snarled, "Butt out, Andrew."

"Oh, for god's sake," Adam howled, "my name is Adam Alexander Aloysius Verlain. Not a bloody Andrew anywhere in it!"

"Aloysius?" said Orisi. "Like on *Sesame Street*?"

"No, after Lady Penelope's chauffeur on *Thunderbirds*." Now everyone gave him a confused look. He rolled his eyes. "It was a marionette program on the telly, back in the Sixties. As for the book, I showed Casey's images to Jeremy, our resident Photoshop expert, and he laughed at how obvious a forgery it was."

"Bullshit," said Veronica.

"No, really," said Adam, fascinated that she was the one arguing with him. "The title page was replaced — very expertly, I might add — but what gives it away is the spine. *Appleton* was erased and Macmillan was laid over. You can see shadows of the former's name under bits of the latter."

"No, I checked that," said Veronica.

"You?!" Casey snapped.

"Of course! You think this idiot knows anything about antiquarian books?" She cast a derisive thumb at Lando.

He blinked and cried, "Ronnie!"

Adam grinned. "Then you should have checked more carefully. Jeremy had to increase the image's size in order to tell the differences in the tone of the cloth's color, but — "

"No, no, no," said Veronica. "It fits all the parameters of a true first impression *Alice*."

"Did you check to make certain the Quires were uniform?" Adam asked.

"Nobody does that!"

"Yes, we do, especially if a leaf might have been added."

Veronica hesitated.

Lando glanced between her and Adam. "Ronnie, what the fuck? You said it was real. That's why Christopher Meillon's backin' my movie!"

"*That's* what all this is about?" Casey snarled.

"Casey, Casey, Casey!" Lando's tone was conciliatory, now. "I — look, I'm sorry but he's willin' to guarantee fundin' for *Ilithium Four Point Two* with this really great director — "

"Don't think so," Casey sneered, "once he sees he's got a forgery."

He dove into a gym bag, muttering, "No, no, if this ain't right — "

"Lando, don't!" Veronica screamed.

He pulled out a bundle wrapped in a towel that was just the right size.

Adam jolted, unable to believe how easy it had been to get him to reveal he had the book then, on impulse, shoved between Veronica and Casey to yank it away from Lando and bolt back to the door.

Veronica grabbed at Adam, but Casey pushed her back as Julie screamed, "NO CAT FIGHT, YET!"

The flight attendant was blocking Adam's way, like a

defensive tackle, so he spun into a lavatory, slammed the door closed and locked it before anyone could think about what he was doing. Then he dropped onto the toilet to brace his feet against the door. Lando pounded on it and pushed and howled, "I'm gonna beat your fuckin' head in," as Veronica cried, "Open up or I'm calling the guards," and Casey screamed, "Leave him alone, you two bastards!"

Adam hated to leave Casey to deal with them, but he needed to be sure. Had to be sure. Had to see it, for himself. So he pressed against the door with every bit of strength he had and damn the pain in his butt, then he unwrapped the towel, even as Casey was screaming, "He's got all rights to that book and you, Lando — you got used by this slut and you're still helping her?!"

"Casey, I have to!" Lando cried. "You gotta help me with this!"

Adam finally revealed a plain hardcover book bound in worn red cloth with gilt inlay, just like the *Appleton* and the facsimile.

Casey was snarling, "After you got me dumped from the movie?! Are you loco?"

"The director got you dumped," Lando cried. "Said you'd be too much trouble, but I'll make him put you back in!"

"I don't want back in!" Her voice was filled with anger and pain and uncertainty. "I'm glad I know you're a shit."

Veronica screamed, "You don't talk to Lando like that!"

Adam forced himself to stay focused on the book. He had to be positive. He looked at the spine.

It had Macmillan at the base.

And the tea stain.

His breath grew quick and sharp.

"I won't, anymore!" Casey was snarling. "I don't want a thing to do with him or you, you plastic bitch."

He made himself open the book to the title page. A sheet of aged onion-skin paper sat between it and the frontispiece — an elaborate sketch of the Queen of Hearts holding court — and at the bottom of the title page was 1865.

It was not tipped in or affixed. It was original.

Adam could barely move.

Casey was snarling, "You fucked me over for a fucking movie, Lando, and now she fucked you over for this book, and that's karma enough for me, baby!"

Then he saw it — in the upper left corner of the frontispiece — a small tear.

The screaming voices vanished into a cold, crisp fog of nothing. He finally had no choice but to accept that this was the same book his father had shown him.

But how could it be? How? It couldn't be. It wasn't possible...

Unless...

He noticed a note wedged in the center. He took it out to read —

SOMETIMES PLANS GO AWRY AND INTENTIONS ARE NOT GOOD ENOUGH. I HOPE THIS WILL HELP, IN SOME SMALL WAY.

Adam stopped breathing.

It *was* the same book.

Oh, dear God, it really was.

Casey's grandfather must have tried to win the book at that auction, but he was outbid by Da's client, so he'd arranged to have it stolen. Only things had gone horribly wrong and Da had died. Not by design, it looked like, but still...Casey's grandfather had caused his death.

And what was worse — he'd let Da's shop be sold and done nothing to help his family after causing them so much grief.

What could Adam do about that?

What could he say about that?

He couldn't tell Casey; he did know that much. Not after what she had been through with Lando's lies and her father's corruption and her grandfather dying. He couldn't add to that. Not now.

But this new truth overwhelmed him. Tore into him. He had to slam his head back against the wall to remind himself to keep breathing, then he gulped in air to keep any sense of control. His eyes filled with tears. He took a tissue from a slot by the sink...

And the whole box popped out.

Perfect. Not what he needed, not at that moment.

The door started to give way, even with his feet propped hard against it. That caught his focus. He snarled a smile and pushed against it even harder, ignoring the howling voices and thanking rugby for giving him legs powerful enough to hold the jackals at bay.

He pulled the green box from his inside jacket pocket and removed the facsimile of the book. He gently laid the *Alice Sixty-five* into it and gazed upon her, whispering, "I can't believe he was going to carry you without a protective case."

Then he heard more voices. "Okay, folks, let's calm down, here." It sounded like Veronica actually had called the guards.

"Not till I get my book!" Casey's voice was raw. Near the edge. It was time to end this.

Adam made a couple of last-minute adjustments then stood up and rubbed his sore rear. No one was pushing at the door, so he unlocked it...but it was off its runner and took some effort to open. Once it was, he saw the two guards standing by the exit, to his right, with Tito, the flight attendant, and what seemed like the entire group of people from the terminal behind them. To his left, Casey, Lando and Veronica still faced off, Julie, Orisi and his crew behind them, packing up.

"Get this story, baby," Casey snarled, "I'm calling the cops and having this plane grounded and — "

"Casey!" Adam called, cutting her off. Then he continued in a gentle tone. "Jeremy was right; the book's a fake. But I have your note." He held it up. "So let's go."

Veronica turned to him, saying, "No. No."

He nodded. "Yes. You can have it back." He tossed a towel-wrapped bundle onto a chair.

"You mean I went through this shit for nothin'?" Lando whined.

Casey beamed. "Oh, Adam," she said as she jaunted over to him. "My ex-boy-fwiend's unhappies 'cause he gots screwed by hisself. Got. To. Love. It."

Adam smiled and turned to the exit. The crowd of people blocked their way so he calmly said, "Stand aside or we *will* call the police, and no trip for you."

They hesitated...then opened a passageway so Adam and Casey could pass.

"Hold it!" Veronica cried. She grabbed the bundle and whipped it open. Then she held up the facsimile copy and snarled, "This isn't the same book! What d'you think you're pullin', Andrew?!"

"Look at his jacket!" Lando gasped.

Everybody looked, including both pilots in the cockpit.

Part of the green box was peeking out of Adam's side pocket.

BAM! Lando leapt over to grab Adam in a wrestler-like hold, and they slammed into Tito — who slammed into the guards — one of whom then slammed into the cockpit — and slammed the two pilots against the massive array of monitors and consoles and switches, smashing several of them and making the jet shudder. Alarms sounded.

The lobby group shrieked and scrambled out and down the steps as Orisi's minions squeaked and backed away from the fight. Veronica tried to help Lando, but Casey pulled her back while the flight attendant screamed and clawed at Adam. He howled and twisted around to shove against Lando, making him crash into the attendant. She fell on her butt, still screaming.

Then Adam realized the plane's engines had roared to life.

Both pilots were lying against the controls, unconscious!

And the second bodyguard was roaring back at him!

Adam's time in the rugby scrums took over, so he rolled aside to kick Lando back against a wall. Tito's arms whipped around Adam's neck and twisted it and yanked him up, and the box slipped from Adam's grasp to bounce off a chair and careen against a table leg and skitter down the passageway, out of reach.

Tito and the guard tried to shove Adam out the door, but he gripped its frame and kicked at them. From the corner of his eye, he saw —

Casey grab the box and Veronica grab Casey. They tumbled into Orisi's minions as the man howled, "Jumpin' jeebus, you don't want Orisi in this fight."

Julie just sighed and shook her head at Veronica. "You've ruined my best work, Sweets."

Adam cried, "Casey, no!" then struggled more with Tito as Lando jumped in to help him and the second guard piled onto the near-naked movie star. Lando pushed at Adam's face and Tito punched at his fingers so they could throw him down the steps. Adam howled and let go to swoop under them and roll across the floor, tripping the first guard to send him head over heels out the door. The flight attendant almost tumbled out, too. The second guard piled onto Adam, but he was able to crawl out from under the man to see —

Casey and Veronica struggling over the box. Then Lando grabbed Adam's leg to pull him back as Veronica swung around and flipped Casey over the pile of men. She tumbled into the cockpit.

Adam fought to free himself from the tangled mass as Veronica tripped over one of Orisi's minions and lost her grip on the box. It bounced farther back in the cabin.

Lando and Tito tried to pull Adam back to the door, but he grabbed the lavatory's doorframe and kicked at them. Then he felt a bump and the jet began to roll. He heard brakes groaning and could smell burning fluid, and he saw the flight attendant was screaming and the first guard was scrambling back up the steps.

He cast a quick glance at the cockpit to see the pilot was still unconscious, the copilot was groggy, and Casey was just getting to her feet...

And the jet was headed for the terminal!

Adam couldn't free himself from the pile of men so he cried, "Casey, the plane!"

She looked around, saw the building growing closer and closer, and twisted to move the pilot aside and make the jet turn before it could connect with the building.

The copilot finally shook off his grogginess and snarled at her, "Get out! Out!" She did. Then the copilot began hitting buttons and panels, to no effect, and tried to pull back the throttle...but it was jammed forward.

Adam twisted around, again, and tumbled away from Lando to land face down. He looked up and saw —

Veronica grab the box, again. She climbed over the seats to an emergency exit.

Casey flew past Adam, jumping after her and screaming, "That's my book, bitch!"

"Don't know what you're talking about!" Veronica howled back as she pulled at the door's handle.

Adam cried, "Casey, let her go!"

The emergency door hissed open and Casey slammed into Veronica and both of them nearly tumbled out through it.

Adam scrambled to his feet and leapt over the chairs to yank Casey and Veronica back in, then Lando and Tito crashed against him and they all collided with Veronica, making her lose the box. Adam grabbed it and flipped it out the emergency exit as Lando punched him, so he almost followed it but managed to hang on...and see it bounce off the wing...and get caught by the air current and be drawn into the jet's turbine and —

BOOM! The engine exploded.

Bits of shrapnel clipped Adam and he lost his grip and tumbled outside to roll off the wing and crash to the ground.

His world shattered. Every pain he'd felt in the last two

days roared back with a fury. He could barely breathe, and his head threatened to come off his neck and roll away. His world was filled with flashing stars and glittery bits of paper whispering around him as Casey screamed, "You stupid bitch!" and the engine spewed fire and smoke and groaned and alarms sounded until —

The engines died and the jet shuddered to a halt.

Adam managed to roll over and look around. He caught sight of the paparazzi twins on the tarmac, their cameras firing as whispery bits of paper drifted down to settle over him, and he fought the urge to laugh because for some reason all he could think was, "They got the cover of *People*."

Then his world went white.

— SIXTEEN —

Adam heard Casey screaming from a thousand miles away, "Adam! Are you all right? Adam?!" and forced his eyes open to see her running around the jet.

He put up a weak hand and murmured, "Please don't shout."

She dropped to beside him then Orisi appeared beside her, to check his head. "Jumpin' jeebus, son, you just tripled the size of that knot on your noggin. Good thing we didn't shave it." Adam started to get up but Orisi shoved him back, snarling, "Don't! EMS is on the way."

Distant sirens were screaming closer, so Adam decided it was better that he wait for them and not risk having Orisi beat him to a bloody pulp for ignoring his instructions.

The next few hours were spent having the medics check Adam's head and re-bandage his old wounds as he explained what happened to the police. Lando ranted with anger and demanded Adam be arrested for assault, while Veronica expressed horror at his *deliberate destruction* of an irreplaceable book. Casey just stood to one side gazing at nothing.

The police were getting so many conflicting stories from the lobby crowd and guards and Orisi's minions, they were close to arresting everybody so they could clear things up at the police station, but Adam finally got Lando alone and said, "You need to end this, now."

"No, you little shit, you're going to jail and — "

"Then I will make certain the full truth of this comes out, and you will be destroyed."

"What the fuck're you — ?"

"I can prove you stole the book," Adam growled, "and dumped Casey to hide the fact. The tabloids will love making money off the revelation that Hollywood's perfect *hero* is anything but."

Lando sneered and motioned to Veronica, who was watching them, wary. "I got nothin' to worry about. She'll back me up by sayin' I — "

Adam put on an innocent expression. "Not if she's the one who exchanged the *Alice Sixty-five* for a fake. I mean, it was she who came to you with the idea, to gain backing for *I-Four-Point-Two*, wasn't it? Just swap a couple of books, which you had no idea was wrong. A nice copy for a poor one? It was like...like *new lamps for old.* Made perfect sense."

"She won't go along with that..."

"If she doesn't, then Christopher Meillon would be exposed as her backer and therefore the one truly to blame, and he will *not* allow it. The rich hate to take responsibility for their actions; too many legal entanglements. The best way for this to end is, you were also used by Veronica, and in the argument over what happened...Casey's book was destroyed, *by accident.* Stupidity is always a good defense."

Lando hesitated, looked at him for a long moment, then sighed and nodded. "You're right, it was her idea. But I'll handle it my own way."

So it was officially decided no charges would be pressed by either side, and Lando agreed to pay for the jet's repairs so the studio would lend him the other jet for his junket.

And he said not one word to Veronica, throughout.

Adam was released and allowed to head for his flight.

Which was set to leave in just under an hour.

He called ahead to let them know he was running

late...then the rest of the ride was in complete silence. Casey did not look at him, once, and he felt it best to say nothing so she could focus on slamming through LA's traffic and ignoring roadway etiquette.

It wasn't until she had literally screeched to a halt in front of the International Terminal's departures doors that she was able to sit back, for a moment, and take a breath...and finally manage to say, "I — I keep thinking I ought to ask you if you've got everything, but I — I dunno what you had." Her voice was soft. Quivering. Traffic growled around them.

He held up his rucksack and pulled at the door's handle.

"Adam!" He stopped and looked at her. She turned to look straight into his eyes and continued with, "Don't you — don't you think you ought to stay? Get yourself checked over? More carefully?"

He hesitated. "I will. In London."

"But..."

"Casey, if I don't leave now, I never will."

"I could live with that." Her voice was a near whisper. "I've got five bedrooms in my crib. You could — "

"What would I do? Be another man who lived off you? Used you?"

"You wouldn't," she said. "You pay your own fare."

"Thank you, for that, but — "

She cut him off with, "But you — you're right. You're right. I — I'm little Miss Beverly Hills and you — you live with your Mom and I've got my Mom and the Moms'll probably hate each other and I'd give it six weeks and — "

She looked at her lap, in tears.

He desperately wanted to make things right for her but he knew it wasn't possible; he had nothing to offer her...even as there was no way he could leave her like this...so he reached across to her...put a tender finger to her cheek...and let it drift around under her chin...and guide her sad, lovely face back to look at him...

210

And he leaned in to kiss her.

Gentle. Easy. Lips barely touching lips. The light taste of salt from her tears. The soft warmth of her breath. It felt so right...so nice...he didn't want it to end...but it had to...it had to...it had to...

He made himself pull back, just a little, and look deep into her eyes and whisper in a voice meant only for her, "You know, you drive me to madness, and I've no idea what to think, from one moment to the next, but the mere fact that I have met you has enriched my life beyond measure. .and filled my heart to bursting. And I know it shall always stay so."

She softened, and her expression shifted from hurt and confused to simple understanding. She leaned back in the seat and wiped her eyes, and tried to smile at him...and he sort-of smiled back.

One of his eyebrows had gone wild so she caressed it into place and he leaned into it, like a kitten. Then she said in a voice low and tender, "You'll miss your flight."

He hesitated then opened the door and slipped out of the car, not letting go of her till he had to. She did not move and —

Horns sounded and drivers cursed and people yammered and a police whistle blew, bringing Adam back to the moment. He looked to his right to see —

Sean and Shawn sitting diagonal to her car, blocking traffic and recording their farewell. Well, Shawn was; Sean was weeping.

Adam had to go. Had to leave her alone in that horrible, open city, and he hated himself for doing it, but the final boarding call was blasting over the intercom and he had to run...had to hijack a ride to the gate...and made the flight moments before the doors closed. Being First Class, they held off just long enough.

He remembered little of what he did or thought while sitting in his luxurious cubicle. Just murmured over and over, "It was for the *Alice*. It was for the *Alice*. It was for the *Alice*." A flight attendant brought him a tray of lovely cheeses and fruit and crackers, and a fluted glass of champagne. He knew he smiled his thanks but barely touched them. His world had broken apart, and he feared if he let himself have one coherent thought, he would break, as well.

And at that moment, he would happily have welcomed it.

****

He took a taxi from the airport straight to Merryton, and as he approached the main entrance, he saw a printout of Patricia's photo of him taped to the chapel's door with *ADAM, THE LAD* scrawled over it. He shook his head, smiling, pulled it off, and continued inside.

Then he saw another copy on a cubicle wall — his image worked into a downpour of confetti. Printed under it was, *FOR A GOOD TIME: SHRED ADAM.* Beside it were the day's news stories and photos of him in the door of the jet, where it looked like he had tossed the book out, and another showing the second after the engine had exploded. The various headlines read variations on — RENT BOY DESTROYS TWO MILLION POUND BOOK. What could he do but add a shrug to his smile?

Then Hakim bolted up, snarling, "Way to go, you bloody bugger. Vincent wants you, straightaway." He had his overcoat on, ready to leave.

Adam nodded and said, "Thank you, Hakim. Nice to know you're on top of things, for once."

Hakim just huffed.

As he approached Elizabeth's cubicle, he saw Jeremy in it with her. He had his rucksack on his back while she was in her heels and her hair was loose. They were streaming a video on her monitor — of everyone in the jet as the book exploded into confetti. She saw Adam and stopped it just as he hit the wing, then closed it, embarrassed.

Jeremy, however, hopped right up.

"Musical chairs, it is," he said. "I'm gettin' me own cubicle, thanks to you. Turn my whole room over to photography."

Adam chuckled and said, "Glad I could help, Jere. Though you do understand, you'll need a wash every day, now."

Jeremy jolted and blinked and said, "Oi. Says who?"

Adam was about to say, *Says anyone who has to work next to you,* but he saw a picture taped to his monitor.

Of his face pasted onto a donkey.

With Casey kissing it.

At the wrong end.

He growled and grabbed it, shoved it in Jeremy's face, and slammed him back against a slim window, his voice vicious and low. "You ever do anything like this to her, again, I'll hit you so bloody hard you'll wind up back inside your Mum, you will!"

Adam's furious scowl scared Jeremy into saying, "Just a joke, mate. Jeez..."

"Adam?" Vincent appeared at his side.

Patricia came up behind him, the green cloth clamshell case in hand. "Ah, here's the little sneak," she said, trying to be jokey.

Adam just glared at her. She stopped.

Vincent guided him away from Jeremy, saying, "Come straight from the airport, have you? Touch of jet-lag?"

Adam gave himself a shake as he said, "I'm fine," but returned his glare to Jeremy. Who edged closer to Elizabeth. Who looked at Adam as if wondering who he was.

"I — I suppose you've heard," Vincent continued. "Word's come down. From on high. Sooner you pack up, the better."

Adam nodded. Of course. The mantra of the Governors — Act first; think later, especially since Sir Robert had come aboard.

He set his rucksack on his desk and said, "You'll want

this, then."

Everyone watched Adam, wary, as he pulled out a tissue box that held his own pair of white briefs wrapped around a pair of Orisi's sequined briefs, which were wrapped around —

The *Alice '65*.

"In glittery-bitty Y-fronts!?" Jeremy all but screamed.

Adam sighed, giving him his weariest look. "Jeremy, this is designer underwear made from Egyptian cotton, with a thread count of twelve-hundred and barely worn, but once. Then very well-laundered; believe me, I did it."

"But we saw the book shredded on YouTube," said Elizabeth.

"Facebook," said Bill.

"BBC World News," said Hakim.

Adam looked at them as if to say, *Do you idiots really not understand?* "Books are my life," he finally croaked out. "I'd sooner cut off my hand than let one be harmed. My jacket has an inside pocket, so I hid her there. Then substituted a mass of facial tissues, some brochures, and a generic Solander box whilst dealing with people too busy fighting to verify what was in it."

"But how the devil did you get this in the country?" Hakim snapped. "Customs will — "

"The book's already been imported. Hasn't it, Vincent?" He looked straight at the man.

Vincent nodded, saying, "My dear boy, of course I'll speak with Sir Robert — "

"No," Adam said. "No, don't." He kept his eyes on Vincent and continued, "But before I go, I want to do the provenance on this beauty. I — I have a deeper understanding of her history. Her meaning."

Elizabeth jolted and said, "Vincent, I'm much better versed in — "

Adam all but snarled, "*Quid est quod Schedel*, Elizabeth?"

She glared at him. She may not speak Latin, but she

knew what he was asking.

As did Vincent, who nodded. "An Eighteenth Century facsimile," he said, "last sold in nineteen-fifty-eight. Do the provenance, Adam. Should take you...a fortnight?"

"I'll be done, tomorrow."

Vincent got his headmaster voice going as he said, "Yes, two weeks. No need to rush. Start Monday. Do your usual top-drawer job. Talk with me when you're done. We may have a new position for you."

Adam did not move. "Thank you ..but no. No." He could not work here, anymore, not after Vincent used him. Known what he was sending him in to. While his actions were understandable on an intellectual level, in his heart...he could no longer trust the man.

The others glanced between the two, confused, but Vincent knew what Adam meant and sagged, a little. Then he took in a deep breath and nodded. "Day's done, all. Start again, tomorrow. Good night."

Everyone wandered away. Elizabeth cast Adam an even more confused glance as she pulled on her coat.

Vincent just returned to his office, silent and alone.

Patricia stayed by Adam's cubicle, watching him, then she said, "You ain't the same boy I picked up at the airport, the other day." He would not look at her. She nodded. "How's Casey?"

He hesitated, then sighed, "She understood I had to return."

"And you? How're you?"

He shrugged. "We'll have to see."

A tender smile crossed Patricia's face. "No, I already got a pretty good idea." She turned and headed for the main entrance, leaving behind the clamshell case. En route, she wrapped a hand around Jeremy's arm and said, "Come along, honey; I'll buy you a drink. We've done enough, for today." Then she led him away.

And the room was finally silent.

Adam sighed and looked up at the dark beams of wood bracing the ceiling...and the aged candelabrum...and felt the tender aura of safety they brought...and slowly sank to his knees, barely able to breathe. The green clamshell case sat on his desk, next to the *Alice Sixty-five*. He opened it to reveal the *Appleton*, then pulled the facsimile of the book from his rucksack and set it next to them. The three looked almost identical.

He removed the *Appleton* from the clamshell case and tenderly, lovingly placed the true *Alice Sixty-five* in it. Then he gently folded the champagne colored cloth around her, one flap over the other in near ceremonious movements, and closed the case. Soft. Easy. Tender. He set his hands on top of it. The mandalas, now side by side, became the head of a powerful wolf, gazing up at him and standing guard, as if Julie had known, somehow, this would be the final stage of his journey. The other two books flanked the case, adding backup protection.

Tears trailed from Adam's eyes. His throat grew full. His heart was almost silent, in respect. He felt light and alive and complete for the first time in years...because now he was home.

Finally.

Finally.

Finally, Da was home.

SEVENTEEN

Two of the records Adam needed to complete the provenance on the *Alice Sixty-five* had been lent out for return on Monday, so Merryton set him up a room on campus to keep him sequestered from reporters till a formal statement could be worked up. They were most unhappy he'd gone home, Thursday night, but he assured them he'd ignored all phone calls from reporters, so they had to let it pass. Of course, he didn't bother to mention he had sent Casey a text to let her know the *Alice* was not destroyed but was safe and in good hands. She did not respond. He was not surprised; he hoped she would come to understand the reason he'd kept the truth from her was so he could transport the book in the safety of complete secrecy.

He spent the full weekend archiving books from The Dark Chamber while decorating his cubicle with newspaper stories about the destruction, including photos of him and Casey getting in the limo...and at the premier as Casey took his photo with Julie and Manny...and him nearly being hit by a car...and him climbing the wall...and him in the pool with Gertrude watching (how Sean got that shot Adam did not want to know)...and him storming away from Lando's with Casey following...and Gertrude hugging him...and him and Casey entering the jet...and the confetti from the jet's engine drifting over him...and the most irritating — him kissing Casey goodbye at the airport. It was all quite ludicrous, but served to keep him focused on the moment.

Then just before noon on Monday, the two volumes appeared and he finalized the book's history.

The *Alice Sixty-five* had been purchased by a Lieutenant Colonel for his daughter to read whilst en route to their new post in Natal, South Africa. She remained in the family's possession until 1931, when she was sold at an estate auction for the princely sum of forty-eight pounds sterling to a book dealer on Charing Cross. Then she was fitted with her clamshell case and sold to a collector of Lewis Carroll's works in Belfast. During a bombing raid in World War 2, his house was hit, the library damaged, and the *Alice* was thought lost. But apparently she had been protected by the new case, so she wound up in the hands of a schoolgirl whose father was an air warden. In 1964, she sold all of her books to a second-hand dealer in Dublin who, when he finally got around to cataloguing her in 1969, realized her worth and sold her to a British antiquarian dealer, who had a wealthy client who was a Senator in Canada's parliament who was looking for a copy.

She stayed with the Canadian Senator until 1998, when he passed away; his entire library was sold to the same British dealer who'd sold him the *Alice*. She remained in a carton in his shop, forgotten for years till a new cataloguer was hired and, while updating the files, realized what they had.

When offered for auction at one of the more prestigious London houses, the price she expected to bring in was between two-hundred and fifty and three-hundred thousand pounds. Adam's father had won her for his client...then she had vanished.

It was up to Adam to close the gap. Patricia told him Casey's grandfather played golf at St. Andrew's, and that he spoke of building a library of English Literature to be donated after his death. He would often purchase fine copies of books from dealers in the UK and ship them to LA, in groups. So Adam *speculated* the copy stolen from his father hadn't been thrown away by the thieves but was sold to an unsuspecting book shop in Edinburgh for a few pounds, and *suggested* the man bought what he thought was a facsimile of an *Alice Sixty-five* from that dealer for an unknown sum, then had simply put her in his library. It was only later that he realized the treasure he'd *happened to buy* and kept her for his granddaughter as insurance. A bit more research brought Adam to a recent business retreat where Sir Robert had crossed the man's path, so he used that as the reason Blanchard directed the book be donated to Merryton's collection.

He put this into the provenance with as little emotion as possible. He knew it would cause something of a stir and questions could still be raised about how Blanchard had really got the book — but questions were one thing; proof was another...and by not mentioning that note, Adam minimized the issue.

The one real question now was his mother; she had an excellent case for demanding the book be given to her. Da's insurance and the liquidation of his shop had actually paid for her, and he was sure Connor, once he found out, would push for major financial restitution, possibly even to the point of insisting she be auctioned off to fetch the highest price possible. Which would give Christopher Meillon yet another shot at owning her. Adam could not let that happen.

What solidified his determination was the call he received from Connor the night he got home, while he was breaking eggs for a quick supper before bed. As he told Merryton, he'd been getting numerous calls from reporters wanting a quote for their stories, so the only reason he accepted this one was because he recognized the number. Connor's face came up and without even a *Hello*, he exploded into. "I hope you're pleased with yourself, you bloody little hobbit. You've made me a laughing stock."

"How so?" was all Adam replied, fighting a yawn.

"People in my office now assign your stupidity to me."

Adam propped the phone on the table. "In Paris?"

"We share the same name, Adam! They know you're my brother, and I'm bloody sorry David kept you from drowning!"

Adam just whipped the eggs, waiting.

It took Connor a minute to speak. "Have you any idea

the trouble this caused me? I may have lost a client, thanks to it. An Australian client!"

"I doubt that," Adam said, his voice cool and calm. "You've told me you have a way out. I nearly drowned. Caused brain damage. Make a joke of it. Or be understanding. If you can."

"What're you talking about?"

"Rich people love fake empathy. And since I look nothing like you or David, toss in this hobbit's adopted. That should amuse your mates; perhaps even enhance your reputation."

Connor was silent, then finally said, "That might work."

"Certainly can't hurt."

Connor was silent for another minute before he continued, "I have to go. I'm meeting Catherine at the Louvre, for a function. Lots of investors wishing to be divested of their money. This'll give me quite a story to tell."

"Happy to help."

Then Connor rang off without another word.

An Australian client. Of course. Christopher Meillon had his suspicions so was covering every angle he could.

Adam sighed, turned off the phone and shifted to see his mother standing in the kitchen doorway, watching him. Her face was ashen.

"Adam, I don't think I heard right," she said, her voice deep with meaning. "Did you just tell Connor to disown you?"

"I only made official what he's already done." Then he poured the eggs into the skillet to scramble.

She gave Adam a long hard look then asked, "What happened to you in Los Angeles? Connor used to anger you so, but this time you didn't even go flush. Kept a smile on your face."

"Did I?"

"...Adam..."

His voice grew gentle. "Connor's to be pitied, Mum. He needs his money, position, wife's family, and little comments about me to make himself feel as though he has meaning. That's rather sad, isn't it?"

A slow smile filled his mother's face. "Yes. And thank God you said that. For a moment I thought you'd been carted off and replaced by a pod person."

"Maybe next trip." And he winked at her...then he grew soft and serious. "Mum, can I ask you something?"

She straightened up and nodded. He knew that posture; she used it when she was about to hear bad news. He hoped this wouldn't be like that.

"You know, the book I went to get. In Los Angeles. This is just between you and me...but it was not destroyed." She blinked and looked closer at him. "I haven't started the provenance, yet, but there's a — I think it was the same book Da was carrying. In fact, I'm certain it was."

She slowly came into the kitchen and sat at the table, her eyes locked on him.

"As such," he continued, careful with every word, "you would have a solid claim to her. But I'd like to leave her at Merryton. Da's alma mater. Have her known as the *Verlain Alice*. Clear his name."

She leaned back in the chair. Let out a long slow breath. "What about the insurance...the pay-out? Would they go along with this?"

"I'll ask Sir Robert to handle them; he knows their chairman. But you...you'd have to relinquish that claim. They couldn't afford to pay you. Not what she's worth. It's just...she'd be safe, there. Protected. Revered, even. I think Da'd like that."

She looked from him to his mobile phone, and back to him. Then she rose...and crossed to him...and hugged him. Long and hard. When she released him, tears were in her eyes.

"You have always been my favorite child," she said, soft and warm. "You know why?" He shook his head. "You have your Da's tender way of looking at the world."

"He liked people." She nodded. He smiled at her. "Want some eggs? I had champagne on the flight, and some rather classy crackers, but with cheese and fruit when they said there'd be caviar and...well..."

She just looked at him, kissed his forehead and said, "Find out what papers I need to sign." Then she walked away.

So there it was — the *Alice* would stay at Merryton to be cared for in the best of fashions, with his father's name no longer associated with her loss. A smile crossed his face as he scooped the eggs onto a slice of toast, for he felt nothing but peace at the decision.

****

Adam finalized the provenance at just after two, on Monday. He saved and rose to head for The Dark Chamber...only Jeremy staggered in, unshaven, bathed in lavender, no pins in his piercings, his clothes barely in order, and walking like a little old man. Adam was startled into stillness at his appearance, until he saw the joy in Jeremy's expression.

The boy stumbled up and slipped an arm around Adam, his voice cracking as he said, "Oh, mate, I been to hell an' back an' loved every minute of it."

"I...I don't understand," Adam murmured.

Jeremy grinned and hugged him close. A hint of bourbon still lingered on his breath, despite him obviously having brushed his teeth, as he whispered into Adam's ear, "There is nothing like an older woman. Pat knows tricks you never even heard of. I ache all over. Feel drained. And oh-so-bloody-blissful. Bloody hell, there's nothing like an older woman."

"Um, Jere — that is far more information than I cared to have shared."

Jeremy leered at him, still more drunk than sober. "You don't want to see the pictures?"

"No!" shot out of Adam. "No, I — I prefer to remember

— um, to think of — um, just — no."

"Too bad," Jeremy smirked. "Some of me best work. Pat says I'd do well in LA. She'd even sponsor me."

"I think you *would* like it there," said Adam. "Have you got your passport in order? Work visa applied for?"

Jeremy gave him a blank look. "I need 'em?"

Adam gave him a sweet smile as he said, "Yes."

"Oh, better check into that." Then he held up a thumb drive and the leer returned. "Sure you won't change your mind?"

"I'll look," came a voice from behind them. They jolted around to see Bill standing by his cubicle, in his jumper and holding a mug of what smelled like soup.

Jeremy cast him a wicked grin and tottered around to the man's cubicle.

It took Adam a moment to recover, then he realized he was holding the *Alice* under his coat as if to protect her. He shook his head and whisper-sang —

I see a book
Who's going to be took
For Jeremy to photograph and put with all the rest.
She's a lovely little book
Who soon will find her nook,
And she will be considered to be one of our best.

— before he could continue on.

As he passed the kitchenette, his mug was thrust in front of him, steaming with tea. Elizabeth was holding it. Surprised, he carefully took it and sipped. Just the way he liked it.

"Brilliant," he said. "Cheers."

"Don't think it means anything," shot out of her faster than a speeding bullet.

He chuckled and started to head on. "I know, I know, I'm not snoggable except at Christmas and my birthday. Never St. Valentine's." The last sentence came out as a chirpy growl.

Elizabeth stopped him, uncertain, unhappy. "Adam, I really was joking."

"Of course you were," he said, then he hesitated and gave her a wary look. "But, Elizabeth, I...I was just wondering something..."

"What?" she asked, just as wary.

"It's just...no one but my brother, Conner, ever called me hobbit. How did you know that?"

Her face took on a deer-caught-in-the-headlights expression.

Adam nodded and continued, "Those trips to Paris. I know you dislike Henry James, but have you tried any Edith Wharton?"

She looked away from him, her face flush.

He sighed. "I suggest you consider *The House of Mirth*. Might give you an idea of what you've set yourself up for."

Then he continued into The Dark Chamber, leaving Elizabeth to herself.

He gently set the case on a shelf and looked around, at peace. Sipped his tea. This room, he would miss. The black shadows. The mystical play of light and dust. The ancient lift in the back. The lines of volumes awaiting their turn before Jeremy's camera, or to find their new home in the stacks. It was like a refuge.

He had still heard nothing from Casey regarding his revelation about the *Alice '65*. She was probably upset with him, and he did not blame her. But what was done was done. He decided to let her know when the book was to be officially unveiled as property of Merryton, to see if she would come for the ceremony. If she did, he would offer his apology, in person. Maybe that would make things right.

He noticed the *Orlando furioso* he'd worked so hard on was still on the shelf. He picked it up and looked at the quires. He knew a leaf had been half torn out of the book, in the back, but this time he looked more closely at the endpaper that would have followed the missing page...and shone his phone-light through it...and could just make out the shadows of ink that could have formed words. He took in a long, deep, happy breath.

"So there it is," he whispered to the book. "I read somewhere that Pope Pius would write notes in his books. He must have cut this one out before giving you to King Victor Emanuel. I wonder if we could reveal what it said, in some way? Compare the handwriting? But whether we can or not, thank you for allowing me to see this. It won't take much to connect you, now, so...would you rather be left in protective obscurity, or shall I update your provenance? Bring you out into the open and — ?"

Tinkling music cut into his thoughts. It took him a moment to recognize it as Paula Frazer's *What Is and Was*.

He chuckled and said, "Well...bright light, it is. Let's do it now."

Then he poked his head out of the room, book still in hand, and looked down the hallway to see if he could locate the source of the music. Hakim and Elizabeth were glancing around, as well. And then he saw —

A big cat creeping down the aisle. A black panther, like Gertrude. But that was impossible. Until he realized it was —

"Casey?"

Sure enough, Casey stopped and looked back over her shoulder at him and said, "There you are, you little sneak." She rose, revealing she was dressed like Catwoman. The music came from her cell phone.

Adam almost bounced for joy. "What're you doing here?" he asked, as she prowled down to him.

"I came to thank you," she said. "You helped me decide that I wanted that Beryl Markham role."

He set his tea in the kitchen as he said, "Me? How?"

"By doing what you said you'd do. By being true to yourself, no matter what. Thought I was doing that...but seems I lost it when I did *Ilithium Four*. Not no more, baby. I called the producer and...well, *talked* him into letting me read for the part...after a few hours of hounding. And I got it. Friday. With some help from this." She showed him her cell phone. It played a video of her in the jet's cockpit, where it looked like she was in control of the plane. "They think I really know how to do this crap."

"Brilliant," Adam said, grinning ear to ear. "Have you time enough to learn?"

She shrugged. "We start shooting at the end of next month. At Leavesden. For three weeks. Then it's off to Kenya. You open to helping me get up to speed?"

"Of course. One of my rugby mates is a pilot. He can show you all the tricks."

"Oh, baby, I do love the tricks." She batted her eyes.

"I'll ring him." He led her to his cubicle. "So how's Gertrude?"

"Bossy bitch love boy cat."

"I'm happy for her."

He set the *Ariosto* on his desk and cleared a chair for her to sit, but she remained standing. "I sat a lot on the flight," she said, stretching just like a cat. "Oh, and I thought you might like to see this. My manager got a copy of the mock-up."

She dug into her purse and pulled out a slab of messy photocopies that had been stapled together — the next *People Magazine*...with Sean and Shawn grinning out from its cover. An *Alice* had been PhotoShopped into their hands. The headline — *The Destruction of a Treasure*.

Adam smiled. "I'm not surprised, but they will be."

"Yeah, got your text, and word's already gettin' around, and guess whose project got tanked, because of it?" Adam grinned. She smiled. "You gonna ask how I found you, so easy?"

He shook his head. Now he understood why Jeremy had stopped to talk with him. "You've seen your mother...and you shared a cab with a tattooed lad...and you have five bedrooms in your crib."

She nodded. "He gets the pool house, which, if I read her

226

subtext correctly, plays into one of her fantasies." Now her smile widened. "I love my mother and I want her to be happy, and I told her to never ever even think of sharing the details." She shivered then focused on him. "She says you're leaving Merryton."

"Yes."

"What you gonna do?"

He shrugged. "Buy and sell antiquarian books. It's what I love — bringing a good tome to a good home. Could be my catch-phrase. I have some savings. Once Jeremy's recuperated, I'll ask him for some decent photos of the *Kristen Lavransdatter* set I've purchased. Put them up on a website. Which would need to be designed by someone who knows how to make it interesting, or I could just post online and with ABEbooks — there's much to think about, still. Plus, I've contacted some dealers I know. Do a bit of freelance for them. Already got a nibble from one in Chelsea, to work on a catalogue, and another in Paris, where Connor lives." Then his tone became as headmaster-like as Vincent's. "Now that I am an Orisi man, I may appear at his office in proper attire and invite him to lunch. Just to wreak havoc on his life. Who knows?"

"I'll want pictures of that," she laughed.

He hesitated before continuing. "I...um, I also need to speak with you about your grandfather's note. It will be a bit surprising."

Casey's eyes went sharp on his. "Adam, sometimes I'm a bit slow on the uptake, but I do know how to add...so don't be surprised if I'm not surprised." And her candid look told him everything. "But let's talk later. Kitty needs her Cat Chow."

"Right you are," he said, rising. "Fish and chips, 'cross the way. Best in England."

He grabbed his Mackintosh and started for the door...but she did not move. He looked at her. She held up the cell phone. The music played.

He nearly groaned. "Casey, no...not really..."

She meowed the words, "You owe me..."

He huffed...and chuckled. She was right. Besides, after all he'd been through? Why not? He took in a deep breath and backed to the main doors, beckoning to her and singing in German —

> *I now see before me...a lady who is lovely.*
> *But do I dare inform her that she is all that I could love?*
> *No, for that would be wrong.*
> *Still she makes my heart strong.*
> *How can I not want her when she is all that I could love?*

Casey paced him as he sang, shooting Elizabeth a hiss as she passed her cubicle, making her jump back.

He hammed it up as he kept singing —

> *I must forget her. She's not right for me.*
> *And yet to see her, brings joy straight to me.*
> *I long to be there when she awakens*
> *From her deep slumber. My love she's taken.*

He could not help but pull her into an embrace and growl, "Mad as a hatter, you are!" Then he kissed her.

When he finally made himself pull away, Casey sighed and looked at him, almost afraid as she said, "Oh, baby, who said you weren't snoggable?"

"Those who never tried me," he said, a smirk in his voice.

"Will you visit me on the set?" she asked.

"If you like. I make my own hours, now. Can work anywhere."

"I thought you said that way of life is dying."

"It's not dead, yet. I've book fairs to attend. I know people at ILAB and ABA and PBFA. There are other dealers my age. Books will always be with us, even if half are electronic. Well, thirty percent. Maybe I'll bring it back from the brink."

She smoothed over one of his eyebrows, murmuring, "I dunno if I like this new you or not."

"Too late; you're half the reason for it."

"Yeah, well — careful, you."

"I will be. It's part of my DNA."

But then he saw something in her eyes. Something that told him what she was really talking about. He could not move. He had to be wrong...to be misinterpreting...but still he made himself ask, "You — you don't mean, with *you*? *You*. Want *me*. To be careful. With *you*?"

Her expression was soft and nervous and wary as she whispered, "Only if it will always be so..."

His heart grew close to bursting. He had to remind himself to breathe. Someone as beautiful and wonderful and irritating as Casey Blanchard wanted him to take care with her. Not just for today or tomorrow or next week, but for who knew how long? And all he could think to say was, "May I tell you, Miss Blanchard, how much I love and adore you?"

A slow smile of the purest happiness spread across her lips. She brushed a strand of hair from his face and said, soft and loving, "Baby...c'mon..."

He drew her into another kiss as long and tender and all-embracing as a cozy chair by a warm fire on a brisk and rainy night, with a fine book in hand offering the prospect of peace and happiness, and he held her as she held him and finally he knew, as his father had promised, he had found his window into a bright new world...

And she was his perfect fit.

— THE END —

About the Author

Kyle Michel Sullivan is a writer and self-involved artist out to change the world until it changes him...as has already happened in far too many ways. He has lived in London, Los Angeles, San Antonio, El Paso, Kansas City, Honolulu, Austin and Houston, and now resides in Buffalo, NY.

He has won multiple awards for his screenplays and has written books of every sort — from sunshine and light (*David Martin*) to cold and dark (*How To Rape A Straight Guy*, which has been banned a couple of times) to mystery (*The Vanishing of Owen Taylor*) to flat out insane (*The Lyons' Den*).

He uses Tolstoy as his guide, and tries to build characters as vivid and real as possible. He has a lot of fun doing it mixed with angst, anger, and amazement...but that's the lot of a writer.

www.ingramcontent.com/pod-product-compliance
Lightning Source LLC
Chambersburg PA
CBHW070524100726
47907CB00004B/974